WATER'S
EDGE

BOOKS BY GREGG OLSEN

GREGG OLSEN

WATER'S EDGE

GRAND CENTRAL
PUBLISHING

New York   Boston

Grand Central Publishing
Hachette Book Group
1290 Avenue of the Americas, New York, NY 10104
grandcentralpublishing.com
twitter.com/grandcentralpub

Originally published in the United Kingdom by Bookouture, an imprint of Storyfire Ltd., in 2020
First North American edition: March 2022

Grand Central Publishing is a division of Hachette Book Group, Inc. The Grand Central Publishing name and logo is a trademark of Hachette Book Group, Inc.

The publisher is not responsible for websites (or their content) that are not owned by the publisher.

The Hachette Speakers Bureau provides a wide range of authors for speaking events. To find out more, go to www.hachettespeakersbureau.com or call (866) 376-6591.

Library of Congress Control Number: 2021945932

ISBN: 9781538706909 (trade paperback)

Printed in the United States of America

LSC-C

Printing 1, 2021

For Paul Marinucci, who lives his best life every single day.

CHAPTER ONE

The streetlights on the corners were dim. Young men—teenagers, mostly—stood in the yards or between houses in small groups, smoking, laughing, staring at her small car as she passed as if challenging her to encroach on their territory. She had heard all the talk about this part of the city. She'd read the newspaper accounts and seen the raw footage on television. And still she came. His invitation had been so shy, embarrassed, charming.

She had rushed home from her shift at the tavern, showered, and tried on several different outfits before she decided on the one that would highlight her figure and accentuate the red of her hair.

Green.

That was her go-to color. She studied herself in the mirror.

She'd been called pretty, even beautiful a time or two.

Yet never by the sober.

Or the especially handsome.

That evening he'd called her beautiful.

She had been working in a coffee shop downtown and just started taking shifts at the tavern. Tips were better at the Sandpiper, but the clientele had bottomed out on the disgusting scale. The coffee shop had been full of New Age creeps and wannabe writers. The Old Whiskey Mill had drunks and more drunks, and it was a cop hangout. Drunks were more generous than coffee sippers.

She ran her fingers through her hair and thought about him.

He looked familiar. Not overly so. Just enough to make her lean in when he spoke. He ordered a Jack Daniel's, straight up, and smiled at her. She'd said something like: "Do I know you from somewhere? Are you famous?"

The moment it passed from her lips she felt schoolgirl silly.

"Afraid not. I'm sure I would remember a beautiful woman like you."

It was a very old, very worn-out pickup line, but he'd blushed. And yet, there it was: a real, honest-to-God blush.

She remembered asking if he worked in town, and he answered with a straight face.

"I work for the CIA."

She blinked and was about to say something, but he laughed and said CIA stood for the Culinary Institute of America. CIA. He was a chef in search of employment. A recent graduate of the Culinary Institute of America in Napa Valley, California. He said he was going to prepare something special for her.

He sheepishly explained he still lived at home with his father and would she mind if his dad ate with them?

That made her mind up. She had felt silly that she had almost turned him down. She hadn't gone out with anyone for a long time. Especially someone she'd just met. She'd said yes much too quickly. She regretted that now. She didn't want him to get the wrong idea.

Or maybe she did?

She knew what her mother would have said if she were still in her life. "Leann Truitt, just what were you thinking?" It was one of her mother's favorite lines, a dart meant to hurt. It was true that sometimes she hadn't been thinking, but she was a grown woman now.

"Shut up, Mom," she said to herself. "We'll find out soon enough what I was thinking."

The house was on the corner and faced north. It was badly in need of a makeover and was exactly as he'd described it. But her stomach dropped as she drove around the corner. The house was dark except for a flickering light behind thick yellowish curtains. It looked empty. She looked at the clock on the dash, thinking she was early, but she was actually a few minutes late.

She parked and walked across the cracked cement of the sidewalk to the side gate. She lifted a black latch and pushed the gate open. A walk of original brickwork led to the door. The bricks were covered in green moss, and she had to step carefully to keep her high heels from slipping. If she twisted an ankle, she wouldn't be able to work—and, even worse, would miss this wonderful evening.

And yet something niggled at her; a little doubt crept in.

She looked for a doorbell but there wasn't one; there wasn't even a knocker. She raised her hand to knock and hesitated. What if his father disapproved of her coming for dinner? This place was older than old. It smelled of mildew and rot. It reminded her of one of her father's rental dumps.

"I'll get it, Dad," a voice said from inside.

She heard footsteps. A shadow appeared behind the glass and the door opened.

He took her hand and led her inside the darkened foyer.

Her eyes adjusted and she could see that both walls of the wide hallway were lined with boxes and stacks of clothing and dolls and appliances and lampshades. There was a narrow path and he was leading her through the clutter. Then she stepped in something sticky. Adrenaline coursed through her. Something was wrong.

"Maybe I should..." she managed to say, before he turned and slammed a fist into her face.

CHAPTER TWO

I sit at my desk at the Jefferson County Sheriff's Office with posters of the craggy Olympic Range on the wall behind me. I can see into Sheriff Gray's office to my left. His door is open and he's leaning back, too far back, in his roll-around chair, the springs squeaking whenever he shifts his weight.

So annoying.

I swear, the chair could be used by the CIA to get confessions from the most hardened terrorist. I want to take a full can of WD-40 and douse the springs.

But I don't.

I turn to the disheveled woman sitting in a chair beside my desk. She is holding a toddler with one arm and attempting to corral her eight-year-old serial-killer-in-training with the other.

"Miss Gamble, let's move to an interview room," I say, partly because I don't want to cause her more embarrassment and partly because her kid can bounce off the walls in there. Literally. In the kids' interview room are soft toys, carpeting, soundproof walls, posters of breaching orcas, the PAW Patrol, lighthouses.

Miss Gamble gladly gets up. Her ears are bleeding also. Whether it's from the squealing made by the chair, the squalling toddler, or the whining, nasal, nasty mouth of her son is unclear. If I thought a can of WD-40 would work on the eight-year-old, I'd use it. But it's not Miss Gamble or her kids that are getting to me. It's her situation. It sparks memories. I try to set it aside. Sparks can be bonfires.

Miss Gamble is unmarried, trying to raise three children by three different fathers, and trying to do it alone. She is on public assistance, living in public housing, using food stamps in an unwise manner—for example, trading them for illegal substances—and I deduce from her belly bump she might have another baby on the way.

She leads the ones she already has into the children's interview room. The interview room for adults is not like this space. Not even close. This one is meant to soothe and mollify. The adult side is designed to irritate and get them to confess just to get out of the room. I can testify that it works. At least, some of the time.

I take a seat, pick up the paperwork provided to me by the Port Hadlock Fire Department, and look at Miss Gamble, then at the eight-year-old.

She remains silent.

"Did you know your son was setting things on fire?"

It's a straightforward question. Yes or no. She doesn't answer. Just gives me those big brown eyes. I can't sympathize. I don't know enough about the family dynamics. Maybe the kid's been abused?

When I ask the question, her little firebug's eyes light up and a half smile plays at his lips. The sheriff is in the next room. I want to continue the questions, but I get up, go into the outer office, shut the door behind me, and return to my desk to clear my head. I wonder if he's a bedwetter. If so, I know how the textbooks would classify him, and it stings me. I know from experience that while bedwetting often indicates a child's future behavior, the trajectory is somewhat changeable.

I hear the sheriff's chair give an emphatic squeal and know he's gotten up. The floors vibrate under his plodding gait as he comes over to my desk.

"You okay?" he asks.

"Why wouldn't I be?"

"Is that kid really setting animals on fire?"

"Fire marshal says so." The fire marshal actually said more than that, but Sheriff Gray doesn't need to hear the descriptive language he used. The man was very upset. I've never seen a grown man cry, but after seeing the pictures of a family's beloved pet, I don't blame him. I felt queasy thinking about it, and it takes a lot to make me queasy.

"Well, I'm going to do you a favor," Sheriff Gray says, handing me a Post-it note.

I read and look back at the kids' interview room. I can hear banging on the wall. "What about them?"

"I'll take care of them," he says. "I'm the sheriff. I can do a referral to juvenile court the same as you, and I've done this job longer."

Outside of a multiple murder in the Snow Creek area, the cases I've had lately have been thefts and high-dollar vandalism. The note the sheriff handed me has eight words printed in his perfect, steady hand.

It reads like a telegram.

Marrowstone Island.
Mystery Bay State Park.
Cove.
Floater

A floater is a tasteless but accurate descriptive term we use for bodies found in water. I haven't been on the job very long—two years—but this is the first time I've heard of a drowning in the little cove of Mystery Bay, Marine State Park.

"Homicide?" I ask.

He gives a little shrug. "They want a detective. You tell me after you get there."

I grab my windbreaker that doubles as a raincoat, thinking the sheriff is done.

He's not.

"Detective Carpenter, meet Reserve Deputy Marsh."

A younger version of me, but with red hair instead of blond, steps in front of my desk with her hand held out. A smattering of freckles high on her cheekbones are visible through the makeup she's applied. The hand is perfectly manicured.

Those nails won't last the day, I think.

I can't help but notice my own hands just then. My skin is dry, tanned from spending time in the sun. Nails somewhat chewed but practical for this kind of work.

I already don't like her, but, to be fair, I don't know her.

I remind myself to get to know her first and then not like her.

Her grip is like water, soft. She is wearing a blue pinstriped suit with a white silk blouse billowing out in front. She probably got the idea for her getup from a television show where all the female cops are busty, with longish styled hair, and dressed in high heels. Her ridiculous outfit will last about as long as her nails before it's ripped or covered with mud or puke or blood.

"Ronnie Marsh," she says.

"Nice to meet you, Ronnie." I don't mean it. I've got a case to work, and in my mind I'm already heading to Marrowstone Island. I let her hand drip through mine, and I slip into my windbreaker. As I turn for the door, Sheriff Gray stops me with a hand on my shoulder. I don't like to be touched, but I'll make an allowance for him.

"Take her with you, Megan."

I work alone. Always have. I work alone for a reason. I don't want complications. I don't want relationships. Working together qualifies as a relationship. Relationship equals abandonment. That's what life has taught me. My brother Hayden hates me because I left him in Idaho with a veritable stranger. My mother betrayed and lied to me in the worst way.

Everyone does eventually.

Reserve Deputy Marsh can ride along with me for today, but that's it.

"You've got her for a week."

I shoot him a look. I don't care if the reserve sees it or not.

"I'm swamped, Sheriff. I can do today. Maybe you can give her to someone else?"

"Swamped with what?"

I stay mute. He already knows the answer. I'm tempted to say, *Sheriff, you and I both know I'm not working shit right now. So why don't we save some time here and you hand her to someone that wants to work her.* But I don't say that because Sheriff Gray gave me a job when probably no one else would. Because he knows things about me. Because he has helped me erase some of my past mistakes. And, more than anything, because he is about the only person I can trust.

He doesn't remove his hand from my shoulder. "You might as well take vacation time, Megan. It's so dead around here."

I wish he wouldn't use that word: "dead." It has a way of multiplying trouble. Like a virus.

Just then, Nan, Sheriff Gray's assistant, shows up. She is also wearing a suit. She and Marsh could be twins. I change my assessment of where Marsh got the idea for her attire. She must have seen Nan.

That doesn't bode well for her.

"Sheriff," Nan says, "Marine Patrol wants to know if they need to respond to the drowning." She's looking at me, smiling at Marsh, and talking to the sheriff. She's perfected multitask ass-kissing. "Should I tell them you're both with a suspect and can't be disturbed?"

Reserve Deputy Marsh speaks up. "I just completed my rotation through Marine Patrol. Captain Martin gave me a good write-up. He said I was his best intern yet."

I'd met the captain one time during *my* academy rotation. He was good-looking, in a Ted Bundy sort of way. I remember he was always partial to the female cadets. The guys, no matter how adept they were on the water, barely squeaked by with a passing grade.

"I can see that," I say.

Nan and Marsh were exchanging looks and giving each other a knowing smile. It's no secret that Nan has a picture of Captain Marvel—that's what I call him—displayed on her desk. He is at the helm of his boat, bravely sailing into a perfect sunset. I remember a while back he gave Nan a ride on his personal boat. The next day she came to work in wrinkled clothes, messed-up hair, no makeup.

I just rolled my eyes when I saw her.

Sheriff Gray looks at me for a response.

"I won't know if I need the Marine Patrol guys until I get there. What's their location?"

Nan gives me a stare. "The captain didn't say. He just asked if he should respond."

"I'll call Captain Marvel when I get there." Then I change my mind. "I'll call the captain on my way," I say, and try to leave.

Sheriff clears his throat. "Aren't you forgetting someone? Take Deputy Marsh with you." He says this like I should stand to attention and salute.

I head to the parking lot, and Deputy Marsh trails behind me with her high heels clacking all the way. I get to my old Taurus and hit the unlock button on the key fob. I forgot that the key fob doesn't work anymore. The good thing is the car is old enough that it still has a regular key on the fob. The bad thing is the car is old. I've asked for a new car. I won't get one until I have to drive with one arm out the window holding the door shut.

The day just gets better and better.

I open the door with the key and hit the inside unlock button. Nothing happens. I lean across and unlock the passenger door. Ronnie Marsh waits until I pull out of the parking lot before she starts what will become stream-of-consciousness chatter. I tune out somewhere around her graduating from middle school at the top of her class.

CHAPTER THREE

The drive to the scene isn't a long one. We cross over the narrow causeway to Indian Island and a second causeway to Marrowstone Island. I turn left on State Route 116, which is also Flagler Road. Every now and then a cut through the thickets of ferns and old cedars reveals the sun reflecting off the waters of the bay. It reminds me of my little brother, Hayden. In Port Orchard we lived not far from a little creek, where he would look for salamanders. He was seven. I was fifteen or sixteen. I read *A Tale of Two Cities* for English class. Charles Dickens said what I was feeling about those times in Port Orchard. "It was the best of times. It was the worst of times." There's enough time and distance from those days that I choose to remember the good. The bad is too painful. Hayden remembers only the worst of days and my screw-ups. He has little contact with me, and that is more painful than the memories.

Mystery Bay is to our left, the state park straight ahead. I see a sign for the boat ramp and slow down. A state patrol car is parked several hundred feet down the road with the emergency lights on. In front of it is one of our Sheriff's Office vehicles.

Further down is a relic: a red or oxidized brown Ford Pinto.

A young man, teens, early twenties, stands behind the deputy's cruiser, one arm wrapped around his chest, his free hand twisting the hair of a skimpy beard and stuffing the end in his mouth. His hair is long and black and curly and looks like it hadn't been washed in ... well possibly, *ever*. He wears camouflage army boots with the laces tied so loosely, I can't imagine how they stay on his feet. His faded jeans are cuffed and tattered.

The trooper's corfam dress shoes are dirt- and mud-free. So very shiny. If I'd been inclined, I could use the toes for a mirror. There's not a fleck of lint or dust on his sharp-enough-to-cut-you pressed trousers. I look at the statie's name badge: *MacDonald.*

"Your deputy is down with the body," he says flatly. "No need for both of us to get dirty. Besides, one of us had to stay up here to keep the road closed to civilians."

I glance at the pair of cruisers with their emergency lights flashing and then return my gaze to him. I want to say that I would have totally missed the police cars with the Christmas lights going and driven right past. But since I have a trainee with me, I shift gears.

"That's what I figured. Good thinking." I give him "the look" so he knows he didn't pull a fast one on me. To my pleasant surprise I hear my trainee giggle.

Maybe she'll be okay.

"Is that the person that found the body?" she asks.

The young man stopped twisting his beard long enough to offer his hand. He says nothing and I don't take the hand. I doubt anyone would.

Trooper MacDonald speaks up. "This is Mr. Boyd."

I nod. "I'll need a statement from you, Mr. Boyd. Why were you down there?"

I didn't see a boat trailer or any fishing gear. He isn't dressed for anything outdoorsy.

He appears surprised by the question. I half expect him to ask if he is a suspect and then invoke his rights. To which I might respond that he has no rights until he becomes a suspect. The truth is everyone is a suspect until they're not. I have learned that from experience. He doesn't disappoint.

"I'm not a suspect, am I?"

"Absolutely not," I lie.

He looks skeptical. "On TV the person to find the body is always a suspect."

That was also true in real life.

"That's TV, Mr. Boyd."

"Robbie," he says. "My name's Robbie. I go to school at Olympic College. I'm taking criminal justice."

"Great choice," I tell him. "So you know how this goes. Tell me: why were you down there?"

He stuffs some of his scraggly mustache in his mouth and chews on it.

Gag.

"I heard about this place from a friend at school," he finally says. "I don't have to give you her name, do I?"

"No," I say.

Not right this minute, anyway, I think. I'll let him tell me all he knows and then I'll get the name out of him.

"Okay," he starts. "I was looking for a new hiking trail. I'm parked right over there." He turns and points at the Pinto as if I hadn't noticed it or it might have mysteriously moved. "I'm a hiker and a rock climber. I was looking for some cliffs. I'm very strong."

"I can see that." He looks all skin and bones in his grimy T-shirt and well-worn jeans and hiking boots.

He smiles and warms to me. Everyone does. I can charm when I need to.

"So," he goes on, "I headed down to the bay—to the boat ramp, I mean—and I started looking for a trail."

He stops a beat.

"This isn't going to be on the news, is it? I'm supposed to be in class. I skipped a test and told them I was sick."

It's going to be in a full-length movie if you keep asking stupid questions, I think.

"I don't think your name will come up," I say.

He seems a little disappointed, so I pivot again. "But I can't promise the news media won't track you down."

He brightens a little. That was the correct response.

"Well, I guess if I have to talk to them..."

"Finish telling your story," I say.

"Okay, so I walk that way"—he points—"and I come to a place where I found a trail. I went into the trees and followed it a bit and that's when I found the place."

Ronnie interjects: "What place?"

"The rocks," he says. "I'm a rock climber. You ever been rock climbing?"

She shakes her head.

I want to shake her for interrupting the interview.

"Mr. Boyd," I say, "you found the body. Can you tell us about that?"

"Okay. Sorry. I just really like rock climbing."

I gave him a stern look. I am running out of patience.

"Anyway, I came up to the little cliff, bluff, whatever." Boyd has warmed to the subject. "It was only, like, thirty feet high, but it was sheer, man. I mean, it was straight down: 'Do not pass GO, do not collect $200,' if you know what I mean."

He gives other expressions of this stupidity and I let him talk until he runs out of "likes" and "you knows" and appears to be wrung dry as far as skirting the subject.

"I was going to climb down. I left my climbing gear back in the car, but it looked like I could make it. Then I saw I didn't have to. Someone left a perfectly good rope tied off to a tree. It was coiled up and I almost tripped over it. I pitched it over, checked the knot, and over I went."

"The body," Ronnie says.

I can see she is getting impatient too.

Good girl.

"So I got down to the bottom and there's a bunch of big rocks and a tiny strip of sandy beach. I pulled on the rope to make sure I could climb back up. I didn't want to fall down in those rocks. Some of them are sharp. Anyway, I was about to climb back up and I saw what looked like a foot sticking out between the rocks. I couldn't see any way to get to this beach except by climbing down. I thought maybe the person had fallen off the cliff. At the same time I wondered how they could have, 'cause the rope was coiled up at the top of the cliff."

He stops and looks at us.

"Aren't you going to take notes?"

"I have a very good memory," I say. "Go on."

He sighs. "Okay. Fine. I go over and look and it's a woman. She ain't moving and looks banged up. I thought maybe she had fallen but then I see she's not wearing anything but her panties and a bra. So I think maybe she tried to swim to the beach and got tossed up on the rocks. I climbed back up and called 911. Then I thought maybe she needed help and I got in my car, but it wouldn't start. Then the officer showed up and he called for a deputy and, well, here we are."

I question him again, walking him through his story. It doesn't change. He climbed down, saw the body, climbed up, and called 911. Boyd swore he didn't touch anything or take any pictures, although I don't believe him, because he still has his phone. He'll probably hightail it back to campus and show pictures to his buddies or sell them to the news media.

I say to him, "So when CSI gets here and takes fingerprints and collects DNA samples, yours won't show up anywhere?"

He swallows and I hear his Adam's apple click in a dry throat. He shakes his head. "I don't think so. You can't get fingerprints off a rope and that's all I touched. Honest to God. And the rocks where I was climbing down."

"We have a new technology that's called Touch DNA. You probably heard about that in class."

He stays silent.

"And it's what the name says. When you touch something, part of your DNA gets on the item, body, whatever. Then, using the FBI and Homeland Security database, we can then trace it back to the person through family lineage and down to a specific individual."

Boyd stops chewing on his beard and begins rubbing the side of his face.

"Well, to tell the truth, I might have walked out in the water to see better. But it was too deep, and I didn't want to get that wet. I didn't never touch her, I swear."

The bottom half of his jeans are still damp.

My rule of thumb is that when someone says, "I swear," what follows is going to be a big fat lie. I believe he didn't touch the body but maybe he took pictures. Maybe even a selfie. People are sick. I should know.

"Can you let him sit in back of your car?" I ask MacDonald.

MacDonald does so reluctantly.

As he is getting in the back seat Boyd says, "I'll give a full statement to your partner, Detective Marsh." He smiles at Ronnie. She smiles back, turns to face me, and scowls.

"I'll take his statement if you like, Detective. They taught us how at the academy. I've got a voice recorder on my cell phone."

I've used my phone recorder to take confessions too. But the person giving the confession didn't know I was recording them. Tricking them didn't bother me.

MacDonald is cold. I need to turn on the charm.

"I'm Megan," I say. "Can I call you Mac?"

"No. It's State Patrolman MacDonald."

CHAPTER FOUR

Seriously.

He wants me to call him *State Patrolman MacDonald.*

Not a chance.

This is going to be a long morning.

"Okay," I tell him. "Is the rope still there, or did Deputy Davis have something of his own to climb down with?"

"He used the witness's rope," MacDonald says.

I was afraid of that. It's too late to collect the rope. I follow the beaten-down grass path through a stand of huge big-leaf maples to a smaller fir where a climbing rope is tied off. The rope extends down the side of the cliff. I step out as far as I can but don't see a body or my deputy. I return to the cars and MacDonald.

"Deputy Marsh will stay up here to wait for Crime Scene. Do you have crime scene tape?"

He nods.

"Can you help me out and string some along both sides of this road? We'll need to search both sides for any evidence or tire marks." I look directly at him.

He doesn't say anything. He goes behind the car and opens the trunk.

"Unless you have hiking boots and work clothes in your handbag," I tell my erstwhile deputy, Ronnie, "I want you to stay up here and take a statement from the witness."

She looks down at her shoes. "Sorry. I thought we'd be staying in the office today. Tomorrow I'll be better prepared, ma'am."

Ma'am? Seriously?

"Don't call me 'ma'am,'" I tell her. "I'm Megan for today. Okay?"

"I'm really taking Mr. Boyd's statement?" she asks.

"Might as well get your feet wet. I want you to write his name and personal information down. And get the license information."

She takes a notebook and pen from inside her jacket. It was so tight fitting I didn't see anywhere she could have hidden them. "And while you're at it, search his car."

"We don't have a warrant. Is he a suspect?"

"No," I lie again. "Just see if he'll let you. If it makes you feel better, you can ask him to let you search his car while you're taking the statement. If he says yes, it will be on the recording."

She doesn't look convinced.

"I've been at this awhile, Ronnie. Trust me."

"I do. Trust you, I mean."

Now, that's a start.

"I'm going down to see what we have." I go to Mac's car, open the door, and ask Boyd, "Are you sure there's no other way down there besides climbing?"

"I guess you could swim around."

Smart-ass.

I return to Ronnie.

"Are you going to call Marine Patrol?" she asks.

"I'll call from down there." Mac approaches with a roll of yellow-and-black tape. "Thank you for helping. This is Reserve Deputy Ronnie Marsh."

Ronnie offers her limp hand and he takes it long enough for it to drip through his fingers and says, "Nice to meet you."

"She will be taking a statement from Mr. Boyd."

I know Mac will gladly let Ronnie take the statement so he can avoid going to court or testifying. I don't warn him that once Ronnie starts talking, there is no off switch. The witness is on his own.

I follow the trail through the trees again and stand at the top of the cliff. It's about thirty or forty feet to the bottom. Rocks ranging in size from a football to a dinner table cover most of the beach. I scan for the body again, but I can't see it from here. I turn around and start descending hand over hand, shoving the toes of my boots in any crack they can find. I get about ten feet from the top and look down again. Can't help it. I don't care for heights. I can't even see the deputy. I start down again and don't dare look anywhere but straight ahead. I hang on to the rope and try to lean away from the rock face like they taught in the academy.

"Watch out for…" a voice comes from below.

My foot picks that exact moment to find probably the only loose shale on the side of this cliff and I slip. Two things save me. There is a small sandy area where Deputy Davis is standing four or five feet below me.

And I land on top of him.

We look like a Jenga puzzle game, all arms and legs askew. The breath is knocked from me, and I can hear Deputy Davis grunting. He'd better not be enjoying himself. I roll off and he helps me up. He begins brushing the sand and dirt from the back of my jacket while I use my fingers to comb the sand out of my hair. He brushes the back of my butt and I move away.

I'm armed.

"I owe you one, Deputy Davis," I say.

Actually, I owe him two—black eyes—if he touches me again.

"Not necessary, ma'am. I mean Detective Carpenter."

Deputy Davis is a year younger than me. He has thick brown hair and a mustache that screams vintage porn star. Or maybe cop. Cop is much better. He's not particularly overweight, but his stomach somehow manages to roll over his coaster-size buckle. He's a good cop and a total pleaser as evidenced by his willingness and ability to make the climb down. I've tried, unsuccessfully, to break him of the habit of calling me "ma'am" and he tries. I have learned to accept it. He is being a gentleman. It's the way he was raised. He explained to me that his mother taught him to call all ladies "ma'am" and all men "sir."

My mother taught me to lie, manipulate, betray, and worse.

"Show me what we have, Deputy Davis," I say. He likes to be called "Deputy."

He climbs over some of the bigger rocks and I try to keep up. I can see the water lick at the rocks thirty feet away. I still don't see a body. I wonder how Boyd saw a foot. I reposition myself on a large rock and look toward the water and I see it. A bare foot, ankle, and part of a lower leg. Toes pointing up.

We make our way closer until I can see the body. A woman. White. On her back in a small sandy area, a twenty-by-ten-foot stretch of beach. Her legs are pointed toward me, her head toward the cove. Her legs are spread with the rock between them. I look to the left and to the right. Boyd was correct: the rocks block any entrance to the body without going into the water. I will have to go over the rocks to get to the body. Or swim from the boat ramp.

I climb on top of another rock and look directly down on the body. Long reddish hair covers half of the face. My guess is she's in her mid-twenties. Just as Robbie Boyd said, she's wearing only a bra and panties. I look around but don't see clothes. Her face is battered; her bottom lip split so much that I can see teeth through the cut. Dark, indented marks circle her wrists and ankles. A wider one encircles her slender neck. Her skin is light blue, but I see deeper blue or black marks on her torso.

It appears she's been beaten or kicked.

I take out my cell phone and breathe in. I've got two bars. I'm tempted to call Ronnie and ask her to climb down. Instead, I call Captain Marvel of the Marine Patrol and advise him of the situation. It will take half an hour for the patrol to arrive.

I also phone Jerry Larsen, our coroner. Since he's in his sixties, he won't be able to make the climb. When he answers, I tell him to meet me at the boat ramp where Mac is parked. He can take the boat. I'd rather not get on the boat with Marvel.

"Do you have a camera, Deputy Davis?"

Davis reaches for his backpack and proffers a digital Nikon.

"Take all the pictures you can," I tell him. "Some of where we climbed down and from there to where I'm at now. How high do you think that cliff is? Thirty feet? Forty?"

"Over thirty, ma'am." He starts clicking away. He doesn't have to be told to get close-ups or to tell me if he saw something unusual. Davis has worked crime scenes before.

"Captain Martin will want to take his own," Davis reminds me, and I say nothing.

Captain Marvel can do whatever the hell he wants as long as he gets the body out without destroying evidence, and gets it someplace where I can get a better look. I always assume homicide until I know different.

Davis says what I'm thinking.

"I don't think she was swimming."

"And she didn't fall from the top of the cliff unless she was running about forty miles an hour before she jumped," I add.

"How long do you think she's been here, ma'am?" he asks.

"Long enough to be dead," I say, and immediately regret being smart with him. "We'll have to wait for the coroner."

I trace a way to move from rock to rock and maybe get down to the body, and I go for it. I slip only once and bang a knee. That's going to leave a bruise. I'm on the gravelly, sandy shoreline now. Ten feet from the body. Her legs are pointed inland. She had to be brought in by boat. Pulled up into the rocks. Dumped. Posed. The tide has erased any drag marks in the sand. The body is at least fifteen, twenty feet from the water, but she has been pulled in between some rocks large enough to hide her body from the water. If Boyd hadn't climbed down the cliff and spotted her, it might have been some time before she was found.

"Damn," Davis says, and I turn toward him.

"What?" My heart is pumping a little.

"I ran out of film," Davis says.

"That's a digital camera. Stop fooling around."

"Sorry, ma'am."

He doesn't sound sorry, but I forgive him. It's the first time he's ever shown any type of humor. He's usually so focused and eager to please that I want him to loosen up. Humor is law enforcement's way of pushing emotion away so you can function under pressure. I wonder what is stressing Davis out. He has worked horrible scenes with me before and seemed okay. I would ask him, but I don't want to see another grown man cry today. I had that earlier with the fire marshal.

As I look over the body, I wonder how she got there. Maybe she was kidnapped, beaten, taken on a boat to be dumped at sea. Then she jumped overboard and ended up here. She would have had to have been pretty desperate to do something like that. I don't even want to step out into the cold water.

The more I look at the position of the body, the more I see a dump site. She was brought here by someone.

I'm punching the sheriff's number into my phone to update him when my phone rings. I answer.

"This is Nan. I've been trying to call you for half an hour."

Nan is an administrative assistant, not my boss. Not anyone's boss, for that matter. Even so, she acts like one.

"Sorry, Nan. The reception is sketchy here. I was just getting ready to call Sheriff Gray to tell him there are body parts everywhere and . . . oh, crap!"

"What?"

I say with a wicked grin, "I just stepped on a finger. At least, I think it's a finger. Or maybe it's a small—"

"I don't want to hear," Nan says. "I just want to tell you that a state patrolman named MacDonald has been calling and asking for your phone number."

"Did you give it to him?"

"I didn't think I should. I told him I'd pass the message on to you. Do you want his number?"

"Yes."

She provides the number.

"Is the sheriff done with the Gamble family?" I ask.

"I can go ask him."

I know she's lying. She knows everything about everybody. Except me. "Never mind. Tell him to call me," I say. I disconnect before I yell at her. I don't know if she's really stupid or if she's just trying to get my goat.

I call Mac.

"I hear your Marine Patrol is coming here."

"In a while," I say. "Where are you?"

"I'm with my car. Do you need me to stay?"

Now I'm getting pissed. "Is there anyone else up there with you?" Besides my brand-spanking-new reserve deputy, I don't add.

"Roger that," he says, and the phone goes dead.

Jerk.

"I looked around the rocks, ma'am, but it might take a couple more guys to do a thorough search," Deputy Davis tells me. "I saw a couple of soft drink and beer cans and put down flags to mark them."

I don't have to ask if he has crime scene flags in his backpack. He probably has a full forensic kit in there. I didn't think of bringing anything. I didn't even want to bring Ronnie of the blue power suit with me.

CHAPTER FIVE

Captain Marvel and one of his crew show up. They anchor the *Integrity* outside the cove and make their way to the shore in a bright yellow Saturn inflatable boat with a five-horsepower motor. The captain eases the inflatable near the rocks at the east end of the beach while his crewman jumps out and ties it off.

Captain Martin comes ashore last. He checks to see that the boat is tied up securely before heading in my direction. If this were a movie, there would be golden sunlight behind him. He's wearing faded cargo pants, but his boots look as expensive as my car. He doesn't say anything to me. Just looks the scene over. He smiles, and I can see why Ronnie is hung up on him. He has a square jaw, piercing cobalt-blue eyes, perfect white teeth, and wavy blond hair cut stylishly. The cargo pants are tight on his triathlon-built frame. I expect him to pose with a hand on his hip, his cape billowing out behind him. I unconsciously smooth my hair.

He nods toward the other deputy, who is wearing an almost identical getup. He's the same size and build as Captain Marvel except he has long, curly brown hair.

The captain introduces us: "Deputy Floyd, Detective Megan Carpenter."

"Floyd."

"Detective."

At least he didn't call me "ma'am."

Floyd digs into his backpack and pulls out full-body waders. They cover his legs and chest with straps going over his shoulders.

He takes out a camera—not as nice as the one Deputy Davis has—and begins wading out to photograph the body from the water, then wades forward until he is only a few feet from it.

"Floyd brought a scuba outfit," Captain Martin says. "He'll check around out in the water while Crime Scene is working the beach."

"That will be good."

I call Mac again. "Has my crime scene guy arrived yet?"

"Yes," he snaps. "I've been trying to call you, but your secretary wouldn't give me your number."

"Hold on," I say, and ask the captain, "Can you go to the boat ramp and pick my guy up?" He nods and goes back to the inflatable.

"The coroner just got here," Mac says.

"Captain Martin is going to meet them at the bottom of the boat ramp. Can you give the phone to Deputy Marsh?"

Ronnie gets on the line. "Deputy Copsey and the coroner are here, Megan."

I hear the barely contained excitement in her words. "Captain Martin is coming to the boat ramp to pick up everyone. Are you finished taking the statement from Boyd?"

"Yes. Should I come with them?"

I ignore her question. "Did you let Boyd leave?"

"He let me search his car. I took pictures of the inside, the outside, the tires, and the plates. I got the information from his driver's license and his address at the school. He wanted to leave. Said he had to get back to school, and if he wasn't under arrest—"

"Okay, I get it. I would have you come with Crime Scene, but you'd have to do it barefoot."

"They always have an extra pair of rubber boots on the boat."

"Hang on." I turn and raise my voice so Deputy Floyd can hear. "Does the captain have an extra pair of rubber boots on the inflatable?" He gives me the thumbs-up. I turn away again and say to Ronnie, "You can come, but you're probably going to ruin your nice outfit."

"It's an old one."

She says that like it's disposable.

"What's your cell phone number?" I realize I never asked that. She tells me. I don't have to write it down. I'll program it into my phone later. "Can you put Larsen on the phone? The coroner."

Larsen gets on the phone. His voice never ceases to amaze me. He's well past sixty, with longish white hair, a six-inch white beard, and laugh lines at the corners of his eyes—all topped off with a merry tone in his voice. He's taller than me, which isn't surprising, and thinner as well.

"I'm coming down, Megan," Larsen says. "I haven't been rock climbing in years. An adventure is in the making."

"You don't want to come that way." I say this nicely. He can be grumpy if I try to tell him what to do. "I've sent a boat to pick you and Crime Scene up at the boat ramp."

"Oh. Okay." He sounds disappointed. He can be pigheaded too, but I can't let him get hurt. Sheriff Gray would disapprove, and Larsen is the only one with authority to order the autopsy.

"I fell on the way down," I say.

Not a lie.

"You would have to be lowered down in a sling," I go on. I know he won't go for that. He stays quiet.

"What is it?" I ask.

"I don't do boats," he says. "I get sick. Don't repeat that to anyone."

"We'll bring the body to you, then." It will be a while. He'll have time to go home, have lunch, watch television or take a nap, then come back. Jeez. I really don't like being in charge. I almost always work alone. This is why.

"How am I supposed to examine the scene from here?"

Good question. I want to tell him I can have him airlifted in, but I don't want to get that sarcastic. He's a good guy. I can count on him to give an honest off-the-record opinion.

I hear Ronnie start to chatter in the background.

"I can use FaceTime on my phone. I can hold the phone where the coroner can view the scene and the body."

"Is that okay with you?" I ask him.

"If I can get a cell phone that has that Face-do-hickey on it."

"Put Ronnie on." I hear him asking in the background if she is Ronnie. Then she comes on the phone again. "Ronnie, give your phone to the coroner."

It's not long before Captain Marvel is back with Deputy Copsey and blue power suit girl, who is becoming my appendage. She is smiling and chatting everyone up, especially Captain Marvel, who is favoring her with his strong profile in tight pants. I reluctantly admit he's a good-looking man.

Deputy Copsey is the first off the inflatable and helps Ronnie onto the shore. She's wearing bright orange rubber boots at least four sizes too big. Captain Marvel hands off several plastic cases of gear to Copsey, then jumps off himself.

My phone rings. It's Larsen wanting to know what's going on.

Ronnie has gotten Larsen fixed up and I have her give the phone to Davis. I don't want her to get too close to the body until they have cleared the scene. Larsen gives Davis directions where to point the phone. Davis moves the phone around to different angles and up closer, then farther away. Larsen says something about very little blood and tells Davis to gently feel around the victim's neck and head. He does.

"There's a knot on the back of her neck, Jerry. Feels like the bone is sticking through the skin. I'd have to move her to tell you more."

"Lift the face up a little and hold the phone so I can see it."

Her long red hair is partially covering the face. Davis smooths some of it away and gently lifts her head. He holds the phone close to her face.

Her lips are deep blue, her eyes open. Davis cants her head to the side. She is younger than me.

Open contusions on her cheeks and chin and several big splits on her lips mar what was once a pretty face. If she washed ashore, the rocks might account for almost every injury. However, it can't account for the dark blue ligature mark around her neck or the positioning of the body.

She was strangled and deliberately posed.

CHAPTER SIX

I have no doubt this is murder. Larsen agrees, although he won't say it officially until he examines the body in person. Crime scene techs lay out a black body bag. It takes Floyd, Captain Marvel, and Deputy Davis to wrestle the victim into the bag and then onto the floor of the inflatable. She can't weigh much, but it's awkward carrying a body. Ronnie and I ride back to the boat ramp with them.

The only thing worse than being in a small boat made of rubber is being on the same boat with a dead body.

At the ramp, Floyd jumps out and pulls the front of the boat up on the concrete. He ties the front line off, and he and Captain Marvel lift the body bag out of the boat and lay it on the ramp. Larsen wheels a stretcher up to the top of the ramp. Next, Captain Marvel and Floyd each take an end of the body bag. Ronnie and I take a side to help carry her to the stretcher.

I watch as Larsen unzips the bag and inserts a rectal thermometer into the victim. Her core temperature is 71.5 degrees. After death, a body generally cools one degree an hour until it reaches the temperature of its surroundings. The outside temperature is in the high sixties. Larsen lifts one of the victim's arms to test for rigor mortis. I see that Crime Scene bagged her hands to protect evidence: broken fingernails, skin under the fingernails, blood. Her arm moves freely. Rigor mortis, or stiffening of the muscles, sets in about two to four hours after death. It can last from twenty-four hours to four days. She has been dead for three or four days. Any longer than that, seagulls would have started snacking on her body.

Larsen uses his thumb and forefinger to spread the eyelids open. Broken blood vessels are etched into the whites of the eyes.

"Petechiae," Ronnie says. "She's been strangled."

"That's quite observant, Deputy," Larsen says, and she swells up like a pufferfish.

Larsen turns the victim's head to the side. The crunching of bones is audible. "Not just strangled."

"Broken neck?" I ask.

He looks in my direction for a split second. "Can't say. Probably." His gaze returns to the body. "Help me roll her to her side. I want to look at her back."

Captain Marvel and Floyd roll her on her side until Larsen holds up a gloved hand.

"Okay," he says. "You can lay her back down." He zips the bag down as far as it will go and looks at her legs and the bottoms of her feet. He examines the skin on her knees. He lifts her arms up one at a time and looks at the backs of her elbows. Then, quietly and solemnly, he zips her up.

Larsen has a windowless white van that he uses to transport bodies to the morgue near Bremerton, an hour away. It is rigged like an ambulance and will accept the stretcher and lock it down. A pathologist will perform the autopsy. Possibly Dr. Andrade, whom I'm familiar with.

I know Larsen saw what I saw.

"The marks on her wrists and ankles," I say. "Were they made by handcuffs?"

"Can't say that for sure. Could have been a rope or a cable. I'd rule out electrical wire, though."

"What about her throat?" It doesn't look like a manual strangulation. There would have been fingermarks, thumb marks in the skin under the chin where the thumbnails cut into the flesh.

He doesn't answer.

"But you agree she was tied up? Rope? Cuffs?"

"I don't want to guess, Megan. I can tell you this: it wasn't a rope. Rope would have left burns in the skin. Abraded the skin."

I didn't have to guess. I am almost certain the marks on the wrists were made by something narrow and metal. I saw deep impressions in the skin but no cuts like wire would make. I have seen this before. Up close and personal. The mark around the neck was something different. It was not as wide as a belt, but the edges were defined.

A collar?

"Can you give me a guess on the time or cause of death?"

Larsen is shaking his head and peering up at me beneath his snowy eyebrows. "More than twenty-four hours. Strangulation, most likely, but I can't rule out drowning or some other preexisting medical condition. I think her neck is broken. Maybe some ribs too. She was beat all to hell."

He leaves with the body and promises to have a preliminary report ready for me in the next few hours. I will have to wait for the postmortem results as well.

Wearing a wet suit, Deputy Floyd searches the water off the cove for fifty yards out from where the body was found. I call Sheriff Gray to update him, and he dispatches a Jefferson County deputy to relieve MacDonald.

Captain Martin takes Ronnie and me back to the boat ramp, where we get in my car.

"Before we go back, can we look at the pictures of the scene again?" I ask.

"Sure."

We trade phones. She set my phone to record the video of Larsen's remote viewing of the scene. I watch and listen to her video interview of Robbie Boyd. She set the phone up in such a way that it caught him from the waist up. I can see most of his movements and expressions as he answered her questions. She asked good questions.

We finish about the same time and exchange phones again.

"Any questions?" I ask.

"Lots of them. This is my first crime scene."

I can tell, but she handled herself pretty well. She didn't throw up on the body, or run screaming out into the cove, or start crying like the fire chief did when he saw the charred remains of someone's beloved pet.

I start. "What do you think we should do next?"

"Me?"

"Yes. What would you do next if it was your investigation?"

"Well, I would try to identify the victim."

"Okay. How do you do that?"

"Missing persons. Circulate her picture," she says, stopping for a moment. "No, that won't work. She's pretty messed up."

I intend to circulate the picture of her face, messed up or not. Someone in law enforcement may recognize her.

"How about give a face shot to all the law enforcement in the area and then get a forensic sketch to put on the news media?"

"That's smart." I smile. "While we're waiting to identify her, what do we do?" I ask.

"See if there are any witnesses around the area where the body was found."

"That's a good idea. But how about we start with the last person to see the victim?"

"You mean Robbie Boyd?"

"He was the last person to see her."

"But the coroner said she's been dead more than twenty-four hours. Would he stick around that long?"

"Plenty of killers want the bodies to be found." I reference the two types of killers: organized and disorganized.

"We learned that in the academy," she says.

"Which kind of killer do you think this guy is?"

"Organized," she says. "He must have planned it. The clothes are missing. He left no visible evidence behind. He hid the body, but not so well that it wouldn't be found. He made it hard for us to identify her by messing up her face."

"Do you think Boyd could have killed her?" I ask.

She thinks a minute. "I don't know. He's pretty creepy."

I go into teacher mode. "Killers enjoy the kill. Sometimes they come back to where they've hidden a body. It gives them a sense of power, control. They know something no one else knows. The posing of the body means something to them. Maybe they're mimicking another killer. Robbie said he was a criminal justice student."

"So he would know about some of this stuff. He told me to either arrest him or let him go. He knew I couldn't arrest him, didn't he?"

She is catching on.

"But he's still a suspect," I say. "What did you think about his statement?"

Ronnie doesn't hesitate. "His story about why he was there in the first place stinks. And he never told me who told him about the place. I don't believe he was just hoping to find somewhere to climb rocks."

"Did he have climbing gear in the car?" She took photographs of the inside and outside of the car but didn't look in the trunk as far as I could tell.

"He had some rope in the trunk. I might have forgotten to take a picture of that. There were gloves on the back floorboard that might be for climbing. I didn't see any carabiners or other equipment. He said he was just checking it out, so maybe he was going to come back?"

Maybe. But he seemed squirrelly to me.

"You said he lives on campus at the college?"

"That's what he told me."

"Did he show you a student ID?"

She looks down at her lap. "I didn't ask for it. Should I have?"

"Not necessarily," I lie, because in her defense, I did kind of throw her to the wolves.

"We'll call the campus when we get to the station to check him out. But you're right: the first thing is to identify the body. Hopefully, someone is missing her."

CHAPTER SEVEN

I start the car to leave and immediately run the case through my mind while Ronnie looks through her phone. I have near perfect recall. Always have. It's a blessing and a curse. A blessing when I need it. A curse when I don't want to think about something bad in my life. I concentrate on what I saw from the cliff.

Rope tied to tree. Coiled. Look down side of cliff at rocks and beach. Can see only rocks and sand and water.

The rope was coiled when Boyd found it. He almost tripped over it. He threw it down, climbed down, saw the body, climbed up. Then Deputy Davis arrived and climbed down before I got there. I didn't know if that meant anything, but it bothered me. I'll call Deputy Davis and see how he found the rope. I should have asked.

I climb down. Turn to see if I can see the body and end up falling on Davis. I climb over several big boulders and see a bare foot like Boyd said. Why was he climbing over the boulders? I'll have to ask him.

I fast-forward. I envision Davis video conferencing with Larsen.

Lift face. Skin. Pale. Blue-white. Lips deep blue. Eyes open. Blue or hazel. Staring at me. Early twenties. Contusions on cheeks. Black circles around both eyes.

I forgot the racoon eyes. Blunt trauma to the head or face causes that.

Split lips.

Ligature marks on both wrists, both ankles, throat. Dark blue. Deep bruising.

I fast-forward again. Crime scene deputies are putting her in the body bag.

I notice the ligature mark around her neck isn't dark blue. It's black. Deep tissue.

At boat ramp. The body is on the stretcher.

Petechiae are present in the eyes. Strangled.

No rigor. Hands are bagged.

Captain Marvel and Floyd roll the body to her side for Larsen.

Lump on back of neck. Not a lump. Something cut to the bone. Half a square in shape.

Wider than ligature. A buckle. Ligature was a collar? Belt? Inch wide? Livor mortis is fixed in her back, buttocks, shoulders, but not her arms.

She was lying on her back after death, but her arms were not stretched out like we found her. The arms must have been suspended above the body. Not touching anything. How is that possible?

Handcuffs? Wrists still handcuffed?

I zone back in and Ronnie is talking. It's nothing important or even about the case. She is complaining about issues with her parents and yada yada. I tune her out and concentrate on what else I saw before the body was placed in the back of the coroner's van.

I watch Jerry Larsen with the stretcher at the top of the boat ramp.

The body bag is laid on the stretcher. Larsen unzips it. I'm thinking how uncomfortable being zipped up in that bag must be.

Then: "She's dead. She doesn't feel a thing."

I've seen a lot of dead bodies. Made a few that way. I was never concerned for the ones I killed. I hope those assholes suffered after death and burn in hell. My heart goes out to this victim. I don't know anything about her. Yet.

Larsen is examining the body. I am too.

Stretch marks on her lower abdomen.

Similar stretch marks on her upper thighs, and when they roll her to the side, I see them on her lower buttocks.

Lost weight? Had a child?

Deep tissue bruising on her upper chest, back, and the right side of her jaw, around both eyes. Some the size of a big fist. Some on her arms and cheeks like fingermarks. She was grabbed by the face.

Some are older injuries that were healing. She was held captive awhile.

The split lip is more recent. I didn't open her mouth to see if teeth were missing. I didn't have to.

The marks encircling her wrists are narrow but deep indentations. Skin was abraded from struggling. Handcuffs. Not likely steel cable or nylon rope. Autopsy will show.

Deep blue bruises encircling ankles in shape of chain links. Reminds me of chain used to hold up a porch swing. Or tie a dog outside. Or chain someone to something. I've seen that. Can't unsee it.

One other thing passes through my mind. I didn't see any rings or jewelry or signs of it. White circles where rings would have been. She might not have been married.

My phone rings. It's Davis.

"Ma'am, I found something."

Do I have to ask? I guess so.

"What did you find, Deputy Davis?"

"I tripped over a rock and there was something scratched into the bottom of it."

"Okay."

"It looks like some kind of devil worship symbol. I'm not good with that stuff."

"Can you send a picture to my phone?"

"Will do."

"How far from the body was it?"

"About ten feet. I must have walked over that rock twenty times. Good thing I tripped, huh?"

"Yeah," I say. "Good thing. Send the picture."

I hang up and my phone dings. I pull over to the shoulder. The symbol was crudely scratched into the rock. Davis took the photo with a ruler to show size. The rock itself is about the size of a toaster. The symbol is a circle with a triangle inside and an oval shape inside the triangle. I have no idea what I'm looking at.

I show it to Ronnie.

"Any ideas?"

Ronnie gets on her phone and taps and slides and taps her finger over the screen until I'm ready to scream. I hate it when people do that. She turns her phone toward me. "The Internet says it's the all-seeing eye of God or the Eye of Providence."

The Internet is never wrong.

Ronnie goes on. "It represents the eye of God watching over humanity."

Organized killers plan their killing. They stalk a victim, decide when, where, and how to dispose of the body, and cover their trail. Disorganized killers are more likely to kill in the heat of the moment or on impulse. They select a target of opportunity, leave them where they kill them. Minimal attempt to cover their trail. No planning. This killer was definitely organized. He left the body where it wouldn't be discovered quickly but knew eventually it would draw attention. He posed it. Maybe he left behind the symbol as well. After all, the posing of the body was symbolism. What it meant to the killer I don't have a clue. It may mean he is watching out for the body. Watching the body. Was he watching us find the body?

Possibly.

Killers also get a kick out of seeing people horrified, or in pain, or at their worst.

I'm pulled out of my thoughts by Ronnie tapping my shoulder.

"Are you okay?" she asks.

"I'm just thinking about this case."

"I looked up news media accounts of other deaths that occurred around the area."

I'm slightly interested but now she doesn't speak. I'm not playing this game.

"Ronnie, you have my permission to tell me things before I ask."

She smiles, missing my point by a mile.

"I've jotted down the details, but the long and short of it is they are mostly boating accidents and accidental drownings, RV fires, stuff like that. Nothing ever happens on Marrowstone Island."

Something has happened now.

"Should we go back and see what Crime Scene and Captain Martin come up with? Maybe they found some new evidence."

Ronnie doesn't give up very easily. Both are characteristics of a stalker and a good detective.

As I drive, Ronnie sits back and is silent for a change. No doubt planning my demise and imagining being swept off her feet by Captain Marvel and living happily ever after. I know there isn't any happily ever after, but I don't tell her. Instead, I notice that her suit is wrinkled.

For some reason that makes me smile.

CHAPTER EIGHT

The mattress is lumpy. Something is jabbing into her ribs. Sharp pain. She doesn't know where she is. Her eyes fly open and she swings her legs over the side. She intends to get up but lands flat on her face. She can't lift her legs. Something is tight around her ankles.

She pushes herself up from the floor to see and pain shoots through her ribs. She sucks in breath through clenched teeth and doesn't dare move until the pain subsides. She wonders if she has broken her ribs. What is happening?

She twists her head and looks around but even moving her head causes a throbbing pain behind her eyes. Her first thought is that she's been in a car wreck. But this isn't a hospital room. The floor is sticky, grimy linoleum that was a light marbled color at one time but is now cracked all over and ripped up in places. A rotting wood floor peeks out from underneath.

She tries to draw her knees under her to get up. She can't move them more than an inch. She lies on her chest again and is immediately sorry. She was right about the broken ribs.

"Where am I?" she says, first to herself and then louder. "Where am I? Is there anyone there?" She listens. No answer. Not even footsteps. A chill runs through her. She's alone, hurt, unable to get to her feet. Even breathing causes lightning bolts of pain to shoot through her side and head, paralyzing her.

The pain subsides a little and she opens her eyes. Carefully, without moving her head, she looks around. She's in a room with a high ceiling. She's in an older home. There are piles of things stacked against the walls and rows of junk surrounding her. Piles of clothing, plastic packaging, dolls, picture frames, blankets, rugs, cloth that may be coats or more clothing or just bolts of material with narrow pathways between them. A portable sewing machine is half buried in one of the piles. The piles are set so close together, it would be impossible to get between them unless she moves sideways. Straight ahead, she can see part of a boarded-over window.

"Hello! Is anyone there?"

She screams this as loudly as she can, but her breath is short, and it comes out no louder than conversation.

How did I get here?

A dim light plays in the room.

She shifts her chin toward her left shoulder. Despite the pain, she moves a little more, feeling a crack in the linoleum scrape her cheek. Her vision sweeps a side of the room and there are more and more junk piles, some that must be over eight feet tall, with only inches between some of them. Boxes everywhere. Some are nothing but boxes of kitchen appliances, a FryDaddy, a Mr. Coffee, a Crock-Pot, a tall box for a Dirt Devil vacuum with an extra-long cord and twelve extra bags included. Randomly, Lego blocks of all sizes and colors are embedded in the floor, as if someone stepped on them, pushing them into the deep black grime.

She lifts her eyes toward the ceiling, ignoring the pain. She is looking for the top of a door or a window that isn't boarded over. What she sees makes her breath catch in her tortured lungs. The tops of the walls and the ceiling are covered with Styrofoam sheets several inches thick.

The room has been soundproofed.

Hot tears run down her face, and her chest seizes up. She lies still for a time, afraid to move, afraid period. She starts to call out again but stops herself.

What if whoever answers is not there to help her?

The young woman has always been independent. She knows that the way to overcome any threat to her survival is to get angry. Angry enough to fight back. She's a fighter. Her mother taught her that. But that was before. In the life she used to have before she became pregnant. Before she went against her mother's wishes and gave the baby away. She made the right choice. Her mom didn't understand. Disowned her. She has been totally on her own since. Moved to another town. Gotten a new job. Made new friends. Dealt with the loss alone.

Her thoughts bring another round of tears and she gives in to it, sucking up the pain. She is crying for her baby. The one she never knew and now doesn't think she'll ever know. She has always thought she can fix things with her mother, given enough time. She defied her mother but is still a good daughter and a good woman. Unlike the father of her child. That man was a ghost. She got a new phone number and changed her appearance. It was enough. He wouldn't look for her too hard. He wanted nothing to do with a child. He made that clear. He looked trapped like an animal when she told him she was pregnant and then said—like he was doing her a great service—that he'd pay for the abortion.

She hears a click from somewhere just out of her field of view. She couldn't even turn her head to look if she dared. She lies still, closes her eyes.

"There you are," he says.

Last night comes rushing back to her.

"I won't tell. Please," she begs.

"You're right. You won't."

CHAPTER NINE

Sheriff Gray is outside, standing on the side of the building, lighting up a cigarette as I park in the lot at the Jefferson County Sheriff's Office. He takes a drag and, while exhaling, fans the smoke away. His wife disapproves of his smoking. He is overweight, eats too much greasy junk food, doesn't exercise, and is a poster boy for bad lifestyle choices.

The sheriff spots my car and tosses the cigarette, crushing it under his shoe and kicking the tobacco around to destroy the evidence. As I approach, with Ronnie following like a duckling, his cheeks suddenly redden.

"I can stop anytime I want," he says.

"Sure."

"I can," he insists. "I have."

"I can see that."

He diverts my attention by addressing Ronnie.

"Did you learn anything?" he asks.

I answer for her. "She was a big help, Sheriff. She took a statement from the guy who found the body."

"Detective Carpenter said I could search his car without a warrant," Ronnie says, looking to the sheriff for clarification. I guess she didn't trust that I'd told her correctly.

"You don't need a warrant if he consented," he says. "Megan should have told you that."

Ronnie's face colors and she keeps it directed downward. "Uh, I meant to say she told me I could search if he gave me consent. He did and I searched."

Liar. Liar. Blue suit on fire.

"Let's go into my office and you can fill me in," Sheriff Gray says as we follow him inside.

I want to keep Ronnie where I can see her. Sheriff Gray brings his office chair out into the room so we can sit in a circle. His chair's seat is mostly duct tape.

I pull my chair out of the circle and into a corner so I can face the door. Never sit with your back to the door.

I fill him in on everything except my observations of the body. It doesn't matter what I thought I saw, except to me. I finish and the sheriff sits for a long time, hand under his chin in thought. He gets up with a squealing of springs and pushes the duct-taped monster back behind his desk.

"So what are you going to do?" he asks.

"I'm going to type up my reports and wait for the Crime Scene, Marine Patrol, and the coroner's reports. I'd like to attend the autopsy if possible." I don't really want to attend, but I want to get another look at the stretch marks. She didn't just lose weight. A baby. Maybe. There may be a child out there somewhere that just lost its mother.

He looks at Ronnie. "Do you want to see an autopsy?"

"Sure," she says with her mouth, but her face says no.

"Take Deputy Marsh with you. She needs the experience."

I've seen my share of dead bodies and death, but I haven't attended a postmortem. I haven't been required to attend one yet and I am sure Ronnie hasn't, either. I'm not sure how I feel about doing so now. I only know I need answers.

A little later Ronnie is behind me, looking over my shoulder at the screen of my laptop. I must have been so deep in thought I didn't notice she was there. I'd forgotten that I pulled up a Google search for Marrowstone Island.

"Why are you researching the island?"

"I was thinking I'd buy it. Build a casino. Retire somewhere warm where it doesn't rain all winter. Buy a yacht."

She giggles. *Really.* "I'm not a big water person. I'll go out on bigger boats, like your yacht. But I don't get in the water unless it's a hot tub or a spa."

Of course not.

"I just want to see how Boyd was able to find the cliff. There wasn't a path to it."

Boyd claimed to have experience climbing, but he didn't seem built for it. Maybe it was nothing. Maybe I was just reading something into his behavior at the scene. He willingly volunteered that he was a criminal justice major in college and immediately asked if he was a suspect. Why would he think that from being asked why he had gone down the cliff? It is a fact that some criminals will insert themselves into a police investigation in order to get the full effect of their kill, a second rush, information. And he was right. The person to report the crime was always the first in line to be a suspect. Then on to someone close to the victim. Spouse, significant other, friends, kids, coworkers, and the like.

I tune back in. Ronnie is saying something, and I have been only half listening.

"Do you want me to call Captain Martin and see if he's found anything?"

She is single-minded. But I haven't checked in with Captain Marvel, nor has he checked in with me. I guess I assume if he finds something, he will call.

"Call him."

Ronnie already has his number punched into her phone and hits the dial button.

"Ask him his opinion on how the body got there."

I think I already know, but he's got more time on the water than I do. My water travel is all by ferry.

"And ask him about the all-seeing eye. See if he's ever seen that on any other beaches before. Maybe it's kids doing that."

"Do you think it was left by the killer?" Ronnie asks, and I'm saved from answering when Captain Marvel answers his phone. I mouth "Speakerphone." Ronnie taps the screen and I can hear voices in the background and then Captain Marvel says, "Ronnie. Good to hear from you."

Oh, please. He has her number in his contacts.

"I'm at the Sheriff's Office with Detective Carpenter *on speakerphone.*"

"Hi, Megan," he says.

"Where are you, Captain?" I ask.

"Still at the scene. We're using the Humminbird—that's for underwater imaging—and radar to see if there's something out here we missed. It's slow going."

"Oh, be careful. You have the other deputy there, don't you?"

"Don't you worry about me, Ronnie. Tell Detective Carpenter that I found something."

I take the phone from Ronnie. "This is Carpenter. What do you have?"

"I don't know if it's important, but you said to let you know if we found anything no matter how insignificant."

I am losing it. "And?"

"I found a couple of light sticks about ten feet out in the water from where the body was. They were floating but they were used up. Like I said, it may not mean a thing. Could have come from anywhere. I've got a box of the same brand on the *Integrity* for night-time illumination in an emergency. I just thought you should know."

"Actually, I have a couple of questions," I say. "Honest opinion. How do you think the body got there?"

"Had to be by boat. Why?"

"Just confirming. Another question: Deputy Davis found a symbol scratched into—"

"A rock," he finishes for me. "I saw it."

"Have you seen any graffiti or markings like it before?"

He's quiet for a few seconds. "Can't say that I have. Maybe. Is it important?"

"Just covering bases. Would you think of a symbol like that as a cult thing?"

"Oh, I don't know. But it's odd finding something like that near a dead body."

I agree.

"Thanks, Captain."

"You bet. And, Ronnie, you did a good job out there today."

"Thanks, Captain," she says. Her cheeks are pink. I hand her phone back.

"You did good today," I add.

It doesn't thrill her as much.

I'm thinking about the light sticks. There would be no chance of fingerprints or anything else and I doubt if Captain Marvel protected them as evidence. He would have told me.

CHAPTER TEN

Ronnie is sitting in the visitor's chair by my desk. Even though she isn't a detective, she witnessed everything that I had seen today. "Find an unoccupied desk. You need to type up your report before you go home."

"But you have a secretary. Can't I just send the audio file of Boyd's statement to Nan?"

I almost laugh. Nan? I'd like to see that. Actually I wouldn't. I don't want Nan in on the little details. Some things are not meant to be leaked. Nan is like a bucket with a hole in the bottom.

"You should type it yourself," I say. "And don't talk about any of this with anyone. That means you give your finished report to either me or the sheriff. No one else unless you get permission."

Nan chimes in from around the corner. "I'll be happy to type the statement, Ronnie."

She has sonar-like hearing.

Nan has never offered to type anything for me. Half the time she doesn't even tell me when I've had a call. Of course, I've never asked her to type anything because she's the queen of gossip. "We've got it, Nan. Thanks."

"Anything else?" Ronnie asks.

I'm thinking of her skill in researching on the Internet. "Start out with the date and time we got the case, when we arrived, who we talked to, and what you did at the scene. You can get our dispatch and arrival time from our dispatcher."

I give her the number.

"But I really didn't do much besides take Boyd's statement," she says.

"That's not true. You were a big help."

Now write a big report. I hope to keep her busy and out of my hair.

"Okay." She gets up and looks around for a computer. "I'll have to call Roy and find out when he and Deputy Floyd arrived."

Roy? "You don't need that in your report. The captain will do his own report." She just stands there. I don't have time to hold her hand. "When you're finished, let me read it before we give it to the sheriff. Okay?"

"Okay."

I pick up the desk phone and start to dial Jerry Larsen's number. Ronnie is trying to get my attention.

"What?"

"What time do I get off today?"

We get off when I say we get off.

"Whenever your shift is over, you can leave. If it's important, you can leave whenever."

Deputy Marsh is not going to make it as a detective. She may not make it as a deputy. But that is her problem. I didn't want to take her on this morning and my gut feelings on her were right on target. Her shift ended an hour ago, but I would have thought she'd show a little interest in this. She sulks off and I get on the phone and call Larsen.

No answer.

I finish my report and collect what Ronnie has typed up. It's actually pretty concise; I have to give her that. We have to wait for Crime Scene's report. They will be working on it for a while. Crime Scene will run the victim's fingerprints through our database and IAFIS, the Integrated Automated Fingerprint Identification System—the national fingerprint and criminal history system kept by the FBI. I have a thought just then. Maybe she isn't in IAFIS or the local and state database. If she commits a crime that is minor enough, some jurisdictions don't enter fingerprints. In Jefferson County, if we arrest someone for a minor vandalism, for instance, we don't require the suspect's prints be put in any database. We keep them in our records, but that's as far as it goes.

I check a few things on the missing persons database and get nowhere. I tell Ronnie she can go home, and she bolts. I check in with Sheriff Gray. He's playing solitaire on his computer.

"I want to catch you up."

"Do you have a suspect?"

"No."

"Have you identified the victim?"

"No."

"Have you done everything you can for the night?"

"Yes."

"Go home and leave me to my solitary pursuits."

I smile politely at his pun and head for home thinking I should have asked Ronnie to get a drink with me. On the other hand I was hoping that I'd seen the last of her. If Sheriff Gray sees us getting close, he will keep us paired.

Not going to happen.

CHAPTER ELEVEN

I sit, engine running, in front of my place in Port Townsend, lost in thought. The thing about being a detective is that you never stop detecting. You don't write a traffic citation or make an arrest and then go home knowing tomorrow will be different. What's on my mind is the preliminary coroner's report. He faxed it over, but I need to clarify what he found. Her hand was broken. There were scrape marks on the wrist and bruising on the heel of her right hand. The trapezium and metacarpal bones were dislocated. The metacarpals are the bones in the palm of the hand, which the fingers are connected to, and the trapezium is the bone that connects the thumb's metacarpal to the wrist. He said my hunch about handcuffs was the most likely cause. She had pulled or tried to pull her hand out of one of the cuffs. The bruising down the side of the hand, from wrist to little finger, indicated she was successful. As if that weren't enough, the metacarpals of both hands were broken, and half-moon-shaped bruising suggested someone stomped on them. He also saw scuff marks on the backs of both elbows. He didn't touch them but indicated it in his preliminary for the pathologist to confirm. To him it looked like she'd crawled on elbows and knees across a rough surface. He didn't see fiber but didn't rule it out.

I figure this is punishment for trying to get out of the handcuffs. He stomped both hands to be sure she wouldn't be able to do it again. She crawled on her elbows because her hands were broken. A pathologist can determine how long ago the bones were broken. That may give me an idea how long she was held captive and possibly when she was murdered. Jerry Larsen isn't a forensic pathologist. He doesn't cut the bodies up to see what made them stop ticking. But he has spent more than half of his sixty years of age doing the job, and with that he's developed some damn fine instincts. Still, I need to talk to Dr. Andrade.

Crime Scene wouldn't have collected a rape kit. That will be Andrade's job in the morning. The rape kit is important for DNA, but the turnaround time for DNA testing and comparison is weeks. The sheriff can request the rape kit be expedited, but it will only tell me if the victim had sex and not with whom. DNA may do that. I know what the crime lab will say. They are always backed up and busy.

It is only one case. For now. I worry that it's not a lone murder. Tomorrow I'll attend the autopsy. Dr. Andrade will be expecting me. Depending on how late Crime Scene works tonight, I don't expect her fingerprints to be run through the local and national database before late morning. If that doesn't give me an identification, I'll just have to continue poring over missing person reports. There are an average of about three hundred murders each year in Washington. Unless I can spotlight this case, the sheriff's request for expedited DNA analysis will go to the back of the line or not see daylight at all, and she will just be a Jane Doe.

I shut off the engine and head up the walk to the historic Victorian. Historic usually equals quaint, but there's nothing quaint about this place. It's a big house divided into two units. At the moment I'm the sole tenant and I like it that way. The other unit is currently, and probably always will be, unoccupied. The last renter gave up because of unreliable heat in the winter and sweltering heat in the summer. The ancient wood floors are dangerously uneven, causing me to trip some nights on my way to the bathroom.

I drop my purse and keys on the table by the leaded glass door to my bedroom, the only part of the house that has any style from the bygone era. I expect someday the place will be razed and the door will end up in some fancy home in Seattle. I have a little office area tucked in one corner and a gun safe in the closet. I lock my gun in the safe and sit at my desk, staring at the blank screen of my laptop.

I think about the dead woman. The nameless woman. The woman who was tortured, probably raped, chained up somewhere like a dog, then dumped on a beach to be found.

I get up and take down a box from the top of my closet. The box contains dozens of mini-cassette tapes of my sessions with Dr. Karen Albright, my psychologist. I place the box on the desk. It's heavy. *Who knew words could weigh so much?* I sit down, pick out a tape, and put it in the little recorder. I get up and go to the fridge to get a glass of wine and bring the box and a plastic tumbler from an Idaho motel back to the desk. I twist the knob on the wine box and white zinfandel fills the tumbler.

Sipping wine, I think about how Dr. Albright brought me back from the precipice that had been my world since I was born.

I recollect how her blue eyes scared me at first. Such a pale blue. Almost otherworldly. How her office smelled of microwave popcorn. How much I grew to trust her. I was twenty when I first saw her. Defensive. Closed off like a street barricade. I had never let anyone inside, but I was smart enough to know that everything inside of me—from my experiences to the bloodline of my birth—had to be exorcized somehow. I'd been traumatized, and while I couldn't see it in the mirror, others did. Night terrors in a college dorm are traumatic and uniquely embarrassing. You don't know what you said, if anything. You don't know if anyone heard your screams.

I open the windows and drink the wine. The box is calling me.

"You'll want these someday," Dr. Albright said.

I refused the gift at first. "I can't see that happening."

She smiled, a warm calming smile. "Trust me. You will. The day will come and listening to the tapes will make you even stronger."

She put her arms around me. We both cried. We held each other for a long time. I knew it wasn't goodbye forever, but it was the end of therapy that had spanned a year and a half. At that time I was graduating from college with a degree in criminology and had plans for the police academy in suburban Seattle.

I draw a breath and peer inside. A boxful of cassettes, each numbered with the dates on which they were recorded. I switch to Scotch. I've taken to keeping a bottle of Cutty Sark in a drawer in the desk. It's cheap but fair. I used to buy a more expensive single malt. One of the "Glens": Glenfiddich, Glenmorangie, Glenlivet. Then I discovered that after the first drink it all tasted the same. I order the real stuff only when I'm in public.

I know I'm stalling. I was drawn to listen to the tapes of my sessions with Dr. Albright, but this case brought the anguish from the past back with a vengeance. Still, I'm curious. I turn on the player.

I hear a short hiss while the audio begins.

Karen Albright starts off with a reminder that I'm not alone on the journey. She tells me I'm strong. This is the path to healing. I remember I wanted to believe that, but my gut told me it was complete and utter bullshit. Deep inside, I knew beyond any doubt, I'd never heal.

Dr. A: Close your eyes, Rylee. Tell me about meeting Aunt Ginger.

She calls me by the only name she knew. Her voice is full of concern and sincerity. I know, or I *feel,* that she is a good person. She believes she can help. I didn't want to close my eyes, but I did.

And I close them now. Thinking about the tortured body of the woman who is now a piece of evidence on the stainless steel table. Being dissected by a pathologist after being bound and beaten, abused, like an animal. Her life was taken, but, worse, her

dignity and worth as a human being was stripped away by force.
Helpless, becoming hollow, drawing into the mind to escape the
horror of what was and what was to come. I think of my mother
and how she lived this nightmare.

I stop the tape. I punch the "play" button and force myself to
concentrate on the words. I can hear myself take a deep breath.

*Me: There was no air in the room. I let out a gasp and Aunt
Ginger is all over me. I don't need CPR. I push her away. I
understand what she said but I feel like the room is spinning
and I'm unable to grab ahold of the meaning of her words.*

I think about the autopsy tomorrow. I push it down deep and
listen to my words.

*Me: Aunt Ginger asks me, "Honey are you all right? Put your head
between your knees." Of course I'm not all right. In the last twenty-
four hours I've lost my mom, pulled a knife from my dead stepfather's
chest, found out that my biological dad is a serial killer. And not
only did he want my mom, he wants me. Upset doesn't cover it.*

Dr. A: You're safe here, Rylee.

Me: Am I? Am I really ever safe anywhere?

I can hear myself let out a breath. I'm calming down. I don't
know this woman, Ginger, the sister of my mom, the aunt I never
knew I had, but I knew she meant well. I remember she had lines
around her eyes that underscored the anxiety she's held inside
since her sister, my mom, disappeared.

*Dr. A: What did you mean when you said your biological
father wanted you?*

Me: He found out my mom was pregnant. He kidnapped her, held her like a toy, raped and tortured her, but she escaped. And she had me. My aunt said he'd made it known that he felt I belonged to him. That my mom still belonged to him. I felt a rush of bile. I could never belong to that rapist. That monster. I belonged to the dad that raised me. The dad that creep of a bio father murdered. My hands were shaking, and my aunt looked me right in the eyes and said, "Rylee, I was there when he came for her... and for you."

Dr. A: Go on. What happened?

Me: I asked my aunt what she meant. Was she there when I was born? I was a little angry that she knew me and I didn't know about her. Aunt Ginger said I was born in the hospital there in Idaho. She had volunteered to be Mom's birthing coach. Mom was just sixteen when I was born. The same age I was when I found out all of this. My mom didn't want to look at me, then she said she was glad she had a girl. I found out she said that because if it—if I—had been a boy, she was afraid she'd see her kidnapper's likeness. Aunt Ginger told her I didn't look like him. I wondered how Aunt Ginger could know that, but she told me later that a policeman had showed up at the hospital and brought flowers. He was my biological dad. The serial killer. A cop.

The tape player shuts off. My mind instantly switches back to the case—a defense mechanism, I'm sure. I need to send a full-face photo and physical description to all the surrounding law enforcement agencies to see if they have any record, had any contact, with my Jane Doe.

I hate calling her that. Depersonalizes her. I'll give her a name and decide to call the victim Jane Snow.

I get on the phone and call Dispatch. Someone new answers the phone and I don't want to talk with someone new. I finally get Susie.

"Susie, I need you to put out an all-points bulletin."

"Nice to hear from you, Megan. I don't think you've called me lately. How am I? I'm fine. What has been going on in my life? Well, you don't want to know."

"Susie," I say. "Please don't make me come over there and get nasty."

Susie chuckles. "I'm teasing, Megan. What can I do you for?"

This is another slang cop line that never made any sense. She couldn't *do me* for anything. I play along. "You heard about the woman we found on Marrowstone this morning?"

"We were just talking about that," she says. "Do you have a name?"

"No. That's why I want you to use whatever you have at your disposal to get her description out to every law enforcement agency in our county and the surrounding ones. If we don't get a response, I may want to go wider."

Susie's all in. "What should the message say?"

I give her a complete description of the body and add the possibility the victim might have had a child. I don't want to give out too much information, but I want to get some serious responses. Washington has the fourth-highest missing person rate in the country. A study was funded by taxpayers called the National Missing and Unidentified Persons System, or NamUs. Now every law enforcement agency uses it, including those in Oregon and Washington. I have the app on my computer and had run the description that afternoon. I got forty-two possibles, but none were close to the dates I wanted except two. I found nothing else on those two. Not even a Facebook page. I give Susie the names and other information on those two just in case something was entered since I last checked.

Susie says she'll call me if she gets anything. I ask her to send me an email instead. It'll be faster. And I want to listen to the rest of the tape. I disconnect and drink some Cutty.

The tumbler has somehow emptied itself. The Scotch is doing its job. I take the tape out of the player, put it back in its case, and return the case to the box. I put the tape player in with them and put the box back on the top shelf of my closet and crawl under the covers.

My eyes closed, I breathe in and exhale. Each deliberate breath is meant to calm, soothe me to sleep. Scare away the bad dreams.

It never works.

Nothing does.

It's her.

She comes to me like a scorpion crawling up the stairs. Her eyes are red. Red, like an albino bunny. But not cute. Horrible. Full of terror. I turn from her eyes to the sound of cutting, gnawing into the wood of the steps. It's her, of course. I don't scream. I just get ready. Lifting herself by her muscled arms, she reminds me of Wyeth's Christina's World. *I hate that painting.*

I hate helplessness.

I will myself to wake up. I sit up shivering, staring at the darkness outside my window. I hold the feeling I had in my dream and I wonder if it is anything like how the victims in my case felt when confronted with their killer's eyes. Did they fight or accede?

CHAPTER TWELVE

A light rain mists the trees and grass this morning, sending dewy diamonds into my view as I make the drive to the office. A pair of deer stand in the roadway, taking their sweet time to cross. I live in a beautiful part of the country. Mountains. Lakes. Salt water. Sometimes I wonder if the beauty of the Northwest is a mask covering the ugly that lurks inside. Peel back the image. See the dead girl. Seal it back up.

Go on a picnic.

When I arrive at work, the sheriff has his door closed and I can hear laughter inside. A woman. Her laughter is penetrating. Forced.

Ronnie.

I don't knock on the door, although I am tempted to break up whatever she is trying to do. No way am I going to be stuck with her again. I know Sheriff Gray wants me to take her to the autopsy today, but when she starts talking, the corpse will get up and run. I pick up my files on the case, check the basket for new reports from Crime Scene or the Marine Patrol, then head for the door.

I don't make it very far.

Sheriff Gray calls to me from his doorway.

"Megan. I heard your car pull in."

"You did?" I purposely parked in the farthest parking spot.

"It's about time we upgraded you. The mufflers on that Taurus sound like they belong on a diesel truck."

"I hadn't noticed. The Taurus is fine. I'll talk to you when I come back."

"Not so fast." He reaches in and brings Reserve Deputy Ronnie Marsh out by one arm. She doesn't look excited. She's not laughing anymore.

"Sorry. I forgot, Sheriff." I nod at Ronnie. "Coming?"

She looks at the sheriff and he gives her a serious look.

"You've got to get the whole experience, Deputy Marsh," he tells her. "You might want to work with Megan one day. Not that Motor Patrol's not important. Or the jail. You could always work with the corrections officers at the jail. Have you rotated through there yet?"

Ronnie snatches her coat off a peg by the sheriff's door and hurries over to me.

"We should get going," she says. "Wouldn't want to miss the autopsy."

Ronnie looks pale. Sheriff Gray grins. She doesn't see it, but I do. *The sly dog.*

Outside the Taurus we go through the same routine. Me trying the key fob, remembering the fob doesn't work, using the key. When we get settled, I see that Ronnie is wearing her uniform. Brown twill pants with a light brown stripe down the legs. A light brown shirt with a sparkling new gold sheriff's badge. New brown lace-up boots too.

She sees me appraising her.

"I thought I should wear something I could work in today," she says. "I hope it's all right."

I wonder if vomit will come out of the shirt very easily. Where we are headed, she may need a hooded raincoat.

"Perfect," I say. "It will give you more authority until people get to know who you are."

Ronnie adjusts the shiny badge on the left front of her shirt. Most of the deputies have opted for the embroidered badges. The shiny steel badges make for a good target, and they tear your expensive uniform shirt when they are ripped off during an arrest.

She'll learn the hard way.

"I see you have your hair pinned up," I say.

"Yeah," she says. "I took the self-defense classes at the academy and the instructor kept harping on not having long hair."

I wonder if she thinks I've been harping on her as well. I don't care.

"Oh. I forgot to give you this." She opens her purse and takes out an envelope with my name printed on it.

It is already opened. It's the crime scene report I've been waiting for. I read the report and it more or less backs up what Larsen said last night. It also indicates they checked the cliff for one hundred yards and found no evidence of someone scaling down besides us. It documents every soda and beer can they'd found. The all-seeing eye is in the report and they collected the rock. I may want to keep it after this case is over.

"This envelope was sealed," I say. "It had my name on it. Did anyone else see what's in here?"

Ronnie says nothing. She just sits and looks out the passenger-side window. I prefer the silence but I don't want to start the day out pissed off at her. Besides, there was nothing new in there that she didn't know.

"Okay, Detective Marsh," I say. "What did you make of the report?"

Ronnie straightens in the seat and turns to me. "We didn't find any clothing except what she was wearing. I don't know if you noticed, but the panties were put on inside out."

I didn't.

I urge her to continue.

And she does.

"No purse. No identification. No jewelry. Not even those white bands you get on your fingers when a ring has been on there for a while. Her face wasn't messed up to the point someone wouldn't recognize her. All the bruises and cuts show she was beaten. I think this killer has done this before. It was too thought-out. Except for the panties being inside out."

"Why do you think the killer put the panties and bra back on her?"

"Maybe he didn't want her to be found naked."

Seriously. That's the best you've got?

"Okay," I finally say. "We'll keep that in mind."

"One other thing," Ronnie goes on. "We're convinced the killer brought her body in by boat. But what if he lowered her over the cliff in a sling?"

I jerk my head toward her. *Sling.* But who would bring a sling? How much planning would that take? To get the body over those rocks would take an enormous effort. It took two crime scene guys to put her in the boat.

"Robbie Boyd said he's a rock climber," Ronnie says. "He might have been able to do it."

"He's not as big as we are." I say it but know not to discount the possibility completely. "Keep talking."

She nods. "Okay. Then there's the rock with the symbol on it. Robbie struck me as a little bit of a freak. He immediately wanted to know if he was a suspect. He brought up the criminal justice stuff. I just have a bad feeling about him."

"All good thinking," I tell her.

The truth is, I have a bad feeling about him too.

Ronnie beams at me and faces front again, placing her hands in her lap like an excited child. She has totally forgotten where we are headed and I hate to spoil her mood, but we have to go.

I put the crime scene report in the folder with the coroner's preliminary report and my own summation of yesterday's events. The sheriff has copies of everything except the crime scene report.

"Did you give the sheriff a copy of the crime scene report?" I ask.

She looks confused. "Should I have?"

"I'll give it to him when we get back." I start the engine and pull out of the parking lot.

Ronnie is quiet until we reach the turnoff for the highway south to Bremerton, Kitsap County's largest city and the location of the morgue shared by three counties. "I've never traveled."

"Where do you want to go?" I ask.

Ronnie lets out a sigh. "Oh, I don't know. Anywhere, I guess. I've never even been to half the places around here. Yesterday was the first time I was on Marrowstone Island. I've been to some of the state parks, camping and boating. I guess I'm not adventurous like you."

I wonder what she means by that. What does she know? I think of how my mom used to say that our midnight moves from one place to the next were a big adventure. How we'd renamed ourselves so many times that I probably couldn't remember them all. How we had a code word that would ignite our most unexpected adventure. RUN. The word that told me life as we knew it was over. I stay quiet. I'm good at quiet until I get really pissed off.

Ronnie carries on. "I mean, you've probably traveled all over the United States. The world, even. You seem so..."

She stops and I press her.

"So *what*, Ronnie?"

"I don't know. So worldly, I guess. You're not afraid of anything. You told that state patrol guy what to do and he didn't argue. And you made detective pretty quick. I heard you're the youngest detective with the Sheriff's Office. Guys are jealous of you."

My thoughts go back to the beauty of the Northwest and how I was musing that morning that the pretty mountains and thick forests of evergreens is a mask.

Peel back the layer. See what's underneath.

I'm a lot like that. Underneath the veneer of my tough personality is a girl who would rather strike at a compliment than take it and be grateful for it.

"No one should ever be jealous of me," I say.

My tone is final. Not harsh. But it plants a big period between the two us, and Ronnie stays quiet for the rest of the ride to the autopsy.

CHAPTER THIRTEEN

A pickup basketball game is going on in the lot behind the morgue and I recognize Dr. Andrade dribbling across the court and pulling off a perfect layup. I notice him because he is so out of place surrounded by the twenty- and thirty-something lab and comm center workers. Dr. Andrade is wearing scrubs and lace-up shoes where everyone else has stripped off their shirts and are in shorts or sweats with tennis shoes. He is kicking their young asses by the looks of disbelief on some of the faces.

Good for him.

I park near the door to his office. He sees me and comes over. Not a drop of sweat on his brow.

"Detective Carpenter."

"This is Reserve Deputy Ronnie Marsh," I tell him. He and Ronnie shake hands.

"Nice to meet you," she says.

"That's some grip you have there, Deputy," he jokes, then grins at me. "Are you attending?"

Ronnie looks nervous, then draws herself up. "Yes. I am."

Dr. Andrade begins walking and talking as he leads us inside the building. "Have you ever attended a post before?" Ronnie stays quiet. "I see," he says. "Well this will be quite the experience. I hope you haven't eaten this morning."

Again he grins and gives me a conspiratorial wink.

"I don't think you've attended one yourself, have you, Detective Carpenter?"

"Not here."

I leave the answer vague, so he won't pry.

I don't know Dr. Andrade all that well except from phone conversations and trading emails. One thing I do know about him: he's very thorough in the actual autopsies but not as thorough in his reports. I've caught him on a couple of occasions leaving out pertinent information. In one case a victim was missing her little toe. That didn't make it into his report. It would have helped identify the body we found, because the toe wasn't the only thing missing. The victim had been missing the little toe for a few years, but when I found her, her face was completely burnt off. I don't generally handle the bodies at the scene enough to count their toes.

The door to the autopsy suite opens and my sinuses are immediately assaulted by the acrid smell of disinfectants. This part of the building is painted that color of green I like to refer to as puke green. The hue is fitting for what we are about to view. A long hall, also that stomach-turning shade, opens in front of me and is dotted intermittently with doors. One door is marked with the likeness of a gingerbread man and his gingerbread wife. Under that it reads, "His *and* Hers." I don't find that amusing but apparently the doc does.

"This is the most popular room with visitors."

Very funny.

A continuous row of naked fluorescent bulbs runs the length of the hallway and buzz overhead like a hundred dragonflies. I follow Andrade to a door marked "Examination Room 1."

Ronnie leans over to me and whispers, "I don't think I can do this."

"You'll be okay. If you think you need to leave, you can go. Just give it a try."

She tries to smile. I feel some compassion for her. If she can't, she can't. It's that simple. You never know what you can do if you don't try. Rolland, my stepfather, taught me that. Myself. I've seen plenty of dead bodies. Some in not as good shape as Jane Snow.

I should be fine.

Dr. Andrade hands us paper masks, caps, booties and latex gloves, all in fashionable green.

"Put these on and we'll get started."

I look across the room to where the victim's naked body is laid out on a stainless steel table, arms at her sides, a wooden block propping up her head. An operating room light on a swivel arm spotlights the body to the point where even the pores in the face can be seen. There is a reddish tint on one cheek that looks like smeared-on blush makeup. The nose isn't straight. An assistant wearing a white Tyvek suit with a hoodie and goggles is washing the body down, removing what detritus remains.

Her eyes are still open and fixed.

"I've taken X-rays of the victim," the pathologist says. "She has several broken ribs and broken bones in both of her hands."

I walk with him to the table. He turns one of the victim's hands palm down on the table.

"See this semicircular mark here?" He points to the top of the hand, and I can see what looks to me like the impression of the heel of a shoe or boot.

"Heel mark?" I ask.

"Look closer," he says. "See the little intermittent spaces in the mark? It's some kind of lug-soled boot. I can't see it as well-defined on the other hand, but this one also has a broken metacarpal and a bone in the wrist."

"Could she have broken the metacarpal pulling her hand out of handcuffs?"

"That's what the coroner said. I agree with his assessment. I need to open her up to see how and how long the ribs have been broken, but I can tell you without a doubt that her neck has been broken. And not by a fall. Someone twisted her head."

He puts up his hands like he's holding a basketball and twists quickly. "It was intentional. He knew what he was doing."

"Did she die from that?" I ask.

He keeps his eyes on mine. "Not necessarily. It could have been done after death."

I lean closer and study her head and neck. The neck doesn't look straight. I see the same bruising and busted lips as at the recovery site, but under the bright light they appear darker, deeper, as if they hadn't yet started healing.

"How old would you say the bruises are?" I ask.

Andrade looks at them and touches several. "They're all different ages. Some, like these," he says, and puts his finger on the bruising on a rib, "are maybe a week old. Maybe less. But some are only a couple of days old."

I look at Ronnie and her eyes are scrunched up.

"You don't have a name yet?" Andrade asks. "Any idea when the last time someone saw her alive was?"

I shake my head. I don't want to jinx myself by saying something negative.

"My best guess without opening her up is that she's been dead at least forty-eight hours. Cause and manner of death are undetermined for now. A broken neck would do it."

I know that time and manner of death is guesswork unless someone sees you die. In most cases it's an educated guess. I have to find out who she is, who saw her last. Besides Robbie Boyd.

Dr. Andrade's assistant uses a piece of dampened gauze and removes the blush from the cheek. I walk around to the other side of the table. Ronnie stays glued to my side. Jane has been kicked in the ribs several times. The marks that encircled her neck, wrists, and ankles are more pronounced under the lights. The skin had almost been rubbed off the side of the neck where the bruise is. I take one last look at the body, starting with the feet. No portion of her body is without injury.

"Did you take a rape kit?" I ask the assistant.

"It was collected and sent to the crime lab yesterday," she says.

I don't ask her if there are signs of sexual assault. Dr. Andrade would check for that in great detail. Rape is a given in my mind.

Ronnie grasps my arm and apparently has quite a grip when she wants. *I* will be bruised.

Dr. Andrade puts on clear goggles. He steps on a pedal under the table. I look up and see a microphone suspended from the light.

He begins by giving the date and time of the autopsy, lists the names and titles of each person in the room, and then indicates that he is performing an examination of an unidentified deceased female. He gives her height, weight, hair, and eye color, then says there are no deformities or tattoos or scars. He states the body has been X-rayed.

"There are several contusions on the head and face," he says, then goes on to describe down to the centimeter the cuts on the lips, the scrapes near the cheeks, a cut on the head, the broken nose, and the broken bones in the hands, all in colorful detail. He stops the recording and separates the hair to examine the scalp. He steps on the pedal and records more findings. The assistant is instructed to shave some of the hair from the right side of the scalp where a deep, sharp-edged bruise can be seen. It resembles the wounds on the ribs. Dr. Andrade postulates the injuries to the scalp and ribs were caused by the same instrument.

The X-ray also shows the maxilla, or upper jaw, on the right side has been fractured and corresponds to the split lips.

He glances at us and says this injury could have been done with a fist, but the person would have had to have been very strong. There are three broken ribs on the right side of the upper chest, two on the lower side of the left side.

"Okay," Dr. Andrade says, "let's turn her."

He and his assistant turn the body over on the table, her fore-head is placed on the wooden block, and her arms are laid loosely at her sides. Dr. Andrade continues looking for cuts, tears, bruises, punctures, or other abnormalities. The bruises here are numerous. I count three places along her spine that show fist-sized bruising. The bony prominence at the base of the neck looks enlarged.

"See this," he says.

"You mean the shape of the bruise?" I ask.

"What does that look like to you?"

Before I can answer, Dr. Andrade's assistant hands him a ruler and he calls out the measurement of the angles. He answers his own question: "A buckle, perhaps. Yes. Definitely a buckle." He measures the width of the bruise encircling the neck, partially blocking out the buckle. "Two point six centimeters wide. Approximately one inch."

He measures several areas on the back and sides of the neck.

"What's one inch wide and has a buckle?" he asks Ronnie. For some reason it sounds like the opening line of a joke, and an inappropriate one at that.

"A collar or belt," she says.

"Give that girl a gold star. We'll have to open her up to see if she's been strangled."

Dr. Andrade holds his hand out. His assistant puts a scalpel in it, and he moves to the top of the table. He pulls the lamp above the victim's head and puts the tip of the blade against the skin behind the left ear. He slices left to right, starting at the bony prominence behind the left ear, ending behind the right ear. He hands the scalpel back to the assistant and uses his fingers to peel the scalp up toward the top of the head. He has to use the scalpel several times to excise the tissue attaching the scalp to the skull, but eventually he's able to get a grip and pulls the scalp up and over the victim's head and eyes.

It looks like the scalp has been turned inside out and put on the head like a hair-fringed sock hat. I feel Ronnie's fingers, which had been so limp when I met her, dig deep into my lower arm. I feel nauseous myself. The sides of the table are angled at the bottom to form a semi-drain that runs into an industrial double-size steel sink. Attached to the faucet is a long hose with a spray head. The assistant uses the sprayer to wash blood away and I watch it run down the steel table in rivulets and pool against the angles before running into the sink.

The blood triggers me.

I'm back in Port Orchard. My little brother, Hayden, is on the kitchen floor. He's crying. His shirt is covered in blood. Rolland is on the kitchen floor beside Hayden. A large hunting knife is buried in his chest. He isn't moving. His eyes are fixed in a thousand-yard stare. The room starts spinning. Spinning. I can't breathe.

"Are you okay, Detective?" A male voice, faint, like it's coming from far away.

"Megan, what's wrong?"

A woman's voice.

"What's wrong with her?"

"Help her to a chair," says the male voice.

"Come on, Megan."

The woman's voice is close in my ear. Too close. Touching me. I jerk away and something catches me in the back of the legs. I sit down hard; my teeth clack together and I bite my tongue. I put my hand over my mouth and zone back in.

"Are you all right?" Ronnie asks.

I look across the room at Dr. Andrade. He has a look of concern on his face, but his assistant looks tired. She's seen this too many times. No doubt thinking that I'll throw up and she'll have a mess to clean up.

"I'm sorry." I get up and start for the door. "I'm going out for a breath of air."

"I'll take notes," Ronnie is saying as I go through the door and almost run to the elevator. I hit the button but it's too slow. I look for the stairs and see the door marked with the silly sign for "His *and* Hers."

I rush into the bathroom, throw the latch, and hurl into the toilet.

CHAPTER FOURTEEN

I clean up the best I can and look in the warped steel mirror above the sink. My eyes are puffy, like I've been crying. I splash water on my face and dry off with paper towels. Pushing my hair back into some order, I stand up and flick the latch open. I walk to the stairs and go up and outside. The fresh air revives me, but I still feel like I'm on the verge of reeling.

I sit on the concrete steps in front of the building. I'm embarrassed. I brought the new girl and *I* was the one who got sick. I will never live it down if Sheriff Gray finds out.

I wipe my mouth with the back of my hand and smell it. I don't think I smell of vomit. I decide to go back in and finish what I am here for. I can do this. I head back in and go down the stairs. My stomach aches a little and that reminds me of the stretch marks on the victim's abdomen.

Dr. Andrade is moving right along. I can see a section of the skull is missing along with the brain. I don't want to ask where they are. Ronnie doesn't notice I've come in.

She's mesmerized.

I find another mask and pull on a new pair of latex gloves. I'm not going to touch anything, but I don't want anything touching me, either. Dr. Andrade doesn't say anything about my absence, but his assistant cuts her eyes toward me. I nod to signal that I'm okay and her face crinkles behind the mask.

I hope it's a smile.

The autopsy takes an hour and thirty-three minutes. All body parts are packed inside, and the body stitched up. Dr. Andrade gives his assistant some final instructions and motions for us to go to his office. We dispose of our gloves, booties, and masks in the biohazard container by the door and follow him down the hallway.

I'm surprised how small his office is. There's barely room for a small wooden desk, three chairs, and a wall full of tall steel filing cabinets.

"I'd offer you coffee, but as you can see, I don't have room for a coffeepot."

He says this with a grin and I suddenly like him.

I take a chair and Ronnie takes another. She hasn't said a word about my sudden departure, but the day isn't over yet.

"I can tell you some of what will be in my report," he says. "The victim is approximately twenty-two years old." Next he gives us a physical description: height, weight, hair color, eye color.

Then he gets into what I am most interested in.

I lean closer and take in every word.

"Marks on her wrists were from hard bindings. I will say handcuffs could have made those marks, not rope or wire, but I can't be one hundred percent sure and I'll say that in my report. The band of bruising around her neck was caused by something an inch wide, leather, with a buckle. I say leather because I picked some pieces of material out of the scrape it left on her skin. The bruising was different depths on the left and back side of the neck as if it were pulled tightly or yanked at times. That's why the buckle cut into the cervical bone."

He pauses and holds his hands down like he's gripping a golf club. "Imagine a dog on a leash and the dog is straining against it. As to cause of death: strangulation. The ligature around the neck fractured the hyoid bone and the bruising was deep around the larynx. The neck was broken afterward."

"What about the stretch marks on her body?" I ask.

He gives me a quick nod. "She's had a baby. More than a year ago. The stretch marks are healing and silvery in color. That would indicate it has been more than a year from the birth of the baby. Sometimes while pregnant the pubis symphysis will separate, but that won't show on an X-ray at this point, of course. The vaginal walls were very loose. I can say definitely that she had a child."

That is terrible news for a baby out there somewhere, but it is good news for me. If she had a child, she might have a husband, a boyfriend, someone to report her missing and identify her. I haven't had any luck at this point. Her fingerprints have revealed nothing. The fibers on the body and the bits of leather collected will need to be confirmed. I have to call Crime Scene and make sure they've requested DNA testing.

"She was raped very recently before her death, Detective," he says. "There was tearing in the vaginal wall and bruising on the labia and vulva. It may have happened during rough sex or something was inserted, causing the damage."

That surprises me. He didn't mention that during the autopsy while I was in the room. "Are you sure?"

The forensic pathologist nods. "I took scrapings of the area and they're being sent to the crime lab to look for pubic hair, tissue, fibers, that kind of stuff. I swabbed her inner thighs and sent that off as well. If there is semen on her, it didn't show up on black light. She may have been cleaned by the killer to destroy evidence."

Dr. Andrade has been very thorough. I knew Crime Scene swabbed her hands, fingerprinted her, and scraped under her nails. Their report will show any results from the lab.

As we leave, my mind is on overload. I don't even know how Ronnie and I got into the Taurus. I am suddenly driving. I was right about the cause of death, and apparently Dr. Andrade thought the marks on her neck were caused by a belt, even though he didn't put that in his report. She was raped and maybe worse. And there was a baby roughly a year ago.

My mother was kidnapped and treated like Jane Snow. Confined, beaten, raped, left waiting to die.

I wonder how much empathy Ronnie can have for the victim. Probably worst thing that's ever happened to her is not being elected homecoming queen. I know that's not fair. She's been a help. She's been a pain, too, but she came through like a trouper today. She stayed through the entire autopsy, didn't throw up, didn't complain, and, more importantly, when I'd asked her not to mention my loss of composure to anyone, she said, "Mention what?"

CHAPTER FIFTEEN

The sun finds an opening in the clouds and sets the scenery along the highway to Jefferson County afire in a thick splinter of golden light. It's early afternoon, and in another hour the shipyard traffic from Bremerton will crowd the roadway as workers head home after a long shift. The ferry dock isn't far, and I think of the last time I took the boat to Seattle. It seems like eons ago. I definitely need to get out more.

The respite from the case is fleeting.

"Our only suspect at this point is Boyd," I say. "When we get back, let's see what more we can find on him while we wait for the evidence to be sorted out."

"I looked him up on the Internet last night," Ronnie says.

When were you going to tell me?

"Nice. Did you get anything?"

Ronnie punches and swipes like crazy. "Bingo. Here it is." She stops and stares at the phone, her mouth agape. "Oh my God!"

I wait, but not for long. I don't have to.

"This wasn't on here last night."

She holds the screen where I can glance at it. There is a selfie of Boyd with the state patrol vehicle behind him. Ronnie swipes again and there's a picture of me. It's not my best look. I concentrate on the road again. Cell phones have made people crazy. They drive crazy. Texting and driving should be a twenty-year prison sentence. Texting and hitting me while driving should be the death penalty.

She swipes several more times. "Boyd is quite the water lover. He's got his own website. He is a tour guide for whitewater rafting, canoeing, kayaking, you name it. He's got a section in here titled 'Killing Box' and has a bunch of pictures of them. Luckily for him there isn't one of our crime scene."

My phone rings. It's Sheriff Gray.

"You coming back to the office?" he asks.

"We're on the way." I fill him in on what we learned at the autopsy. He doesn't seem surprised. I guess with his years of service not much surprises him.

"Where are you exactly?"

"We're about halfway to Hadlock. What's up?" I can tell it's important or he would wait until we got back to the office.

"I just got a call from the state patrol I thought you might be interested in."

"I already talked to the state guy at the scene. MacDonald. He didn't know anything. His shoes were sure shiny, though."

"Not him, Megan, and be nice. They have a tough job, and you might need them to back you up someday."

He is right, of course. "So who did you talk to?" And why would I be interested?

"Trooper Lonigan. Working out on Marrowstone Island today. He got your APB and wants you to call him. He may have a lead on who your Jane Doe is."

"Jane Snow," I correct him.

"What?"

"Nothing, Sheriff. Give me the number and I'll call from where we are." I pull over and write down the number Sheriff Gray gives me, but I don't really need to. I'm good with numbers.

When I hang up, Ronnie says, "Marrowstone? Maybe she's from there."

"Yep." I dial the number and it's answered promptly.

"State Patrol, Lonigan."

"This is Detective Carpenter, Jefferson County Sheriff's Office. Sheriff told me to call you."

"Okay."

I wait. Why is everyone making me wait today?

"Why am I calling you?"

"'Cause I got your bulletin about the missing woman and a scary photo. I understand from MacDonald you found the body down at the state park. I was in the Nordland General Store a while ago. You know where that's at?"

I don't.

I say, "I think so."

"They got some really good sandwiches there. But anyway, I was reading your bulletin while I was eating an early lunch and I said something to Cass. She's the owner. Makes a mean meat loaf, too, I'll tell you."

I am silent this time. I'm hungry too.

"Anyway, I told her what Mac said, and what you had in your bulletin, and we put two and two together and come up with Joe Bobbsey."

There are hundreds of state patrol officers in Washington State and I had to draw the simple-minded one.

"Joe Bobbsey is my victim?" I ask, confused.

"No. I'm getting to that. You probably don't know Joe. He moved here from Indiana about ten, fifteen years back. He was a farmer but now he owns some land and built fishing cabins."

I say it this time: "Okay."

"Well, Cass says there's a youngish woman that matches your description in the store weekly. She said the lady gets her groceries here. She'd do better to go to one of the new big stores in Silverdale. Cheaper by far and a better selection too."

"Cass?"

"Cass runs the place. Says the woman always pays in cash. Has a pocketful of dollar bills and change. So, anyhow, she didn't come in this Sunday. She matches the description and I thought I'd check it out for you."

"Do you happen to have a name for the woman who rents from Joe Bobbsey?" I ask, thinking I'd better be specific. Yes-or-no questions are best.

"Her name is Leann Truitt."

"Do you have an address for Leann Truitt?"

Ronnie writes in her notebook.

"Yep. You won't be able to find it without Joe Bobbsey. There aren't any roads to his cabins. Just a trail through the woods. Not even a trail to some of them."

"Where are you?"

Lonigan tells me.

"I'm almost in Port Hadlock now. I'll meet you in a bit."

"Go to the Nordland General Store and I'll find you."

I disconnect the call.

"We got our first good lead," Ronnie says. She looks excited. It may pan out. May not. Either way, we have to check.

Then we need to run down Robbie Boyd.

CHAPTER SIXTEEN

On the way, Ronnie gives me an oral history of Marrowstone Island she's pulled up on her phone. If that thing weren't so useful, I'd be tempted to pitch it out the window into Puget Sound.

"Marrowstone is named for Marrowstone Point, discovered in 1792 by George Vancouver, a British explorer. He called it Marrowstone because of the hard clay-like soil."

I don't tell her to shut up. She's excited and this seems to be how she blows off steam.

"The census shows 884 residents. There are no cities. Just a couple of state parks. Four hundred and thirty-two households and only ten percent of them have children under eighteen years old. Can you imagine?"

"Wow!" I say.

I'm totally uninterested.

"No resident is under the poverty line. That's amazing."

"Sure is."

We cross the causeway to Indian Island.

Kilisut Harbor spreads out to our left. I see a sign for beach cottages telling me to turn right onto Robbins Road, but that's the wrong end of the island. I head north where State Route 116 is Flagler Road and follow Kilisut Harbor for a long while before the island makes a big thumb and creates Mystery Bay. According to Ronnie's GPS, the Nordland General Store is right there at Mystery Bay.

Much of the area has been turned into farmland and vineyards, with a scattering of small businesses and its very own RV park. A road sign for Mystery Bay is coming up, and another, bigger sign for the Nordland General Store. I follow the directions and end up in the gravel parking lot in front of a one-level flat-roofed building. The wood-paneled structure has been added on to several times. The general store is on one side, Mystery Bay Sails and Canvas in the middle, and, on the end, is a post office. A boat rental place is across the street on the bay. All it needs is a gas pump, a garage, and a church for a complete community. One-stop shopping.

Next to the Taurus are a couple of vans loaded with camping gear and kids and older couples who must be the grandparents. The grandparents look frazzled but happy. I don't know who my grandparents are. On my mother's side I know my grandparents were awful people that more or less ran my mother off when she was sixteen, pregnant, and scared. I don't want to know them. On my biological father's side, I never went down that path. I never cared as long as they weren't a threat to me or my brother.

Ronnie twists in the seat and looks around. "Didn't Trooper Lonigan say there was a restaurant here?"

I see signs in the window advertising only Port Townsend microbrewed beer. Pass. I also don't see a state patrol car. We get out and go inside to find Lonigan.

Inside is nothing like I imagined from the car. It's spacious, with white-painted shelves and freezer cases stocked with anything and everything a person would need to grocery shop and stock up on beer or wine to boot. There are also household items: toaster ovens, coffeepots, both electric and the old-type percolators, wire potato mashers, hand blenders, dishes and mugs and silverware. Looking out through the front picture windows, I can see the porch with its rocking chairs and benches and a table where kids are playing checkers. On the inside, in front of the window, are a full coal bucket and scoop beside a cast-iron potbellied stove that must date to the nineteenth century. Grouped around and facing the stove and windows are a half dozen wooden chairs. The chairs are heavy, well-made, and well used.

There is no one in the store. "Hello? Anyone here?"

A woman, maybe forty, maybe fifty, shorter than me and heavier than me by about forty pounds, comes up from behind the shellacked wooden counter. She pats her silver hair into place and pulls the loose strands back and twists them into a ponytail.

"If you're looking for anyone, they ain't here." She smiles when she says this, which makes me smile. "Prince Harry and Meghan will be here tomorrow."

She rubs her hand on her apron and holds it out. "Cass."

"Megan. And this is Ronnie." I don't know why I introduced us by our first names. Reflex. She is Cass; we are Megan and Ronnie.

"I know who you are. Lonigan told me you were coming."

"He was going to meet us here. I guess he got busy."

Cass smirks. "Yeah. Busy. Sure. If you say so. I've called Joe. He should be here shortly. He's out breaking arms, collecting rent."

I notice her expression is more serious when she talks about Joe Bobbsey. She doesn't like him.

"Do you know about how long he'll be? We need to show him a picture."

"You can show it to me if it's of Leann. She comes in on Sundays. Like clockwork, that one."

I exchange a look with Ronnie. "The picture is of a deceased woman. You might—"

"Honey, I've been around. I've seen dead people. Let's see it."

I have brought the file folder in with me. I open it and take out a five-by-seven-inch close-up of the victim's face. Cass barely looks at it.

"Yeah. That's Leann all right. Poor girl. Poor, poor little thing." In the next breath: "I forgot my manners. Lonigan said you might want to eat. Even detectives have to eat lunch."

"We really just need to see Joe and ask some questions." When I say this, I can see the disappointment on Ronnie's face. There is a plastic display case filled with pastries and, best of all, big cinnamon rolls smothered in white icing. "But maybe we can have one of the cinnamon rolls you have there."

"You'll have time to eat if you want to talk to Joe. He's on Joe time. He'll get here when he gets here. I told him to hurry up, but he won't." She mutters something I can't quite hear. "Let me get you a proper lunch."

Cass disappears through a door. I hear plates clack and smell something heavenly. She's back in less than a couple of minutes and carrying two platters filled with food.

"Have a seat over by the stove. You'll have to eat on your lap. Everyone does. It's kind of a thing here." She laughs again and I find myself chuckling along with her. I can't help it. I've eaten on my lap in cars for years. Ronnie sits down and accepts her platter and silverware like she's holding a baby for the first time and doesn't know quite what to do with it. I dig in.

Meat loaf, gravy, mashed potatoes, corn fried in butter that tastes like it was cut fresh off the cob. Lonigan didn't lie. It isn't exactly a restaurant. It's better than a restaurant.

"How about seconds?"

I wave her away. My mouth is full. My stomach equally so. Ronnie keeps her fingers over her lips and shakes her head. I look at the wall clock. We've been here for twenty minutes. Still no Bobbsey. Cass returns with more coffee, and a bell dings over the door.

"Joe's here," Cass says, and goes to the counter.

Joe Bobbsey isn't anything like I'd pictured him. From the way everyone talks about him, I expected a hick farmer with a round belly and thinning hair, wearing a green John Deere cap and chewing on Red Man. Joe is six feet, 170 pounds, and fortyish, with blond hair touching his collar, blue eyes, and a lumberjack's beard.

He looks at Ronnie's plate. "How 'bout a piece of that pie?"

"Fresh out," Cass says, and leans down, elbows on the counter. She looks like a barkeep in an old Western. She motions with her head in my direction. "You have to talk to them."

"I don't *have* to do anything, Cass. I'm here as a courtesy to Ray. I support the police in my own way."

"Yeah. Right. I guess you rent your cabins to honest, God-fearing folks and not to scum of the earth that break into my store or shoplift or get into fights in my parking lot, driving my business away."

"Cass, I don't run a police background check on people that want to rent a fishing cabin. I've got a business to run, just like you."

Cass scoffed. "Like me…"

"I guess you check out all your customers. All the people that rent from me come here for supplies. My customers are your customers. So I guess you're guilty same as me. We've been through this."

"You're right. Go talk to those ladies. I'm busy." Cass goes into the back room.

Joe sits in a chair with his back to the windows. He doesn't introduce himself or ask our names.

"I'm Detective Carpenter. This is Deputy Marsh. If you're Joe Bobbsey, I need to show you a picture."

"My name isn't Bobbsey. It's Bohleber. Joe Bohleber. My brother is Steve Bohleber. We're twins. Moved here from Indiana eight years ago and they took to calling us the Bobbsey Twins."

I stand up and hand Bohleber the picture and say, "It's not a pleasant picture, but I'm told you might know who this is."

I watch for his reaction.

He looks at the photo for even less time than Cass. "Her name is Leann Truitt. She rents from me." His flicker of recognition indicates a melancholy. "What happened to her?"

I don't explain. "Can you give me her address?"

"I'll have to show you, and I'm pretty busy right now. Can you come back later?"

"No."

"Oh. Uh, okay. Do you mean right now?"

"Ronnie will follow you in my car and I'll ride with you." I look at Ronnie. I don't care much one way or the other if she likes it. We have to put on a united front. I can see why Cass doesn't like him.

"Okay. Why are you riding with me? Do you think I'm going to run or something? I'm not a suspect in whatever this is, am I?"

Joe is the second person in as many days to ask if he is a suspect. It must be catching.

"No. You're not." I'm lying now. He just became one. "I just want to ask you questions about your renter on the way. You get us there and you can leave."

"You're not going to tear the place up, are you? I run clean cabins. I check them once a week. If they've done any damage, they're out."

"I don't think Ms. Truitt will be doing any damage," I say. And she's about as out as she can get. It's interesting that he checks them so often. I wonder if he has a key.

Of course he does.

I hand my keys to Ronnie as Cass brings her a to-go box and whispers in her ear. Cass must think Ronnie is too thin.

I do too.

CHAPTER SEVENTEEN

Parked right out front taking up two spots is Joe's Jeep Grand Cherokee Laredo four-wheel drive. A yellow two-person kayak is strapped to the top. The vehicle is coated in a thin, whitish gray dust. The kayak, however, is dust-free. I get in the passenger seat and immediately catch a whiff of marijuana. Probably more than a whiff. Joe notices that I notice. I don't say anything.

He could shoot up heroin as long as he takes me to the victim's house, or cabin, or whatever it is.

We drive north down Flagler for a couple of miles before coming to the opening where Mystery Bay is fed by Kilisut Harbor. I remember what Ronnie said about eight hundred or so people living on the island. I wonder what it would be like to have this type of seclusion. Isolation. Would it help me deal with my life, or socially alienate me even more?

We continue north toward Fort Flagler Historical State Park and turn onto a gravel embankment, then onto a rutted path between farm fields, and then over tall grass toward Mystery Bay.

"Does anyone live with her?" I ask.

He stares straight ahead. "Better not have anyone there."

"Is that a yes or no?"

"It's an I don't know but she'd better not."

"Does she have a rental agreement?"

"Yep."

"Do you require a reference?"

"Yep."

"Do you mind answering with more than a yep?"

"Look," he says, looking at me for the first time, "I took time out to drive you the hell out here. I'll send you the rental agreement. I guess it won't do me no good now, will it?"

"Do you remember who the reference was? Mother? Father? Employer?"

Killer?

"She didn't say, but I talked to a Jim Truitt. I guess he's related somehow. Rich guy. I don't recall how it came about, but I got his phone number and address on the rental papers."

We enter a wooded area and the Jeep slaloms between the towering firs. I can see a blue strip of horizon like dashes and dots in the distance: Mystery Bay.

"And I don't remember the address," he says. "She might have a copy inside if you want to look. I got a key."

He isn't telling me everything, so I press him for details.

"Do you know Jim Truitt?"

"No. Never heard of the guy. Why don't you bother him instead of me?"

"You just said he's rich. How do you know that?"

He doesn't respond. I don't say anything but I'm going to find Jim Truitt. And I'm going to send a deputy to Joe's house to get the rental agreement. I don't want him sending it to me on "Joe time," as Cass put it.

The Jeep comes out on a narrow dirt road. A clearing with a log cabin is dead ahead. I look back to see if Ronnie was able to navigate the rough terrain. I don't see my car but the way through the trees should have new tire tracks through it. I hope my Taurus isn't in a shallow ditch with a busted axle. I'm relieved when she pulls up beside us.

I don't plan to go inside the cabin. In fact, I don't even want to walk around the cabin. This might be where the murder took place. She was bound, beaten, and sexually assaulted. I have personal knowledge of that kind of sicko. Now that I have one victim, I have to search for others.

I take Joe's key to the cabin, and Ronnie writes all his personal contact information in her notebook. He lives on Flagler Road, so he won't be hard to find. She writes his license plate number and vehicle description and asks for his driver's license. He is a little testy but becomes really nasty when I tell him the cabin and area is now off-limits until Crime Scene releases it. I promise he'll get his key back and the place won't be trashed. He doesn't believe me.

While we wait for Crime Scene techs to arrive, Ronnie puts Joe in the Taurus and records a statement. I listen in: she asks all the right questions. She doesn't make the mistake some investigators make and try to be chummy or too authoritative. She lets him ask questions and she lets him answer his own questions.

Smart.

Before I let him leave, I ask, "Where is your twin brother now?"

He shakes his head.

"You don't know, or you won't say?"

"I don't know," he says. "He took off right after Leann rented the cabin. Been a while since I heard from him."

"Did you tell my deputy where he lives? A phone number? Some way to find him?"

Ronnie shakes her head.

"Why not, Mr. Bohleber?"

"I'm not my brother's keeper. He has half this business, but he just packed up and took off. He didn't tell me where he was going and, to be honest, I don't want to know. He's left me with all the work and he's still getting half the proceeds."

"What bank?"

He just looks at me.

"I'm not going to ask again, Mr. Bohleber. If I have to get a warrant, I'll have to consider you a suspect and this will get much messier."

Ronnie hands him her notebook and he writes it down.

"There," he spits out. "Is that all? Can I get back to work?"

"Sure," I say. "After my deputy gets some images of your tire treads."

He makes a face, and Ronnie does as she's asked.

When he drives away, she takes more photos of the tire tracks in the damp earth.

I call Sheriff Gray with the update. Ronnie gives me the exact GPS coordinates from her phone, and I pass them on. I ask the sheriff to send another deputy to Joe Bohleber's house to get the rental agreement. I ask if he will run criminal records on Leann Truitt and Jim Truitt. He agrees but he sounds a little hesitant. I give him Joe Bohleber's date of birth and tell him about the twin thing with Steve.

Next I call Joe.

"I thought we were done," he says.

"Not yet," I say. "I've got a deputy coming to your address to pick up the rental agreement. He'll write you a receipt for it."

"I wasn't planning on going home."

"Sorry," I say, although I don't mean it at all. "A deputy is already on his way and you've been so cooperative."

"I'll be at home," he says finally. "But I ain't waiting long."

I end the call, and Ronnie and I cordon off a large area around the cabin with yellow-and-black crime scene tape while we wait for Deputies Davis and Copsey to arrive. It's a surprisingly short wait, which is good. The deputies widen the perimeter with another roll of tape.

Mindy Newsom's white van rolls in just then. The name of her flower shop is on the sides, but she isn't there delivering flowers. She has been my friend since I arrived in Port Townsend. She had just graduated from the University of Washington with a degree in forensic science and was new to the Sheriff's Office when I started there. Sheriff Gray even converted an old conference room into a lab for her. Just when she was certified by the state as a criminalist, the job became part-time. Very part-time. Jefferson County didn't seem to need her skills on a regular basis. She left, got married to a mill manager, and had a baby. While she was on family leave, she opened a flower shop downtown.

"Is this the only way we get to see each other?" she asks, coming right for me.

I give her a hug. I'm not that close to other women. Not really close to anyone. Mindy is fun, smart. She makes me laugh too. If I had a sister, I would want her to be just like Mindy.

But I don't. I barely have a brother.

"Sheriff says this is related to the body you found yesterday," she says, surveying the scene.

"I've got her identified by two people from her crime scene photo," I say. "It will be good if you can get a match some other way. Is the sheriff coming?"

"He just said you needed me." Mindy opens a side door to the van and pulls out white coveralls. "Are you coming inside?"

Ronnie comes over and I make the introductions.

"I'd like to go in," she says, and Mindy and I exchange looks.

"Suit up," I tell her. "But do exactly as Mindy tells you. Don't touch anything. And stay right behind her."

Ronnie gives a comical little salute.

I shake my head and it passes through my mind that if I had a sister, I would not want her to be like Ronnie.

Mindy gives her a set of Tyvek coveralls, booties, and a mask.

While Ronnie dresses, I show Mindy a couple of the crime scene photos from the cove and a good face shot from the morning's autopsy.

It's a face that no longer belongs to Jane Snow.

Leann is her name.

I sit on the hood of the Taurus and read the documents in the file folder while Mindy and Ronnie enter the cabin. Now I have a name and an address, or at least a GPS fix. I have the landlord, who in my book, was a little cold. I have the hiker, Boyd, who found the body. I have a statement from Cass at the Nordland General Store concerning the victim's habits, and she did have habits. She shopped at the general store every Sunday for groceries. Like clockwork.

Patterns are a magnet for killers.

I think of what I haven't done and what I still have to do when Sheriff Gray calls.

"I've got Leann Truitt's driver's license information if you're ready to copy."

I don't need a pen and paper.

"Go."

He reads off the information. The physical description matches perfectly. The address on the license isn't where I am at present, but she moved here a year ago according to the Bobbsey twin. Gray tells me she owns a '93 Subaru. Forest-green. He gives me the plate number.

"The vehicle isn't here," I say, adding, "How does she go to the grocery store like clockwork every Sunday?"

Before I let him answer, I say, "Either she has a regular ride, or her car has been ditched somewhere."

"That's what I was going to say," Sheriff Gray says.

"Sorry. Just thinking out loud."

I wish I'd stop saying sorry. I'm almost never sorry.

Next I get on the phone and call Susie at Dispatch directly. I don't want Truitt's name released just yet. I still have to find Jim Truitt. I have Susie run the Subaru VIN and plate number to see if it has been tagged and towed. If it was reported as abandoned, officers might have towed it. She finds nothing. I tell her to keep me advised if that license plate or VIN is run by anyone.

"Put out feelers to law enforcement asking them to notify me directly if the vehicle is found. I don't want to make a big deal of it yet."

"Got it," Susie says.

I have sworn to do whatever it takes to find and stop serial killers. This guy isn't one—not yet, as far as I know—but I've got a gnawing in my gut that's about to change. I also don't think Mindy is going to find any evidence of foul play inside the cabin. Call it a hunch.

Leann went to meet someone. And she didn't make it back home.

CHAPTER EIGHTEEN

Ronnie emerges from the cabin, strips off her white cocoon of protective coveralls, and gets into the Taurus. She wears a perplexed look on her face.

"What is it?" I ask as she fastens her seat belt.

"I don't understand. There was nothing in the cabin," she says. "Mindy looked everywhere. Not a sign of blood or a fight or anything broken."

"It's not our scene," I say. "Leann was held captive and killed somewhere else."

"Right, but I hoped we'd find something."

Hope is a nice idea, I think, but it doesn't get a detective anywhere.

I watch the road now as we drive, still thinking about what Ronnie found in Boyd's social media. "Killing Box," he'd called it. The pictures she pulled from his pages were of dangerous obstructions on a river or stream where tree roots or limbs are down in the water. I think of a fish trap in the river: water passes through, but animals and people are caught up in the current and get sucked in. It's nearly impossible for them to fight their way out and get free. Boyd had pictures of small animals and even deer that had drowned there.

A "killing box."

Sick.

I need to concentrate on talking to Jim Truitt, Leann's father. DMV records put him in Port Ludlow. I have to know more about her.

"What did you think you'd find in there?" I ask as my thoughts turn back to Ronnie.

"I wanted to find *something*. *Anything* that would give us a lead."

I smile inwardly. Ronnie is already talking like a detective on television. She isn't wrong, though. I, too, hoped she and Mindy would find a note or something to indicate this woman had a life. A picture of a boyfriend. Or a girlfriend. Ronnie said there were no photos. Not on the walls, the dressers, anywhere.

"Walk me through everything again."

I haven't been listening for a while.

"There was nothing unusual about it."

"Close your eyes and visualize walking in the door. I've found the technique to be helpful. Try it."

It *is* helpful. When I was sixteen, my stepfather was murdered, and my mom was kidnapped. I drove all night, desperately trying to find her. I had only just gotten my learner's permit. My knuckles ached and I pulled into a rest stop next to a minivan. The windows of the minivan were steamed up.

A little girl was in the back, sleeping, and when I stopped next to the van, she opened her eyes and I nodded at her. I wondered if she was on the run too. I'd been that little girl in my past. Sleeping in our car, waiting, always waiting. This girl looked to be four or five years old. The minivan was loaded to the ceiling with stuff. It wasn't camping stuff, but it looked like she and whoever was with her was living in the van. I saw a man behind the wheel and wondered where the mother was. The little girl was pretty. She had dark hair, dark eyes. She saw me watching and moved her finger through the condensation on her window. She made a circle with two dots inside. Then an arch. *I'm sad. I'm on the run.* I couldn't help her. Not then. But later. When I caught the bastard who killed my stepfather and I rescued my mother, I went looking for the girl in the van. I used the visualization from that day I first saw her. I remembered everything. Everything about the minivan, the man sitting behind the wheel, the sad look on the girl's face, the license plate number...

I had to rescue her.

The license plate number was what led me to find her and set her free.

I am still caught up in that memory when I feel Ronnie tug at my arm. I swerve a little across the centerline and a truck blares its horn. I get back in my lane. I'm tired and this case is bringing back ghosts of the past. I had to become someone else to do what had to be done back then. I don't want to be that girl anymore, but I have to be.

Leann needs me too.

"I thought you nodded off," Ronnie says. "Didn't you get any sleep last night? Or are you like me? I eat heavy food and I go into a carb coma."

Ronnie keeps chattering and I don't feel like interrupting her. She was disappointed that there wasn't a note from the killer in the cabin:

Hey. It's me. I killed Leann Truitt and I'm waiting to be arrested. Here's my name, date of birth, and location...

That isn't fair and I know it. Ronnie has tried to be helpful. And she hasn't yet asked when she can get off work.

"I think you saw more than you realize," I tell her. "That's all. I know you know this stuff, but it really works."

She closes her eyes, theatrically leans her head back against the seat. "Okay, but this seems weird."

"What did they say about listening to your training officer?" I ask.

"Uh. They said the training officer is always right. Do what they tell you to do."

"That's good. So I'm your training officer today. I want you to remember everything that you did at that cabin."

"Sorry, Detective. I'm just nervous, and when I get nervous, I talk."

Understatement of the new millennium.

She keeps her eyes shuttered. "I signed my name on a clipboard for the deputy guarding the door. Mindy went in and I tried to stay in her footsteps."

I interrupt. "What is the floor made of?"

"Wood. Planks. Worn smooth."

"Is it dirty? Dusty?"

"Not dusty. Not superclean. I wouldn't eat off of it. For a cabin, it's pretty clean."

"Look around you," I say, my eyes secured on the road. "What do you see?"

She takes a breath.

"There is barely any furniture. A couch. Blue. The arms are padded, but there is a torn spot and stuffing is coming out of one of the arms. An upholstered chair with a high back. Old. Wood legs and arms. Green. A television. Flat-screen. Turned off. A counter separates the front room from the kitchen. The bedroom and a bathroom are behind the kitchen through a door."

"Is there a table in the front room?"

She stirs a little but keeps her eyes closed. "A small one. Beside the chair. Round. Drop-leaf. There's a plant on the table and a glass of something beside the plant. A clear tumbler. Red liquid. I didn't smell it, but it looks like a cranberry gin and tonic. I like them too."

I make a note of that in case I invite her over someday.

"The kitchen?"

"No table. Just the countertop. A coffeepot. Electric. Mr. Coffee, I think. There's burnt coffee in the bottom of the pot. The switch is in the 'on' position. She's left the pot and the coffee burnt up. It must have shut itself off. I don't smell it."

I push for more. "Any papers on the table or countertop?"

"An envelope on the counter. Mindy peeked. It was a money order made out to Joe Bohleber. Eight hundred dollars."

She's doing damn good for not wanting to do this.

"Stove?"

Ronnie cocks her head slightly, remembering. "Gas. There must be a propane tank outside. I looked at the burner knobs. All off. I was worried. She left the coffeepot to burn up. Nothing on top of the stove. Wait. There was. An iron skillet. The skillet looked like there was bacon grease in it. Old. I didn't smell it. I didn't smell anything except for in the bathroom."

"Go to the bathroom, then."

"No door. It's missing. The sink is rust stained. Formica countertop. A bar of soap...lavender...and a jewelry thingy. You know, one of those ceramic hands with fingers spread so you can put rings and necklaces and stuff on the fingers? There are no rings. A gold chain with a locket."

"Did Mindy see the locket?" I ask.

Ronnie's head bobs a little. "Yeah. She opened it. It was gold. Real old looking. Inside was a picture of an older man on one side, a picture of a baby, a newborn on the other. Mindy let me take pictures of it with my phone. Want to see?"

I do and start slowing the Taurus.

I pull over onto the shoulder to see. The old man's picture is one of those old black-and-white shots. A stern-looking face, sharp nose, and dark, bushy eyebrows. He looks to be in his forties, which I suppose is ancient to Ronnie. The baby is not much more than a face shot. This one in color. The baby looks chubby, but I guess most babies look chubby. It is definitely a newborn. Its dark hair looks like it was glued down in swirls.

"It's odd that she'd have a locket with these pictures, don't you think?" Ronnie asks, her eyes now open.

"Maybe it was her mother's. Or she bought it like that," I say. "What else do you remember? Clothes? Posters? Bills lying around? Anything?"

Ronnie shrugs and looks upward, thinking. "The closet was stuffed with clothes. I mean, she was a real clotheshorse. Anyway, there were several sets of clothes scattered on top of her bed. Three tops, one long-sleeve button-down, beige. One light blue, short-sleeve. One pullover with sequins. A couple of slacks, beige and black. A pair of jeans. They were all pretty old, but still nice. Her house was very tidy. It wasn't like her to leave those lying out. I thought she must have been deciding what to wear. I didn't see a checkbook or purse or anything."

"Why would she be deciding what to wear?" I ask.

Ronnie locks eyes with me and says what I'm thinking.

"She must have had a date."

CHAPTER NINETEEN

Jim Truitt's house is a mini-mansion facing the Twins, two small uninhabited islands that lie between the Bay Club and the peninsula known as Bull's Head. Strike that: it's a full-blown mansion. Nothing mini about it. I can see a dock behind the huge house. Several slips are occupied. Sailboats, a yacht, a cabin cruiser, and some smaller but not less-expensive-looking vessels. I take the twisting, rhododendron-lined drive and come to a parking area off to one side. The driveway continues on behind the house. A black BMW is parked under a covered portico.

"The mah-stuh is home," Ronnie says in a haughty voice.

I ignore her.

I get out and Ronnie opens her car door with a screech that I've never noticed before. Being surrounded by wealth, out in the playground of God's country, the BMW makes my Taurus look like the Beverly Hillbillies have arrived. As I look around, I spot the surveillance cameras. One on each side of the portico. I press the intercom button beside the door and wait. And wait. Finally, a man's voice asks, "Can I help you?"

"Detective Megan Carpenter."

The door opens to reveal a tall man with dark red hair styled in a spiked crew cut. His features are sharp, angular. He has full pouty lips, and his nose is too wide for his thin face. His ears protrude from his head like the handles on a Rookwood vase. He's dressed in blue jeans shredded at the knees and a purple T-shirt with "Priestess Warrior" silk screened on the front. He's also wearing a smile. It doesn't look real. He's somewhere in his mid-forties, and I wonder if we've come to the right house or if there is a cult gathering inside that's passing around Kool-Aid.

Priestess Warrior?

"I'm Detective Carpenter. This is Deputy Marsh." I hold up my credential case again. He doesn't look at it, but he does ogle Ronnie's badge—or her breasts. "I'm looking for Mr. Jim Truitt."

His smile changes to something more akin to a cat spotting a bird.

"Really? To what do I owe the pleasure of a visit from the, uh"—he checks out Ronnie's badge/breasts again—"Jefferson County Sheriff's Office?"

"I'm here about your daughter," I say.

The smile recedes but isn't replaced with concern. It's more like I said something distasteful. "What's she done now?"

"Can we come in?"

He thinks a beat, then steps aside and leads us in to a room the size of my apartment and then some. One entire wall is floor-to-ceiling glass that takes in a sailboat with a candy-striped spinnaker that skims the bay's lead-gray surface. The furniture is expensive and has that unused look of a showroom display. There are framed photos everywhere of Jim Truitt: on the deck of a yacht; with a trophy catch; at the wheel in the cabin of what I figure is his classic mahogany-deck speedboat. Dozens more of sailing vessels, fishing catches, underwater shots; Truitt in diving gear, Truitt in Bermuda shorts, Truitt fly-fishing.

The tableau of photos is a testimonial to him.

None of his daughter, a wife, or any other living being if one didn't include the gasping fish he was dragging from the water. In none of the images, however, was he smiling.

And here I thought money made you happy.

"Is Mrs. Truitt home?"

A shake of the head. "The ex-Mrs. Truitt is living on St. Lucia in the house I bought as a divorce gift."

He doesn't ask about his daughter. That's very strange. I bring her up.

"When is the last time you saw or spoke to Leann?"

"I haven't seen or spoken to my daughter in two years."

A man of few words and lots of toys.

"Do you have other children?"

"What's this about, Detective?"

I open the file folder. "I'm going to show you a picture. It's not pleasant."

I hand him the five-by-seven face shot of his murdered daughter. He lets out a little gasp as he looks at it, but he pulls back whatever emotion he's just exhibited. He passes back the photograph.

He doesn't say, "That's my daughter. That's Leann" or "What happened to her?" The only emotion I detect is a slight change in his voice.

I try to hand the photo back to him. "Can you take another look. I need a yes or no."

He refuses to take it.

"That's her."

I realize that I am being a bit cruel, but I am determined to get some kind of human response from him.

"That's your daughter. Leann Truitt?"

He nods.

I know people process grief in different ways. This isn't one of those. This is almost relief. I want to smack him.

But I don't.

"Can you tell me where she works?" I ask.

He shrugs a little, indicating he's not interested. He says, "I heard she was tending bar in Port Townsend. I don't know the name of the place."

"That's good," I say. "I can find out where." I motion for Ronnie to sit. I take a place on the couch, leaving room for him.

Hoping he will sit and not clam up. "Did your daughter go to college around here?"

He sinks into the other end of the couch and thinks for a minute.

"She was brilliant, Detective. Had a future ahead of her. Then something happened. I don't know what. She wouldn't say. She came home. I guess law school wasn't for her. She said she couldn't see being a lawyer and called them all assholes. She had never used that kind of language in her life. She was angry all the time. And needy. Always needy. I knew something had hurt her, but..."

I wait. He isn't really talking to me. More like he is replaying a tape of the past. A memory that he had to speak to make it real, or to let it go.

"I didn't have a close relationship with Leann. Her mother could get her to open up. That was their thing. But her mother was gone by the time she came back. Left. That was when Leann gave college up for good. I blamed my ex. I didn't know the problem wasn't school or her mother. It was here with her. Honestly, she never made good choices."

"Did you have a disagreement?" Ronnie asks, and I shoot her a look. A rule in investigations is that only one person does the questioning. I don't want him to get defensive and stop talking.

Ronnie gets the hint and becomes invisible.

"Oh, we had a disagreement, I can tell you. Before she left for school, she bummed around the party circuit. There were strong words. On both sides. I convinced her she needed a career. Something substantial to make her mark in life. She wasn't interested in making anything of herself. Then, when things got bad between her mother and me, she agreed to go to college. I had to pull some strings. Expensive strings. But she got accepted and left for school. I don't know if she agreed to get away from the arguments or if she actually saw reason."

He puts his hands together and grips them, closes his eyes, and seems to be repeating some mantra or something, but he's just moving his lips. No sound. He stays like that for a while. Long enough for me and Ronnie to exchange a quick *WTF?* look.

He opens his eyes and notices I'm watching him. "I was making contact. Asking for guidance."

Oh, please, I think.

"I'm afraid I don't understand," I say.

His face takes on a smug expression. "Do you know what a soul contract is, Detective Carpenter?"

I shake my head, not remembering if religious confusion is one of the stages of grieving.

"A soul contract," he says patiently, "is an agreement we have made with other souls before we are born."

I blink. I have no idea where this is going.

"The contracts have a purpose. They teach us important lessons that we choose to learn before we can reach reincarnation. I don't suppose you believe in reincarnation?"

This is all crazy talk to me, but I want to keep him talking.

"I do."

I look at Ronnie and she's nodding her head also.

I'm all but certain he doesn't believe me, but he continues anyway.

"Leann was so much like her mother. They didn't believe in anything spiritual. Anything good that happened was pure luck. Not the result of making a soul contract. They could have looked around at all the things I've provided for them and seen they were wrong. This wasn't all my doing. I was merely a conduit for my future transition."

This kind of nonsense is beyond the pale, but I listen to be polite and to encourage something of use to come out of his mouth. I just want to get some facts about his daughter so I can make a soul contract with her killer and prepare them for reincarnation.

"I can see you don't believe," he says. "It's okay. Not many do."

All of this likely has something to do with the purple Warrior Priestess T-shirt. Maybe he feels guilty about being wealthy. Maybe his will stipulates he's to be buried with his yacht and a gold guard dog. He's just lost the only part of his family that hasn't divorced him. Doesn't appear to matter to him. It does to me.

"It doesn't matter what I believe," I tell him.

That is the correct answer. He smiles. "That's right. It only matters what I believe and what I do."

I use that pause to get back on track before he starts talking to the other side again.

"What were the specific arguments about? Between you and Leann. Money? Religion? The pending divorce?"

Your being a jerk?

"Let me show you something," he says, then gets up and leaves the room. Ronnie is stifling a giggle and I flash her a stern look. He comes right back carrying a folder stuffed with papers. He takes a set of papers out and hands them to me. It's a rental agreement signed by Joe Bohleber and Leann Truitt going back a year. Jim Truitt is listed as her reference and it clearly states he is her father.

Bohleber lied. He said he wasn't sure of their relationship.

There are copies of money orders made out to Steve Bohleber in the amount of eight hundred dollars. Ronnie didn't say whom the money order they found in Leann's rental was written for. Maybe these were something else?

"You're paying your daughter's rent?" I ask.

"I paid more than that. I may not have approved of her decisions—destructive as they were—but she was my daughter. Mr. Bohleber is a cheat. He wanted to keep the baby so he could get more money out of me. I paid what he asked, and he convinced her to give it up for adoption. I wanted it to go to a good family and not a dysfunctional wreck of one. In the end I wasn't told what happened."

Dr. Andrade said she'd had a child recently. Truitt just confirmed it.

"You're talking about Leann's baby?"

"Of course," he says, narrowing his brow. "Isn't that why you're here?"

"Bohleber is the father of Leann's child."

I didn't say it like a question, and I hoped he wouldn't realize how little I knew.

"He called and warned me that you would be coming. He said the police were coming for a copy of this rental agreement. He offered to make it disappear for a price. I told him to go to hell. He gets nothing else from me. Leann's gone. The baby's gone. My wife is gone. But I still have a purpose. I can connect. I can..."

His words trail off and he stares out of the windows at the water. I'm afraid he will ask us to leave. I'm afraid for his sake that he won't ask. It amazes me that he still hasn't yet asked how his daughter died.

It's even more amazing that I can control my temper.

"I just want to confirm that Joe Bohleber is the father of Leann's baby," I say.

He looks confused. "No," he says. "Not that one. His twin. Steve. Steve is the father. At least, he got her pregnant. He would never have made a good father."

He looks down and shakes his head, and for the first time I see what I believe is real emotion.

"She should never have come home."

CHAPTER TWENTY

Ronnie is busy unpacking the interview with Jim Truitt as we make our way back to the office. Nonstop. To be fair, there is plenty to unpack.

I need a Scotch. Make that two.

"So let me see if I've got this straight," she says. "Her father was paying her rent to Joe Bohleber to bribe Steve, the father of her baby, to convince Leann to give the baby up?"

That was too many words, but that was about it. Truitt had convinced himself that he was serving a higher purpose as dictated by his secret soul. He might have loved his daughter, but he couldn't stand the shame of her becoming pregnant by a lowlife farmer turned handyman turned landlord.

"The whole thing makes me sick," I say.

Leann had left school and given up her chance at a career that would have made her father proud—one he could brag about at the yacht club or when he was moored off a private island. Yet he failed to recognize that he had ruined his daughter's life with his holier-than-thou expectations and interference. And his money too. When his wife and then his daughter didn't live up to his standards, he paid them both off. The wife got a divorce and a beachfront property in St. Lucia. His daughter got pregnant and wanted nothing from him but money.

"To top it off," I add, "his so-called soul contract spirit instructed him to do it so he could be reincarnated."

"Remind me not to join his club," Ronnie says.

I give her a smile.

As far as useful information goes, Jim Truitt knew only that she had tended bar in Port Townsend. He didn't know which one. He didn't know any of her friends. He didn't know where she banked. He sent her money orders each month to tide her over, maybe to her post office box or maybe delivered by Bohleber. He didn't want word of his disappointing daughter to spread around the yacht club.

"Deputy Davis picked up the rental agreement from Bohleber," Ronnie says, reading a text. "I guess we'll be working late again tonight?"

I want to see if it was the same one that Truitt gave us. And I want to find Joe Bobbsey and squeeze the truth out of him. But I'm tired. I know Ronnie is tired. I need a drink. I surprise myself by telling her it can wait until morning.

"Do you want to get a drink?" I ask.

Ronnie brightens. "Absolutely. Where are we going?"

"I'm buying, so don't ask."

We get to The Tides and I'm hoping Mindy will be there; if she's anywhere, it's at The Tides. I spot her white van at the corner. She is sitting in a booth by the windows.

"I saw you pull up. I was hoping you'd stop by."

"How did you know I would come here? More importantly, if you saw me pull up, why isn't my drink on the table?"

She laughs. "Because I saw Deputy Marsh with you. I don't know what she drinks. I knew if you stopped anywhere, it would be here."

We sit in the booth. I order Scotch, neat, doubles, all around. The waiter asks if I prefer a particular brand. I tell him anything named Glen will do. Mindy starts to object but sees my mood. Mindy is a white wine drinker. I want to expand her horizons.

And I don't want to be seen drinking hard liquor alone. I have a reputation to uphold.

"What did Leann's father tell you?" Mindy asks.

I shake my head. "He's part of a New Age movement. His spirit guide told him to abandon his daughter and pay the father of her baby to convince her to give it away."

She doesn't act surprised. "That explains why there were no baby things in the cabin. But I did find a partial bottle of multivitamins in the medicine cabinet. So who is the baby's father?"

"Steve Bohleber," I tell her. "He of Bobbsey Twin fame."

Mindy looks confused, so I explain about the twins and the locals giving them the nickname. I now know why Steve wasn't anywhere to be found. I hope he was paid well for betraying his baby mama and child. I wonder if he knew his brother, Joe, was still shaking Truitt down. Truitt isn't the sort of man to part with money easy. He's saving it for his next life. And Joe is a mercenary type. He wouldn't let a rich guy like Truitt off the hook easily. Hence the call to Truitt to warn him I was coming. The offer to destroy the rental agreement. He'll regret that the next time I see him.

"I went over every inch of that cabin," Mindy says. "She wasn't killed there. There would have been some sign from all the cuts and injuries on the body. Plus there weren't any rub marks or scrapes on any surface where she could have been chained. No chain. No rope. No broken furniture. The only thing I found interesting was the clothing on the bed. Ronnie probably told you."

Our drinks come and Ronnie downs half of hers without making a face. She's tougher than she looks. She's beginning to grow on me and I'm not sure how I feel about that.

"Tell me about the clothes again," I ask, although I really don't need to know. I just want to drink my Scotch and not talk.

"There were three sets of clothes laid out on the mattress," Mindy goes on. "I couldn't tell if anything was missing from the closet. It looked to me like she had a date, left, and didn't come back. That's another reason I don't think she was killed in her cabin."

"Do you remember the locket, Mindy?" Ronnie asks.

Mindy sets down her glass and nods. "Vintage. Solid gold. Heart-shaped. The latch was broken."

"Tell her about the pictures inside the locket," Ronnie puts in.

Mindy takes a sip of the Scotch and mulls it over. "Black-and-white photo of a white male, a full-face shot. Late thirties. And a color picture of a baby. Newborn. No way to tell the gender."

Ronnie goes back to the screen on her phone. She's found something. She uses her fingers to widen the screen and turns it for me to see.

"This is the picture of the man in the locket."

It's a black-and-white photo but the hair is some dark color, not black. It's worn down on the shoulders. The man does appear to be in his late thirties. His jaw is angular, the cheekbones sharp. The lips are full, almost puffy. The mouth is set in a scowl.

"That's Jim Truitt," I say.

Ronnie nods. "Now look at the baby," she says. The lips are full, like inner tubes. The ears stick out, and the too-wide nose... "Is it possible...?"

Ronnie then replaces the baby's photo with one of Jim Truitt that she found on the Internet. Then one of Joe Bohleber. The baby looks nothing like a Bohleber.

It looks like a Truitt.

I don't need a photo to remember Leann's face. Her nose was petite. She got her looks from her mother, perhaps, like I did. The baby resembles Jim Truitt's line.

"Maybe Jim Truitt is the father," I say.

We sit there silently. Ronnie downs the last of her Scotch like a pro. She flips from one screen to the next.

"What do you think, Ronnie?" I ask.

I let her give her thoughts on it. It was, after all, her eye that caught this.

"Jim Truitt is the father," she says, holding out her empty glass. "I've earned another I think."

Ronnie matches me drink for drink and neither of us is better for it. Mindy doesn't finish her Scotch and switches back to wine. I switch to coffee. Ronnie, still drinking, wants to go somewhere to sing karaoke. That's never going to happen.

Mindy leaves, and Ronnie and I sit there while I practically force-feed her coffee. She prattles on about how much fun karaoke would be and finally sobers up enough to drive, and I follow her home to make sure she gets in her door.

CHAPTER TWENTY-ONE

Ronnie Marsh lives in an Airbnb rental called the Big Red Barn. It had actually been a barn at one time. The owner remodeled, put a small wooden footbridge over a narrow man-made stream, new tin roof and black barn hinges on the two sets of double doors at the front, and voilà: a city person's dream of life in the country.

I coax her from her car, take her inside, and pour her into her bed.

While she's asleep I take the opportunity to look around. I'm sure she would have given me the tour anyway.

The rooms aren't deep but the bedroom and living room have a walk-out view of Port Townsend Bay along the ferry routes. There's a huge garden tub in the bathroom and a kitchen area off to the side of the living room. A door from the bedroom leads to an outside deck, nicely decorated with Adirondack chairs, potted flowers, and a small charcoal grill. A dirt footpath looks as though it winds all the way down to the waterfront. I'm tempted to go down to the water.

I look out and a passing ferry stirs memories of my brother, Hayden. Our estrangement is never far from my mind. He's in Afghanistan. I look across the bay at the lights and speak to him in my mind. I tell him all the things I wish I could say in person.

Come home.

Forgive me.

I love you.

I pull myself back. The lingering Scotch is talking. I take one last look around, draw in a deep, cleansing breath, let it out, and go back inside.

I shut and lock the door to the deck, then go through the place, making sure the doors and windows are locked. I remember Ronnie's firearm. I return to the bedroom and unhitch her gun belt. She stirs but doesn't wake. I put the gun belt and gun in her closet, where two more uniforms hang, neat, pressed, in lint-free dry cleaner bags. She has an impressive amount of nice clothes in her closet. A cache of designer purses are lined up on the top shelf above the clothes.

Satisfied that all is well in Ronnie Land, I drive home and park in my usual spot. I didn't leave any lights on and I carefully feel my way to the front door, almost tripping once, and let myself in, then promptly trip on the uneven maple floor.

I go into my home office and sit at my desk. Thoughts of the case fly through my mind. Jim Truitt is a world-class creep. Bohleber is a world-class creep. In my book all are suspects. The idea that Truitt fathered a child with his daughter is repulsive but possible. It happens. It says everything about what kind of man he is—and to drive the point home, he not only abandoned her and his grandchild, child, whatever, but he paid a stranger to convince Leann to give up her baby. He didn't even have the backbone to do it himself. He was a zealot, or maybe just pretending to be one as an excuse to himself for his deplorable behavior. He claimed to be connecting with another soul that gave him instructions. While I can't be completely certain, his decision seemed to have ruined three lives and possibly cost his daughter hers.

What would it be like to have a sister-daughter?

Leann had to struggle with that.

And now she was dead.

Thinking of Jim Truitt connecting to his spirits takes me back to the ride to Marrowstone Island with Ronnie that morning. I was so focused on my dislike for the Bohlebers that I wanted them to be the prime suspects. Truitt said Steve was the father of Leann's child. But the similarity between the man in the gold locket and Jim Truitt keeps nudging me in another direction. The worst. The baby *is* his. I didn't see it immediately, but Ronnie did. I have to hand it to her.

I think about Marie Rader and the last time I saw her. She was the wife of Alex Rader, my biological father, which made Marie my stepmother—a disgusting thought. I committed parricide, the killing of parents. Technically it wasn't, though. I killed my father, which was patricide, and my stepmother. That would be considered tyrannicide, the killing of a tyrant.

If only there were such a thing.

I had a session with Dr. Albright where I told her about how I killed Marie Rader.

I get up and find the tape of that session. I've listened to it once and marked it. I put it in the cassette player and hit "play."

My gun is still in my hand as I listen.

I remember perfectly clearly being in her office. Dr. Albright is sitting there with her eyes softening. She sees the passion and confusion in my eyes.

Dr. A: You've mentioned Marie. I know something terrible happened with her ... and you.

Me: It wasn't terrible. It was what it needed to be.

Dr. A: Fine. Tell me. I'm here.

I can hear the anger and anxiety in my voice.

Me: I tell her she's like a Venus flytrap. So pure and tragic in her wheelchair, with no feeling at all below the waist. Marie was paralyzed in a car accident that was her husband's fault. She never lets him forget it. She hates any woman that was more attractive, more desirable, than her. She plays out her anger by using her husband.

I tell her the truth: that she is just sitting in her chair, consumed with bitterness, waiting for the next girl to come by so she can entrap her. She tries to tell me that it isn't like that, but she calls me Rylee. She knows my real name. The name I'm using. She's holding a knife and her face is hard again. I can tell she hates me for reminding her. For knowing what I know. Not about him. But about how pathetic she is.

Dr. A: What did she say to you?

Me: "I should have killed you when I had the chance. I should have tattooed you like the others and then slit your little throat. I know what you are to him." It figures that she was the tattoo artist. The tail of a koi carp peeks out from under the bulging upper sleeve of her light pink T-shirt. Just then she starts coming toward me. She is turning the wheels of her chair with one arm. In her hand is the knife. She is quite the tattoo artist. She's the one that has tattooed all the victims of her and her husband. A small heart on the shoulder.

She is strong. She comes flying at me across the kitchen. I have a gun. I fire but miss. I remember thinking, "Shit!" I have only one bullet left. I fire again, striking her in the kneecap. As if that would give me any hope of retreat. Blood flows from her dead limb and she doesn't even acknowledge it. She can't feel anything. The wheels of the chair spin faster. I take a step back, thinking what to do. How I will stop her. I have no bullets. I drop the gun to the floor, regretting doing so instantly. I should have used it to bash in her skull.

"Alex isn't much," she cries at me. Now her eyes are narrow and full of sorrow, but she's a fraud and I know it. "He's pathetic. But he's mine. He does what he's told. He goddamn owes me."

I think back to what my freak father said before I obliterated him: "I did what I had to do. I had no choice."

"You pulled the strings, Marie!" I scream at her. "You're the pathetic one!" The knife sends a triangle of reflected light into my eyes, and I blink.

"Guilt was Alex's motivator. Revenge on all the pretty girls was mine," she says as she lunges with the blade pointed at me. "Now you've ruined everything."

In a flash she's nearly on me, and I do the only thing I can think of. I plant my foot between her legs and catch the base of the chair. It is fast and decisive. The knife falls to the floor. Marie Rader goes flying backward through the plate glass slider that leads to her patio.

The tape goes quiet. Dr. Albright is waiting. There is a look of concern and support on her face.

Me: Oddly, she doesn't scream. She starts coming toward me again. I don't know exactly how I accomplish it, but I manage to plant my hands on her chair as she flails about. With all the strength that's somehow still inside of me, I push her through the glittery shards of glass on the patio toward her massive koi pond. The one she bragged about while she was poisoning me with her iced tea. The water surges over her head as she starts to sink down beneath the surface. Instinctively, I return for the knife. I stand by the water's edge as Marie flails around. She's coughing and choking, but she grabs hold of the cement edge of the pond. I see her rise up. Those arms of hers. They are like a pair of pine trees. They undulate with muscle tissue. I see the veins in her forearms press upward like a mass of worms under her skin.

"Goddamn you!" she says. Her eyes are wild. She starts to pull herself up and I do what I know I have to do. And partly

because I want to do it. I can't stop myself. I take the knife and slam its glinting edge through her fingers, and she screams. Yet she hangs on. I stomp on her other hand with my shoe like I'm crushing the life out of a scorpion. Which she is, and at the same time she's an insult to the creature. Her severed fingers are lying there on the edge of the cement and the water is turning to blood. She goes under again. The koi are drawn to her. I wish they were piranhas. I wish the pond were a vat of hydrochloric acid. No matter. I am done. So is Marie.

Dr. A: Were the police called?

I notice Dr. Albright hasn't asked directly if I called the police. I answer her question as best I can.

Me: Marie and I made a lot of noise and I'm hoping no one else heard or cared enough to call the police. Since Alex Rader was a cop, my respect for the cops has nose-dived. Rolland once said that the police are limited in what they can do, but I know that there was at least one among them—and maybe more—who did what they wanted, no matter the price. Go to the police? Mom went there for help and look how it turned out for her. It is one thing of two that I know she and I agree on. The other is that Hayden must never know what I know to be true. Like Mom, I carry that burden now. I love my little brother too much to have him live a life knowing that his heart circulates poisoned blood. Like mine.

Dr. A: So what do you remember?

Me: The koi pond is red with Marie's blood, and I feel sorry that the fish have to swim in the filth of her body. Even so, I kick her fingers into the water with the tip of my shoe. Under

the surface I see her face. Her eyes are open and so is her mouth,
in a permanent scream. She was handicapped but she put up
more of a fight than her husband, the worthless pig. I start
for the living room, and though I scan it with speed, I still see
everything and capture it in my memory forever. Like a camera
with my finger on the shutter. Click. Click. Click. *The scene,*
the furnishings. Everything is mundane. A TV sits across from
a sofa. A recliner points toward the set, and a basket contain-
ing needlework sits at the end of the carpet ruts left by Marie's
chair. I grab the wedding photo of Alex and Marie, smash the
glass, and pull the photo from the frame. Folded, it goes in my
pocket. The ruts. My eyes trace the worn parallel lines in the
carpet throughout the house. They stop at the only place Marie
cannot go. The door that leads upstairs. If Alex Rader wanted to
keep a souvenir from the prying eyes of his wife, then it would
be where she could not follow. He wouldn't have to lock it up.
I turn on the light and head up the steps.

The tape goes silent again. I'm replaying in my mind the scene
before I speak again.

Me: Up top is one large room with the dormers looking out
toward the street. Alex Rader had set it up as his office. It is
like no office I could have imagined. Yes, I've seen porn. Never
on purpose. Not really. There have been times when I've gone
online and clicked the wrong link and in an instant I'm in
a world of naked bodies moving and emoting in ways that
indicate great pleasure but frequently make little sense. One
time I saw something so strange I still don't know what they
were doing. Or how many were doing it. And, truthfully, I
don't want to know. The room is paneled in dark oak. Using
the seams in the paneling as a guide, Alex Rader has taped up
photo after vile photo. These are scenes so sickening that I have

to steady myself as I try to take them in without vomiting. I wouldn't mind vomiting right now. But I don't have the time. I move closer to a section of the wall that holds a familiar face. Megan Moriarty does the splits in her cheerleading uniform from Kentridge High School. It is one of the images of her that I saw online. Next is Shannon Blume's picture, the same pretty but sad-eyed photo that appeared in the newspaper—the one that her parents held in their arms as they called out to the world for help in finding their daughter. Leanne is there too. But this photo is not familiar. It was candidly snapped when she was caught down by the marina, unaware. She was being stalked.

I hit the "stop" button. Is it a coincidence that one of Rader's victims was named Leanne? Or is this destiny's way of reminding me of what I'm supposed to do? Rader is dead. Marie, his helper, his leader, is dead.

The picture of Rader's Leanne was candidly snapped. Down by the marina. She was being stalked. I believe my victim—and I think of Leann as *my* victim now—was being stalked too.

I hit "play" again, resuming the tape.

Me: I hear the thumping, louder this time, and I turn around. Using her one good hand and the stump that I made for her with the kitchen knife, soaking-wet Marie has heaved herself up the stairs. She slithers. She can barely speak, but she is as mad as hell and she won't be denied.

"To get out of here," Marie spits out, "you have to get by me." *She has the knife in her hand. I see by looking past her that she used it like a rock climber to hoist herself up the stairway. A trail of water and blood follows her like a snail's trail. Except, she's no snail. Marie is fast. Faster than anyone can imagine. I have been upstairs only a few minutes and she's managed to*

*track me. She pulls herself toward me. Her hair is wet and
soaked with blood.*

*"Do you realize what you've done?" I ask, as though someone
so vile could even fathom it. "Do you realize how many lives
you ruined?"*

*"Try being in a wheelchair," she says. "See how that ruins
your life."*

*"Am I supposed to feel sorry for you? Am I supposed to
think that your playtime photo sessions were the result of some
deep-seated anger you hold at the world because your spinal
cord was cut? Get real, Marie."*

I stop and gather my thoughts. I know what comes next, but
I have to hear it one more time. It's a compulsion I can't abate.

*Me: "You're not getting out of here alive," she says. The blade has
been dulled by its use as a stair climber, but it can still inflict
fatal damage if I give her the chance. Which I won't. I take the
desk chair and I spin it hard and fast in her direction. Marie
lifts her torso from the floor with those powerful arms—arms
that were mighty when she was a swimmer, when she could hold
her breath for a long time. She balances herself with her stump
and tries to lunge at me. I throw my body on the chair and it
smashes into her, sending her screaming backward down the
stairwell. When she lands, I see the tip of the knife. During her
loud tumble, the blade found its way behind her, entering her
neck and protruding through her mouth like a carbide tongue
as she fell back. I can barely breathe. I stand there for a beat,
watching as red oozes from Marie's gaping mouth.*

I don't have to stop the tape. I picture Leann Truitt's body laid
out in a staged pose, neck broken, tortured, raped.

Me: Her light pink shirt is now a bloody red tie-dye. I hear sirens and I know I have to get out of there right away. I gather photos from the floor and skirt past Marie's slumped body, her withered legs, her tree-trunk, arms and that pie-cutting knife protruding from her mouth. By the door I see my mom-style purse. I grab it, stuff the photos inside, and run out of the door and through the hedge to the street. I know my fingerprints are all over the house, but I've never been arrested and there's no trace of me in anyone's system. At least, not yet.

I put my gun in the safe. My tongue still smarts. I take the bottle of Scotch and the used plastic tumbler out of the desk drawer and pour a little, then a little more.

Before I listen to any of the other tapes, I click on my email and scroll downward.

Wallace has written another message.

My heart sinks. It's like a sleeping snake and I don't want to disturb it.

But I do.

It's brief.

I doubt you know what it's like to be hurt so deeply you've lost a part of yourself. I know what it feels like. Soon, Rylee, you will too.

My head spins. It's not the alcohol, of course. Although it could be. It's the sentiment. It's the hate. Someone out there knows my secrets. Someone out there wants me to be made to suffer.

CHAPTER TWENTY-TWO

I slot in another tape, rewind a little and hit play. My voice comes over the tiny speaker in the player.

Me: Courtney is my mom's real name. She hid that from me as well as everything else. Aunt Ginger said my mom was scrunched up in the hospital bed after she delivered me and didn't look at me right away. Mom said she was glad I was a girl. My aunt Ginger said to my mom that she was hoping for that too. She told Mom to look at me. She said I was beautiful. My mom wouldn't look. She was afraid to look. Afraid that if she looked she would see him.

Dr. A: Him?

I fast-forward the tape a little.

Me: So much of what happened in my life was orchestrated turmoil. Orchestrated by my mother to cover the tracks of one lie with another lie and another and another. I remember one time when we were watching an episode of Teen Mom *on TV and the girl who'd just had a baby was talking about giving it up for adoption.*

Dr. A: Your mom considered giving you up.

Me: Yeah. I guess she did. Of course, Aunt Ginger said it was to protect me from him. She pretended to be hidden from him for so long that he didn't know she was pregnant. It was all a lie. While we watched that show, my mom and me, I told her that I could never do that. Never give a baby up like that. She said if it was what was best for the child, it might be what's best for me. She said she knew people who had considered it because it was the only right thing to do.

The tape is quiet for a few moments.

Me: Ditching your kid—how could that ever be right? I mean, they shouldn't have got pregnant in the first place. My mom just said mistakes happen sometimes. Sometimes pregnancies are anything but planned. I knew my mom was young when she had me. She said she was eighteen but now I know she was sixteen. I thought she'd been married to my father. The one that died fighting for his country, a war hero. That was all lies too.

The tape hisses and ends. I eject it and turn it over, insert it, and think of the case. Leann Truitt had given her baby up. My mother had almost given me up. I wonder now where I fell on the spectrum my mother had laid bare.

Had she regretted keeping me? Had I ruined her life?

I hit "play" and wait for the blank portion of the tape to catch up.

Me: Aunt Ginger told my mother that I look just like her. She told my mother that I was her baby and not his. A nurse heard her say that and remarked that it was none of her business, but sometimes it's good to have a man around. For child support if nothing else. My aunt said that would never happen with this man.

Aunt Ginger was right. This man, my biological father, was a monster. As a dad and as a person. Maybe Leann Truitt's kid was lucky to get far away from Jim Truitt. Maybe my mom was right about a baby sometimes being better off...

Dr. A: Your mother came to accept you.

Me: I don't know if she ever accepted me. Aunt Ginger said Mom never filled out the paperwork to give me up for adoption. I don't know if that was on purpose or if she had other reasons for keeping me. She always doted on Hayden, my brother. She expected me to be her replacement when she wasn't there. Maybe she always planned on abandoning us and thought I would take her place.

Silence.

Me: Aunt Ginger said my mom held me and told me she loved me and would never let anyone hurt me. Another lie. Aunt Ginger was sitting and was about to get up, but I stopped her. I didn't need to know that Mom was going to give me up but changed her mind. I wanted to know how my biological father, Alex Rader, knew that my mother was having a baby. Me. I wanted to know why he thought I belonged to him. I told her that I'd spent my whole life thinking I was alone. I had no relatives but Mom and Dad and Hayden. I told her I needed to know everything so I can find my mom. And my stepfather's killer.

Dr. A: Go on.

Me: Aunt Ginger is holding something back. Something big. But I also feel that she cares about me. That's why she told me that right after my mom had me, a policeman came into the room with flowers.

I don't need to hear the rest. Leann was lied to just like I had been. Where was her mother during all of this? Someone who got his daughter pregnant is not a one-time offender. He may have been, probably was, molesting her for her whole life. Did her mom know? Was she so money hungry that she turned a blind eye?

I had checked for a criminal history on Jim Truitt and he was clean. Not even a traffic citation. I didn't see a bunch of alcohol in his house. As far as I know, he wasn't a drunk or an addict. I'm convinced that Leann's mom betrayed her, lied to her, just as my mom had done to me my whole life. We share a similar history.

I'm here to get justice for both of us.

CHAPTER TWENTY-THREE

It's barely seven in the morning. I sit at my desk making computer inquiries while regretting the whisky from the night before. I am wiped out and didn't sleep much. I have no doubt that I'll pay all day for that. I hear Nan down the hall yammering with excitement that the donuts Sheriff Gray brought in include an apple fritter. Her favorite. To bring a dozen donuts without a fritter for Nan was to commit a major offense in an office that deals with homicides and other crimes.

It dawns on me that Nan wields a lot of power in the office. I think the sheriff is afraid of her. She's the passive-aggressive type who gets even without one being even aware.

Silly me. I thought I'd given you that file.

He didn't leave a number.

Oh. I thought the apple fritter was mine. I guess I was mistaken.

I turn my attention to the case. Jim Truitt said his daughter was tending bar in Port Townsend. There are more than a dozen bars in Port Townsend—even more in the surrounding area. Lucky for me, I try the Old Whiskey Mill on Water Street only a few calls in.

That's where Leann worked.

The Old Whiskey Mill started life in the late 1800s as a hotel, the grandest in Port Townsend, at a time when the town was betting on being the terminus for the railroad, a distinction that went to the other side of Puget Sound, Seattle and Tacoma. Several businesses had been tried in the ground floor of the building, but none seemed to draw the money needed to keep it afloat. Then two sisters tried a bar. It was a hit, especially with law enforcement types, and the Old Whiskey Mill was off and running.

I spoke to a bartender who was filling in for Leann and gave him the bad news that she wasn't returning to work. He was sorry, but he couldn't tell me anything about her. Next, I talked to the owner, who told me Leann had worked there for only a month. She'd come to them from a coffee shop somewhere. The owner didn't know which one and she hadn't filled out a job application.

So how did her father know she was working in a bar if he wasn't keeping track of her like he claimed?

I pull up more from the criminal database. Turns out, Steve Bohleber has a criminal record out of Indiana. He wasn't a farmer, unless he farmed marijuana in Indiana, and it's still illegal there. He did three years in Pendleton, a maximum-security prison in Indiana, for aggravated assault. He attacked a policeman. The policeman went to the hospital with a concussion. Steve went to prison. He was lucky to get prison.

The arresting officers were too kind.

Now he was in the wind. No one, including his parole officer, knew his whereabouts. No one cared. Except me.

Joe Bohleber has never been a farmer, either. He was arrested a couple of times for fraud and money laundering. To my way of thinking, it wasn't a big leap to see him blackmailing Truitt. With what, exactly, I wasn't sure.

There is something going on between those two. But what?

I check out Jim Truitt too. Newspaper archives are a great place to look for rich creeps like Truitt. He is barely a blip in the *Port Townsend Leader*. He was involved in some kind of land scheme over near Fort Flagler Historical State Park. The paper mentioned him as one of the investors. Interestingly, Joe and Steve Bohleber purchased the properties where they had their fishing cabins from a company where Jim Truitt was a partner.

They've done business before.

They both lied to me.

Lying to me is a serious mistake.

I also discover a stack of paperwork and get a good start on requesting placement information from Olympia regarding the adoption of Leann's baby. Jim Truitt is a man with connections. Money. He knows people as well as spirits. He may have found a home for the child himself.

It is, after all, his child.

He didn't strike me as a man who gives up anything that he owns. He found a place for his pregnant daughter to live and then paid her rent. He kept her at arm's distance but still controlled her. He bought his wife a beach house in St. Lucia but still keeps track of her.

He is someone I'll have to keep my eye on.

I get coffee from the breakroom and consider a donut from the box on the counter. Pass. I hear Nan regaling the records clerk with a story about her daughter's latest achievement. I tune it out and return to my desk.

I start with the state adoption agency. After thirty minutes or so I realize I'm not going to get into the system without leaving evidence behind. The Jefferson County Sheriff's Office doesn't have clearance to do a search for mothers, much less placement information.

Sheriff Gray comes through the office with a paper cup of something and a greasy bag of fast food. It's a big bag for breakfast, but he is a big man. Or at least his belly is getting that way. He sees me looking at the bag and comes over to my desk.

"I brought breakfast."

Sure you did.

"What's in the bag?" I ask.

He opens the top and the smell of fried onions comes at me. He takes out something wrapped in greasy paper. "I got you a double sausage with onion and pickle from the street vendor. Sorry I didn't get you a malted milk shake, but I couldn't carry it all."

"And I turned down a donut in the breakroom."

Sheriff is married to a nurse he met at the hospital after he had a mild heart attack. He's overweight and, despite his constant complaining about dieting, I've never seen him eat anything resembling healthy food.

He lays the greasy-paper-wrapped sandwich on my desk and says, "Let's keep this to ourselves."

I haven't eaten since yesterday, but I pass. I know about keeping secrets. He has kept enough of mine.

Ronnie comes in the office and looks as if she were fresh from a spa. I feel like I've gone a few rounds with an MMA fighter, but she is alert, smiling, and chattering. When I put her to bed last night she was zonked. If I'd had as much to drink as she had, I would hurl at the smell of grease.

Sheriff Gray looks at the bag, at me, at her, and takes another sandwich out. "I got enough for you too. But don't tell Nan."

Or his wife.

I gesture for Ronnie to pull up a chair. She does, sits, and unwraps the still-steaming hot double sausage, onion, and pickle piece of heaven. Today she's wearing a modest outfit, blue blouse, light jacket, gray slacks, and low-heeled shoes. Her nails are trimmed but now painted a bright fire engine red.

"I'll be in my office," the sheriff says. "Before you go anywhere, I want an update. I am the sheriff. I'm supposed to know what you're doing."

I detect a hint of accusation in his tone and suddenly I feel defensive.

"I updated you yesterday when we knocked off," I say.

"You didn't tell me you talked to Jim Truitt."

"I did too," I tell him. "It's in your box."

I put it there a half hour ago. I just don't tell him that.

"Let me rephrase that. You didn't tell me it was *that* Jim Truitt."

"So what about him?" I am surprised that he is making a big deal of this. So what if Truitt is rich. Sheriff Gray has never pulled his punches—or mine—before.

"Let's just say you should go easy on him, Megan."

I don't like where this is going.

"Is he important?" I ask, already aware of the answer.

"He's a big contributor. He supports a lot of police events. Buys equipment when the county can't."

Or won't, I think.

"Funny you should bring him up, Sheriff. We need to talk to you about him. Maybe we should go into your office for some privacy?"

He gives me a little scowl. Not a big one. Just a touch.

"I think that would be a wonderful idea, Detective Carpenter."

Uh-oh. I've pissed him off. He's never called me that. Ronnie and I follow him to his office. He motions for Ronnie to pull the door closed. We all sit. His chair squeals.

WD-40 isn't the answer.

Losing about fifty pounds is.

"Jim Truitt might be a big police supporter, Sheriff. That's great. We can always use more support. But he's something else too."

I pause. It's like laying down a winning hand, even when the game is just getting started.

"Two things," I say. "He's quite possibly a child molester. He might also be our killer."

"There's a lot to unpack there," he says, narrowing his gaze at me. "A lot of supposition."

"I can't prove he's the father of Leann's baby. But I'm working on it. The thing is, I don't have authority to get the adoption records. If I can find the baby, I can get DNA comparisons with Bohleber and Truitt."

Ronnie pipes up. "If he lied about the baby, it gives him a motive for her murder."

Sheriff Gray is thinking.

"Maybe he hired someone to kill her?" he suggests. "Maybe finding the baby won't matter. And you will still need DNA from Truitt and Bohleber for comparison. Do you think they'll cooperate?"

Hell no, I think.

"Yes," I say.

CHAPTER TWENTY-FOUR

Nan knocks and sticks her head in the doorway of the sheriff's office.

She hates being excluded and uses every opportunity to edge her way into the know.

This time she has a legitimate reason.

"I got something for you," she says, handing a printout to me. She lingers a second, looking at the food on the desk and giving the sheriff a dirty look before shutting the door behind her.

"You're going to get coal in your Christmas stocking this year, Sheriff," I say.

His eyes widen. "Me? I'm telling her Ronnie brought the stuff in."

Sheriff is light on his feet when he wants to be. I look at the printout and my eyes bug out.

"What?" he asks.

I return to my desk, drink some cold coffee, and get busy on the phone. Ronnie is on the computer pulling files on the names from the printout. An hour later we meet up in the sheriff's office again.

He has a worried look on his face. His sausage burger is only half eaten and still on the wrapper on his desk.

"Is it as bad as it looks?" he asks.

I'm holding the printout Nan gave me. Parts of it are highlighted in yellow. I read from it.

"Two confirmed murders. The oldest is from two years ago. Both are bodies they matched to missing persons reports. I only asked for VICAP data from Jefferson, Clallam, Thurston, Mason, and Kitsap Counties. I didn't ask about the other side of Puget Sound. There could be others if we widen the search."

My eyes meet the sheriff's and Ronnie's for a second before I go on.

"Their injuries match what happened to Leann. Both women were strangled. Both had their necks broken. Multiple broken bones. Marks on the wrists, ankles, and neck like in our case. The one from two years ago says the cause of death was exsanguination. Apparently she was pregnant, and the baby was cut from her. I called the detectives working the cases. The old case is in Clallam County. The newer one is from six months ago in Kitsap. I'll set up meetings with them."

I look up from the printout. Sheriff has a sick look on his face. Not the sandwich, I think.

"The case in Clallam is a woman named Margie Benton," I say. "She went missing and her body was found two weeks later. The one in Kitsap is Dina Knowles. She vanished and was found murdered a week later. And get this: both women were around Leann's age and size and had red hair."

I have Sheriff Gray's undivided attention now. For good reason. A serial killer has come to Jefferson County.

"The detectives have been sharing information and it seems that the victims have more in common. Knowles had given up a baby the year before she was killed. They both worked in bars."

The sheriff throws the sandwich into his waste basket. "Do they have any evidence? A suspect?"

I shake my head and drop a bomb.

"They did rape kits on both women. There was physical evidence of rape. There's no suspect."

"Well, shoot," he says, his face growing red. "Why didn't we hear about this before now?"

"I kind of got the impression that the two detectives thought they would have this wrapped up before now," I say.

That was a problem in law enforcement. One jurisdiction didn't want to share information with another. They each felt like the case was theirs alone and they would solve it alone. Make the arrest themselves. I could relate to that. But in this case I had a bad feeling that my killer was the same as theirs. That meant we had a serial killer on the loose.

"Sheriff, I've asked for a DNA test on the rape kit from Leann Truitt, but you know how the lab is. I'll call Marley, but can I tell him you want this one given priority?"

"You do that," he says. "And tell him if they don't get it done right quick, there will be hell to pay."

Seriously? I am proud of Sheriff Gray being so forceful. Now I just wish he'd let me shake Jim Truitt up and see what we get. He must have been reading my mind.

"And you have my permission to turn Jim Truitt upside down if necessary and see what falls out, though I don't think we have enough to get a warrant. See what you come up with on these other murders and I'll see what I can do about getting a court order for DNA."

I plan to pursue Truitt, permission or not. The sheriff already knows this but is giving me protection in case some politician comes after me. I can always count on him. Truitt seems to have some clout and I hope he won't be able to avoid cooperating in the investigation.

"Do you need anything else from me? Any help with this?" he asks.

"I'd like to request Deputy Marsh continue to help with the investigation."

Ronnie looks surprised, then beams in my direction.

"I *insist* she does," I say.

"I'll clear it with the training unit," Sheriff Gray says, a slight smile on his face. "Just keep her out of the line of fire."

I'm not sure if he's talking about political fallout or Ronnie possibly getting killed. I guess one is the same as the other. Political fallout can mean the end of a career and getting blackballed with any other agency. He knows I can protect myself.

I am beginning to think Ronnie can do the same.

CHAPTER TWENTY-FIVE

It will take most of the morning for Kitsap's and Clallam's case files to be couriered to my office. I want to go through them page by page before I set up a meeting with the detectives. I call Marley Yang at the crime lab to see if he received the rape kit. I get the receptionist.

"I'll have to see if Mr. Yang is in," she says. "Can I take a number and have him call you back?"

"If he is unavailable, I guess I'll have to, but our sheriff wants to talk to him. Should I put Sheriff Gray on? He's talking to a judge in his office, but I can get him to the phone."

"That won't be necessary," she says. "I'll put you through to Mr. Yang."

She leaves, the line doesn't ring, and I don't get the usual sappy Muzak, so I think she's disconnected me. Finally a click.

"Yang here," a familiar voice says. "Detective Carpenter. Put me through to the sheriff."

"The sheriff said I should talk to you," I lie. "He wants to know if you got the rape kit from yesterday morning. The body found on Marrowstone."

Marley is the lab supervisor at the crime lab. I've seen him only once in person. He's short, compact, with longish black hair and a wannabe goatee. He is of the generation that believes CSI is all racing around in cars or foot chases, carrying guns, shooting up the bad guys, and going to a bar to celebrate.

It's not like that. Except for the bars, of course.

"You mean *you* want to know. Is that it, Detective Carpenter?"

He sounds a little cross. "You got me, Marley. If it makes it a better trade, you can call me Megan from now on."

Marley laughs, really more of a snort.

"Yes, I got the rape kit," he says. "I know it's a priority, along with thirty or forty other requests. I'm sorry, but you know how backed up we are."

Here we go. I really don't give one whit if you're taking work home to finish it.

"I totally understand," I say. "I get the same thing here. Can you believe a woman came in yesterday demanding that I have her car fingerprinted to prove her boyfriend had been driving it around with some other girl? She wanted the fingerprints tested for DNA. I told her no way. You guys are way too busy with major crimes."

"Seriously?" he asks.

"I went out and threw some fingerprint powder around just to make her happy. Told her I'd get to the bottom of it." I'm lying but he will think he owes me for not dumping something inane like that on him. Also, it sounds cool. Like I did something he'd never get away with because he's part of the administration.

He laughs in earnest now.

"I thought you'd get a kick out of that."

"I have no opinion," he says, chuckling. "In fact, I didn't even hear that. Good for you."

I plead. But only a little. I never beg.

"Can you help me out here, Marley?"

"You said the sheriff wants this done posthaste?"

"He said to call him with the results, and he'll relay them to me. I'm going to be all over the place interviewing people today. Maybe I could stop by later and check with you if I'm out your way?"

"I'll be swamped, Megan."

He's calling me Megan, so my job kissing his ass is done here.

"Just a thought," I say. "I've got a trainee with me anyway. Ronnie Marsh. Know her?"

"Ronnie?"

It wasn't a question.

It was *excitement*.

If I checked his sperm count it would have doubled.

"She was here for a rotation. Smart girl."

Evidently, Ronnie makes an impression wherever she goes.

"Yeah," he says. "If you come by, I'll show you what we've got on your kit."

"See you in a bit, Marley. By the way, how long will that test take? A couple of days? A week?"

"Nah," he says. "We have a new piece of equipment. We can get the DNA in two hours. Trouble is, I'm the only one here that's been trained on it. You'll have to ask for me."

"Will do."

That way you can show off for Ronnie and tell me what I want, I think.

"Bye, Marley."

"Later on, Megan."

I'm glad I can make someone's day. Now I have to get the DNA samples from the Clallam and Kitsap County cases, also a rush job. Maybe I should send Ronnie to hand deliver them to be sure he'll get on it. To be fair, Marley is a good forensic technician. The last case I had involved a locked cell phone. He managed to get it open in an hour and was able to give me much-needed information. And he'll work all night if the case interests him. He's like me in that way. Curious to a fault.

On the other hand, Marley is part of the bureaucracy. He's stuck with having to justify everything. Every penny. Every hour. I only have to get results. I do what I have to and then ask for leniency if they catch me.

Much like I am about to do to Jim Truitt.

Wangling people to get information or favors is a residual trait from a childhood in which I learned very quickly that a trick or a lie is an excellent way to get what you want. I probably cried for a bottle even when I didn't want one. But as good as I was at manipulation, my mother was the undisputed queen. She manipulated me my entire life. I didn't realize it then, but every idea I thought was mine, every move I made, was orchestrated by her. Taking care of my brother while she was gone for days or weeks at a time was all for her benefit. She told me she was protecting the family—protecting me and my brother—but she was really maneuvering, lying bitch that she was. She betrayed us. When my stepfather was murdered, Hayden and I were forced to run. No plan. No money. No shelter. No food except what I could scrounge or steal. She turned me into a predator just like her, and my brother into someone I pitied and tried to protect.

That's not true, I think as I reel in my thoughts.

I love Hayden. Always will. But the things I was forced to do I had to do alone. He thinks I abandoned him, and I don't know if he'll ever forgive me.

In fact, I think he hates me.

Ronnie comes to my desk and dramatically lays a few eight-by-ten photographs in front of me. The quality is not the best because at the moment Jefferson County's budget doesn't include a decent color printer. She puts her finger on the first image.

"Margie Benton. Clallam."

I was prepared for Margie to have red hair. Even to be young, in her early twenties. But I'm not at all prepared for the close likeness to Leann Truitt.

In fact, they could be sisters.

"Dina Knowles. Kitsap," Ronnie says, turning up the next picture.

I feel my heart beating fast in my chest. My mouth is dry, and I feel a little nauseous. Not as bad as at the autopsy, of course. I was overwhelmed with feelings from the past crashing into each other and forcing themselves to the front. I must have zoned out staring at the pictures. The next thing I know, Ronnie is gently shaking my shoulder.

"Are you okay?" she asks.

I force my eyes away from the photos and look at Ronnie.

"I'm okay. I'm fine," I say, and try to lick my lips, but I have no saliva.

Ronnie sees my predicament. "I'll get you some water," she says, rushing away to the water cooler. She returns a second later with a tiny paper cup.

I have part of a pint of McCallum's Scotch hidden in the back of my bottom desk drawer, but I don't think I should get it. I need to be a good role model, although I really could use a drink.

I take the water and down it like a shot, turning the cup over on my desk and giving Ronnie a half smile.

"Feel better?"

"I'm fine," I say.

The truth is I'm embarrassed. She already saw me get sick at Dr. Andrade's stainless steel table. But she hasn't seen a tenth of the things I've seen.

Or done.

Ronnie has several more pictures in her hands and starts to pull them away. I put my hand on hers.

"Leave them. I need to see all of them."

I start with Margie. The description under the photo shows her height at five feet six inches, weight 110, hair color red, eyes blue, age twenty-two, white, female. The date she went missing and the date the body was found are listed last.

The second picture in the stack is a missing persons poster. It appears to be a selfie taken in a car. It captures her from the chest up. The top of the steering wheel is in the picture but can't hide the fullness of her breasts. Not now. She is giving a sexy *You know you want me* look. Her hair shines with a lustrous copper hue. Her face is flushed with happiness.

The contrast is like a negative of the autopsy photo.

Dina Knowles is listed as five feet eight inches, weight 120, hair red, eyes hazel, age twenty, white, female. The dates she went missing and was found are also recorded. I turn to the second page, which is also a missing person poster. This one is captured in the backyard of a home. She is sitting at a picnic table with a large drink in front of her. Maybe an iced tea or Long Island tea. There are several beer cans and bottles on the table. She is smiling and playfully holding a hand up in a fake attempt to block the camera. No rings on her fingers. No jewelry. *Wrong.* She is wearing a nose ring, a small gold hook. I did that once to look like a college student. I was only seventeen and had faked my admissions papers to get into Portland State.

I look again at the "Missing" photo of Margie. She is wearing earrings that look like little gold multicolor butterflies.

They are missing in her autopsy photo.

Margie was killed almost two years ago. Dina six months ago. The dates they were reported missing were not the same months, or even close. The killer wasn't driven by a season or date like some. Instead he focused on the similarity of his victims.

Leann's description from her license matches the description given by Dr. Andrade at the autopsy. Height five feet seven inches, weight 125, hair red, eyes hazel, age twenty-one—one month shy of twenty-two—white, female. She is wearing hoop earrings in the license photo. In the autopsy photo, her hair is washed-out red. Dead looking. Tiny puncture marks indent each earlobe. The earrings are missing from her pierced ears.

Ronnie said there was no jewelry in Leann's cabin except for the locket.

Maybe this guy is a collector?

Margie's butterflies.

Dina's nose ring.

Leann's hoop earrings.

Serial killers frequently keep mementos of their victims. I knew of one guy in Indiana who kept the driver's licenses or ID cards of his victims. The pictures turned him on. They also proved to be his downfall.

"They all have the most beautiful red hair," Ronnie says, bringing me back to the moment. "Mine was bright like that until I put a ridiculous rinse on it. I think I'll change it back."

She's right. They all look like sisters. I don't say it, but it passes through my mind just then: Ronnie looks like she could be related to the dead girls.

CHAPTER TWENTY-SIX

I flip through the remaining crime scene photos provided by the detectives in the Clallam and Kitsap County Sheriff's Offices. The injuries on the bodies are almost identical to our victim's. Dark narrow cuts encircle the wrists, the same marks are around the ankles, and there is a wider, deeper bruise around the throat. A buckle mark cut into the back of the neck. The bodies only differ in the amount of deep tissue bruising from a fist or feet.

Margie also had some bruising that their pathologist stated was caused by a club about two inches wide that had broken some of the ribs in her back. She was the first victim. It's possible her killer changed his method a little in the next killings for some reason.

Refining his techniques.

Anxious he'd be caught.

Playing with his victim.

I couldn't look at the pictures of Margie's evisceration too closely. Just so violent. So unspeakably cruel. I would read the autopsy report findings for that one. The idea of a baby being cut from her made me sick to my stomach. My mother escaped her captor and stayed lost long enough to have me. He didn't cut me out of her.

I see Ronnie is having trouble with it also.

I have an idea and call Cass at the Nordland General Store. The phone rings several times before she answers.

"Nordland General Store. Eat in or carry out?"

"Cass, it's me. Megan Carpenter with Jefferson County Sheriff's."

"I thought it might be you or that friend of yours. The Sheriff's Office number came up on the screen. What can I get you?" she asks, before adding her two cents: "I hope you don't want to talk to that no-account Bobbsey twin again. He gives me the creeps."

I tell her what I have in mind without giving her a reason. She draws her own conclusion and agrees. She promises to call me.

I hang up just as Ronnie makes her way over from her temporary desk.

"I've got the detective from Kitsap on the phone," she says. "He wants to know if we're going to have a meeting here or do we want to come there? He's already talked to Clallam County and they can go either way. He sounds anxious to see what we've got."

I think for a moment. "Give me his number and tell him I'll call him back. I need to see what the sheriff wants." I don't, really, but I need time to think how to do this. I already have a helper. Ronnie has worked out okay, but I work alone. Not out of jealousy, or to guard my case, but more because I do whatever it takes to find the bastard and take him out of play. I don't need partners holding me back or holding me accountable.

I'm not sure how Ronnie will react to what I just asked Cass to do.

Ronnie goes back to her desk and gets on the phone.

My desk phone rings, and I answer. "Jefferson County Sheriff's Office, Detective Carpenter."

"Thank goodness. I thought maybe you'd quit."

I know the voice immediately. "Hello, Dan."

Dan Anderson is a man I met on my last major case, involving multiple murders up in Snow Creek. He lived in the area of the murders and helped with background information on two of the victims. He asked me out, I accepted, and the date went fairly well. And then the case had ended, and I didn't keep up with him. In fact, he left a couple of voice messages that I never got around to returning. I don't think I intended to. I figured he would get tired and give up. Most men would. Apparently not Dan.

"It's been a while, Megan."

Actually it has been two months and some change. I almost ask how he got my desk number but catch myself before the words come out.

"Yes, it has. Sorry." I find myself almost doing the whole *I've been busy* or *It's me, not you* routine. He saves me from babbling.

Actually, he saves me from ruining a potential relationship—something that has been in short supply of late.

As of always.

"I'm sorry for not reaching out before now," Dan says. He doesn't ask if I'd gotten his messages. He's not confrontational or judgmental that way.

"I should have called you," I say.

The line is silent. I'm wondering what to say next and I guess he is too. So awkward.

"Well, I'll let you go. You're probably in the middle of some big case. I just wanted to hear your voice again."

I don't need a relationship right now. Then I feel my resolve melting. "Actually, I am. But if you're ever in the area, we should get together for coffee or something."

It was like the words just escaped from my mouth. Just came out. I didn't mean them. Or did I?

"As it happens, I'm in the area."

"Port Hadlock?"

"No, Port Townsend," he says. "I might as well come clean. I ran into Mindy a while back and she suggested I call you. In case you're wondering, she's the one who gave me this number."

That figures. Mindy has been pushing me to have a life for as long as I've known her. "I'm pretty tied up today," I say.

I am busy, but it's really not you. It's me. I'm sorry.

He lets out a breath. "Oh. Okay. Maybe some other time."

His disappointment is palpable through the phone and I immediately amend my response.

"Dan," I say, "wait. I might be able to meet you downtown, at the waterfront. You remember where Hops Ahoy is, right?"

We had our first and only date there. Mindy came along with me to be an escape route if I didn't like him. He showed up and the two of them did most of the talking. I couldn't share my past and felt horrible making things up. Not that I couldn't come up with lies quick. I just didn't like lying to Dan. He walked me to my car and asked me for another date. It didn't happen.

I didn't let it.

"That's great. When? I mean what time?"

We agree on seven and the call is over. I hope I will be able to put the case aside by then, knowing full well that I'll stew all night. And something may come up. If that happens, I have his number to disappoint him again. Unfortunately, Ronnie overhears my part of the conversation.

"Is Dan your boyfriend?" she asks.

"No," I say. "Just an acquaintance."

I'm not about to explain to her that when it comes to relationships, especially one that might actually go somewhere besides the bedroom, I'm pretty messed up. Or that I liked him almost immediately and I know he liked me. Or when it comes to love I don't have the trust that's needed to water it and help it grow. Instead, I withhold the parts of me that are important and end up lying about almost everything. Nothing grows in salted soil.

Ronnie grins. "Sounds to me like you have a date tonight."

I give her a shrug and return the smile. Yes. It does. Not much scares me, but I'm scared. I need to make a call. I go outside and make a call to another person I haven't talked to for a while.

Dr. Albright is always there for me.

CHAPTER TWENTY-SEVEN

Karen Albright doesn't let me down. She answers almost before the first ring is finished.

"Megan, I'm so glad you called."

She sounds sincere. *Is* sincere. She's my last best friend on earth. She's the only living soul who knows almost all of my past. Enough to label me one of the monsters I've hunted. Hunted and killed. But she doesn't. She listens. I trust her like I never trusted my mother. Or my aunt.

I've never allowed myself to call her Karen. Her first name. She is always Dr. Albright to me. She knows it. I know it. It's what works for us.

"Dr. Albright, I just called to see how you are." Even *I* can hear the lie in my voice. The nervous edge that comes with each word.

"Talk to me, Megan. I'm here."

I knew she would always be there too.

"This is going to sound silly," I say.

"Then why don't you take a moment and amuse me."

I can hear the smile. I don't know why, but I feel a sting of wetness in my eyes. I don't allow myself to cry. It's a weakness. Weakness equals disaster, even death, in my world. I force myself to let out a small laugh.

"I've got a date tonight."

Dr. Albright stays silent. That's one of my tricks. A good one. I fill in the gap. "I guess I'm afraid."

"Afraid you'll have fun?"

I detect the mirth in her voice again. She's not interrupting the flow. She's redirecting it to the real reason I called her.

"I like him," I say. "He likes me. He's been trying to reach me for a month."

"He contacted you today?"

"Just now. He wants to meet me for drinks tonight." I don't admit that I'm the one who proposed that. It's a little miscommunication, not really a lie. Dr. Albright is quiet. I know if I don't tell her what's on my mind, the whole conversation will be me saying one or two words and her staying silent.

"We got together a short while back and seemed to get along. And then, when he was walking me to my car, he asked me to go with him to some kind of art thing. I said yes. But I didn't meet him. And I haven't been returning his calls. And then he just shows up and I have too much to deal with already."

"What are you dealing with, Megan?"

"I'm on the hunt again. I know you don't approve of what I do, or how I see my place in the world, but someone is kidnapping, torturing, and killing young women. I can't... I don't know how to..."

She waits. I get my voice under control, although my emotions are all over the place. Sadness, panic, anger, rage, self-loathing. I don't want to be like my biological father. I don't want to be like my mother. Sometimes I don't want to be like me.

"I see myself as the bad guy—girl—sometimes. It freaks me out, but I know what I have to do. I know it's the right thing to do. Yesterday and today have been a jumble of connections to my past. I attended an autopsy on one of these victims. There are three so far over the last two years. The one I went to the autopsy on happened two days ago. At least, that's when we found her body."

I can feel the darkness edging its way into my vision and my thoughts. Anger is winning out. Soon it will be full-blown rage.

I keep going. No air. No stopping. Just unloading it all.

"The woman he killed two years ago was gutted. He cut a baby out of her. She was four months pregnant. Sick. Disgusting. And the woman I found yesterday had a baby about a year ago. I think she got pregnant by her father. He's a suspect now. He's rich and arrogant and sick in the head. He's trying to get the sheriff to take me off the case."

I take a breath and silence fills the empty space.

"But you don't know if he's the killer."

"Yeah," I say, quickly adding, "I mean, no. I'm not positive he's even the father. And if he is, it doesn't necessarily mean he killed her. Or had her killed. He needs to be in prison. Or a loony bin. But I want to see him take responsibility for at least ruining this girl's life."

"Like yours was ruined by your biological father."

"It's not the same," I say.

"Isn't it?"

I continue to bounce my thoughts and feelings off Dr. Albright's indestructible and nonjudgmental wall of professionalism. I still have one more thing to talk about, but I can't. It's the most troubling thing of all and it has nothing to do with these murders. It has to do with my past. More specifically, someone from my past. Someone I can't identify. Someone who may mean me harm.

I say goodbye, promise to call more often, and hang up.

I lean against the wall of the building, listening to a bell ringing far out in the bay, seagulls screeching and squabbling. The sounds are soothing. The email I received right after I saw Dan the last time wasn't soothing at all. It was like a slap in the face. Unexpected. Painful. A blur.

I had just finished working several murders in the secluded area above Snow Creek, far from where Leann's body was found. I was feeling pretty good. Things had turned out well. I had time to check my emails, as I usually do many times a day, hoping there is one from Hayden. There were more than a dozen new emails, none from my brother. I started to delete them when one caught my eye and sent chills down my back.

The subject line said, "It's you, Rylee."

Rylee wasn't a name many people knew I had used. The sender's name was one I didn't recognize: "Wallace." When I opened it, I couldn't breathe.

Someone knew where I lived. What I did for a living.

More distressingly, I realized, they might know what I had *done*.

A voice next to my ear makes me jump. It's Ronnie. She's eerily quiet sometimes.

"Megan, the detective from Kitsap called again. Have you made a decision yet?"

"We'll have lunch in town and then go," I tell her. "Call him back and see if he's free later this afternoon."

CHAPTER TWENTY-EIGHT

The Ajax Cafe sits in a historic building on North Water Street, which separates the town from the southern end of Port Townsend Bay. The seating is a charmingly riotous mishmash of different sizes, colors, and shapes of chairs and tables. Overhead is a centipede-like row of hats for which there seems no restriction, from cowboy to beret to sequins to garden-variety felt. It looks as if someone has gone berserk at dozens of garage sales. Yelp says, and I agree, the food is excellent. I have a Port Hadlock Haddock Burger. Ronnie has a tiny side salad. I have a large Hadlock Vanilla Gorilla Milkshake. Ronnie has water.

My waistline hates her.

We are just getting back on the road when Cass calls from the Nordland General Store on Marrowstone Island.

I answer. "Cass, did you get them?"

"Sure did. What do you want me to do? Anything to put these bastards away."

"I'll see if Lonigan can pick them up. Did you touch them?"

"I had to. How do you pick something up without touching it?"

"That's okay. You put them in separate paper bags and put B and T on the bags like I asked, right?"

"That's what you told me to do," she says. "I'm not a dumb broad; I just play one on TV."

I laugh. I really like this woman. "I'll get back to you, or Lonigan will pick them up. Keep them safe."

She promises.

"What is Lonigan picking up and taking to the crime lab?" Ronnie asks as I put away my phone.

I don't want to tell her. Or ruin her perception of professional investigations where everything is done perfectly. But she deserves to know, since she will hang alongside me if it goes bad.

"Plates, forks, and soda cans."

"Are they from this case, Megan?"

"Yes. And no."

"How's that?"

"I had Cass collect the stuff after Joe Bohleber and Jim Truitt ate. She might have told them she was giving away free slices of pie and soda today. One-time offer to boost business."

Ronnie gives me a knowing look. "She *might* have, huh? What a coincidence. And she just happened to mark the bags *B* for 'Bohleber' and *T* for 'Truitt'?"

I nod.

"And Lonigan is taking them to Marley for DNA comparison with DNA collected from Leann's case?"

I nod a second time. "I called Marley about the rape kit. He agreed to run it. We're going to have the DNA from the other two cases compared with Leann's."

"Wow! I did my rotation through the crime lab and they are always backed up the wazoo. Marley really agreed to compare all three?"

Now I give Ronnie a knowing look before speaking.

"He will if you ask him nicely."

She grins.

Next I call Lonigan. "Detective Carpenter here. You on Marrowstone?"

"Yeah," he says. "Same as yesterday and the day before."

"Can you do me a huge favor? I'll owe you a meat loaf dinner at Cass's."

"What's the favor first?"

I tell him. He doesn't balk. I don't even have to pay up. He gets his food comped at the Nordland General Store.

"I'll take the bags to the crime lab after I've had my meat loaf."

"You need to ask for Marley Yang."

"Yang, huh?"

"Is that a problem?" I ask.

He doesn't hesitate. "I guess you don't need the stuff processed right away."

I can tell he's familiar with Marley and doesn't care for him.

"I'll give it to him personally, but I don't have any paperwork. He'll want me to sign for it."

"Tell him I'll bring the paperwork today. And don't sign anything."

I put the phone away to find Ronnie giving me a quizzical look, but she doesn't ask me anything. I can see the wheels turning, but they're not getting her anywhere just yet.

I watch the scenery go by. I think about my "date" with Dan tonight. I don't have any new clothes. Not my style. *Clothes.* I think of what Ronnie and Mindy said about the clothes left lying out on Leann's bed at her cabin. She was an attractive young woman. She would probably turn heads in a potato sack. And yet she'd tried on at least three outfits.

God knows, I don't have a lot of experience with dating, and the only thing I know about fashion are the things I've seen on TV or picked up around my old college dorm. Three outfits indicates she was really trying to impress whoever she was going off to see. That makes me think of my date again. And Dan. Should I try to impress him? He already seems impressed or he wouldn't be trying to keep in touch. But where did he expect this to go? If he just wants me to sleep with him, he won't have to break my arm. But what if he expects more? He may want me to share things about my past with him. I can't. I haven't even shared a lot of my past with my own brother. I told Hayden only what he needed to know. So how much do I want Dan to know?

"Earth to Megan."

I'm driving on autopilot and our turn is just ahead.

"I'm thinking."

"About tonight? Your date?"

"No," I say in such a way that she not only knows otherwise but also knows that I don't intend to talk about it.

We follow the coast of Puget Sound to State Route 104, cross the Hood Canal Floating Bridge, past Port Gamble to Northeast State Route 104, and then to the Kitsap County Sheriff's Office substation in Kingston.

The Kingston office is a one-story building, wood-sided, with a wood-shingled roof. There's minimal parking. I pull into a spot marked "Sheriff's Office Only." There are two other spaces. Both empty.

"This is where he said to meet us, right?"

Ronnie takes her phone out. "Kingston office. Should I call him?"

I notice a boy's bicycle leaning against the front. "Maybe that's his police vehicle." I get out and she follows me to the front door. I twist the knob.

"Hello. Anyone home?"

No answer.

Inside is an empty yawning space, no private offices. No interview rooms. There isn't even a counter separating the front from the two desks that have name plates on them. I can hear a copy machine running somewhere and I follow the noise just as a man wearing faded Lee jeans and a purple University of Washington T-shirt stretched tightly across his chest emerges.

He holds out his hand. "Detective Clay Osborne."

His grip is strong and grinds the bones in my hand and I try to give the same back.

Never show weakness.

"Detective Megan Carpenter," I say.

"Reserve Deputy Ronnie Marsh." Ronnie holds her hand out and looks him over.

Clay takes her hand and I see her wince. To him, I suspect, it is akin to squeezing a Nerf ball.

Detective Osborne is in his mid-thirties, six feet something. His weight is hard to guess but it is perfect for his physique. He has thick red hair and a lumberjack's beard. The only thing identifying him as law enforcement is the shoulder holster he's wearing. He has an old Colt Model 1911 in the rig and sees me noticing it.

"Are you familiar with the government model Colt .45?"

"A little," I say.

The truth is I know a lot about it. Rolland, my stepfather, had a Colt M1911A1 semiautomatic. It was old army issue and was carried by soldiers in a lot of wars. My mother said my real father—who turned out to be a fictitious father—had one just like it when he went overseas. I always imagined him charging the enemy with that gun. She told me he was a hero.

Liar.

Clay slips the pistol from the holster, drops the magazine, and makes it safe. He does all this with practiced ease, second nature. He doesn't offer it to either of us but holds it up and turns it so we can see each side.

"This is actually a 1912 Colt government model," he says. "Forty-five-caliber, magazine capacity seven rounds plus one in the chamber. The after-factory magazines hold eight plus one in the chamber. This is the original. My stepfather carried it in Vietnam."

The way he says it makes me think his stepfather is deceased, so I don't ask. He puts the weapon back in the shoulder rig. "You aren't here to talk about my gun, though."

"I brought my file," I say. "What we have so far, anyway. Is Clallam County coming?"

He sets a couple of chairs over by one of the desks and we all sit. Dina Knowles's face is familiar to me. I notice her file open on the desk. A few of the photos from when she was found are in a neat array.

"Larry might be a little late," he says. "He's trying to get his hands on the DNA results. He said he couldn't find them in his case file, and he'll have to get copies from the crime lab."

Of course. Why didn't I think of that? The DNA results would already have been run by the crime lab. I won't have to supply Marley with any of that. All I'll have to give him are the DNA samples Cass collected for me.

"You're talking about Marley Yang, correct?" I ask.

"Yeah," he says. "He's the one that did the comparison of our cases. Have you submitted DNA yet?"

"A rape kit," I say. "They haven't run it yet."

Clay lets out a breath. "I know how that is. Took me four weeks to get them to look at mine, and then another three weeks after I found out about Clallam County's case to get them to agree to compare them. That was about five months ago."

"I talked to Marley today," I say. "He tells me they have a new machine that can run the DNA in less than two hours."

Clay's eyebrows bounce. "I guess they don't want that to get out. They wouldn't be able to put everyone off with that 'I'm covered up with DNA work' routine."

My thoughts exactly. I think Marley is afraid the lab will be flooded with priority requests.

Ronnie speaks up. "He showed me the machine when I did my rotation last month. It's a fascinating and very expensive piece of equipment and he's the only one trained to use it."

And he probably wants to keep it that way. I get it. *Job security.*

I take the case file on Leann Truitt out of my bag.

"I'm sorry I didn't have a chance to copy it," I say. "Can you do that while we wait for Larry to bring Clallam's case?"

"Did someone call my name?" Larry Gray says from the doorway.

I have spoken to Larry Gray only briefly. I look at him, but I see the spitting image of Sheriff Tony Gray. Same features. Same thin hair. Same belly. Same size. The only difference is he's five or so years younger and ten pounds heavier.

Make that fifteen.

"You don't happen to be related to our sheriff?" I ask. "Tony Gray?"

He gives a friendly shrug. "Second cousins on my mother's side. He doesn't claim me and that's the way I like it." He adds with a huge, toothy grin, "Tony's okay. Nothing wrong with him that retirement won't cure."

Thanks for nothing, I think.

Larry is lugging a big accordion folder barely held shut with a string and some rubber bands. Clay kicks a chair out, and Larry brings over his file.

"Clay," he says.

"Larry."

"Megan," I say putting my hand out. His hand is big, but his grip is soft. Compared to Clay's, anyway.

"And this must be your trusty deputy, Ronnie Marsh," Larry says as Ronnie's hand drips through his big paw. "We've talked a few times. I called Yang at the crime lab. You know Marley, don't you?"

I nod and he goes on. "Yeah, he's a pistol. He said I didn't need a copy of the results because he has all of that pulled up already and is looking at our cases. He has high praise for Ronnie here. Said to tell her he's running her case through now."

Her case?

Ronnie's case?

"Let's get busy," Clay says, taking out legal-size notepads and handing them out. "Why don't you go first, Detective Carpenter? You have the newest case, right?"

I know his type. I know it like a fox knows a chicken.

I will always be the fox.

CHAPTER TWENTY-NINE

The Kingston, Kitsap County, substation is silent. No purr of a heating system. No ringing of phones. It's quiet like a prayer. It occurs to me that prayer isn't a bad idea. Finding Leann's killer is about saving another victim. Young. Pretty. Dreaming of the future, while he lies in wait.

I start with the discovery of Leann's body on Marrowstone Island by Robbie Boyd; I look at the men I've just met. I wonder if they will be territorial or if they will understand that serial killers don't care about wandering over various jurisdictions. Indeed, that's what works best for them. We need to unite. Not posture.

I keep my fingers crossed.

"Do either of you have anything on that name?"

"I ran him through the system," Clay says. "I don't think that's his real name."

"Why?" Larry asks.

"I have a friend who's a policeman that works security at the college," Clay says. "I had him run the guy through their files and he said they had a Robbie Boyd, full name Robert Aloysius Boyd. I had Jimmy—that's my buddy—send me a picture from his campus ID. I compared that to the link to the Facebook page Ronnie sent. Doesn't look anything like him. In fact, the Robbie Boyd attending school there is a black male."

That disclosure absolutely stuns me. I had Ronnie call the college and check to see if Robbie Boyd was supposed to have been in a class during the time we were at the scene. He *was* in class. But apparently it wasn't the right Robbie Boyd. I hate being completely wrong about anything. Not a smart way to live. The Boyd at the crime scene could have used someone's name and identification. It was confusing because the license plate on his crap Ford Pinto came back to Boyd.

"He must know Boyd," I suggest. "The license tags came back to Robert Boyd. Boyd showed Ronnie a Washington driver's license with that name. He knew that the real Boyd was supposed to be in class."

Clay picks up the desk phone and punches in a number.

"Hi, this is Detective Osborne. Is Jimmy there? Yeah, let me talk to him." Clay holds the phone away from his ear. "I'm going to have my friend see if he can locate the real Boyd and try to round up the impersonator."

While we wait for Jimmy to get to the phone, I keep going.

"State Patrolman MacDonald was the first officer on the scene, followed by Deputy Davis."

"'Old MacDonald Had a Farm' MacDonald?" Larry asks. "Did he get out of his car?"

Interesting, I think. He knows MacDonald. "Yeah. He stayed with Boyd while Deputy Davis climbed down a cliff to secure the scene."

Larry grins and nods. "Sounds like him."

I pull out photos of my crime scene, taken in vivid color: blood red against the blue of Port Townsend Bay. Shots from the water showing the body's position on the shore. Shots in each direction showing the limited access to the scene.

"Have either of you heard of a strainer?" I ask.

Both shake their heads.

I go on: "It's an obstacle that catches animals or people that are caught up in the current and they die because they can't get out."

They clearly don't know where I'm going.

"Boyd has a website that talks about such things. He calls it a 'Killing Box,'" I say as I tap my finger on the photograph. "If you notice, my crime scene is kind of boxed in. There are only a couple of ways to get to that spot, and all are very difficult. Either down a forty-foot cliff, by swimming, or by boat."

Larry gives me a questioning look.

"You think Boyd's our guy?" he asks.

"He's a suspect."

"I guess you didn't detain him," Larry asks.

It comes across as a dig. I understand: What if I had the killer and let him leave? I should have taken the statement myself.

Clay reads my expression.

"No way you could have known he was lying about who he was," he says. "Some of these fake IDs are damn good. Jimmy told me last year that someone on campus was making and selling them."

My face feels warm. Probably red too. I should have caught that. I am a veritable expert at procuring fake driver's licenses, bogus birth certificates, made-up business cards, anything one would need to disappear or become someone else.

I've done it many, many times.

Clay gets Jimmy on the phone. He puts it on speakerphone and tells him who's in the room.

"What can I do for you, Clay?" Jimmy asks.

"You remember that clown I asked about? Robbie Boyd?"

"Aloysius? Yeah."

"The guy we're looking for is a white guy—" he says, interrupting himself as he catches my eye. "Wait a minute. I'll have Detective Carpenter give you a description."

I offer up a complete description and he repeats it back to me. I also provide the license plate of the car.

"You got all that, Jimmy?" Clay asks.

"What?" he asks, his tone suddenly more playful. "You think I'm just here for my good looks?"

"Nah," Clay says. "If you were there for your looks, they would have fired you by now."

"What do you want me to do if I find him?"

"Hold him and call me."

"Arrest?" Jimmy asks. "Or just detain?"

"Break his legs," Clay snaps back. "I don't care. Just call me."

"Okay," he says right away. "You don't have to get sore. I'll call you."

Clay returns the phone to its cradle. "Jimmy's a good security cop but he's not a hard worker, if you catch my drift."

That's what worries me.

"Will he look for Boyd?" I finally ask.

Clay gives it a little thought, leaning back in his chair. "He will. But not too hard. He used to be with Kitsap Sheriff's. He got passed up for a detective position and pulled the pin, quit and went on to work for Port Townsend PD and on to be a campus cop. He says he's happy doing his shift and working off duty. I guess to each his own."

"My gal, Margie Benton, was hard to get to," Larry says, speaking up. "She was hung up on some rocks on San Juan Island. Almost in Canadian waters. You could see D'Arcy Island from where she was found."

Larry starts digging through the accordion folder.

"I got some shots from the scene, but go ahead."

"My victim was wearing a bra and panties," I say. "We didn't find any other clothing."

I look over at Clay.

Larry is still digging.

"Dina Knowles only had panties on," Clay says. "We didn't find her clothing, either."

Larry finally finds what he is searching for. He puts a couple of pictures on the desk and points with a fingernail that needs some serious clipping. "This was taken beside the body and out across the strait. You can see D'Arcy Island right over there."

I wonder what is so important about that tiny island that he's going to so much trouble to find the picture and point it out. So I ask: "What about D'Arcy?"

Larry leans back again and spreads his hands out like a bishop giving a blessing. "Well, you see what I'm saying."

I don't. Not at all. Clay does and covers a grin with his hand. Ronnie is clueless by her expression.

"It's simple," Larry says. "If she'd been across the strait, she'd have been the Mounties' problem."

"Poor you." Clay pats Larry on the hand. "Always overworked and underpaid. You have the worst luck of anyone I've ever known."

Larry waves him off. "Yeah, yeah."

"No," he says. "I mean it. I think the killer only dumped the body there to piss you off."

"Okay. I get it. No one sees what I mean."

I still didn't see it.

Larry taps the picture again with that fingernail. "Whoever killed this girl had his pick of islands and beaches and inlets. He had to get there by boat, so if he'd dumped my girl anywhere in the Haro Strait, it would have been the same to him. We don't know where the murder took place. It could be any one of a couple dozen islands, but he dumps her on San Juan Island. The killer could be Canadian for all we know."

I wasn't familiar with every island, especially along the Canadian border.

"Larry," Clay says, "all three of these women could have been killed anywhere and dumped in our jurisdictions. The facts are—and correct me if I'm wrong—they all lived alone, all looked alike, all are around the same age, all had babies or were pregnant, and all worked at bars near some type of waterway."

That sums it up nicely, I think.

"Mine was staged to look like she'd drowned there," Larry adds.

I raise my eyebrows. None of that is in the reports I've been given.

"Staged?" I ask.

He taps the pictures again. "No one in their right mind would want to be swimming in the icy water in their birthday suit." With his eyes still on mine, he extracts another picture from the folder. This is one of the victims at the scene. She is on her back, arms splayed out to her sides, legs shoulder-width apart. It is a very unnatural position for a body to have washed up on the beach. For that matter, it is not the way a body would come to rest if it was dumped out of a boat or dragged onto the beach.

It was just like the way Leann Truitt was staged.

"Did you think she drowned?" I ask.

"It's what one of the Marine Patrol guys said. Anyway, Benton was two years ago. Somehow it got leaked to the news that my girl was strangled with a belt. Had been tortured. You two might have a copycat killer. Someone that got wind of Margie Benton's case."

"Was it in the news?" I ask.

"'Course," he sneers. "Those bloodsuckers posted pictures and everything. I don't know where they got them."

Ben Franklin once said three can keep a secret, if two of them are dead. So true. Nothing is secret when it involves law enforcement if more than one person knows about it. Larry himself might have leaked to a reporter.

Clay laughs a little. "Larry, I don't believe it's a copycat and neither do you. This guy is proud of his killings. He marks them."

I turn and face him. "What do you mean?"

Before he can explain, my phone buzzes with a call from Marley Yang. I excuse myself and take it outside. I know that Marley is going ballistic if he's gotten the DNA sample from

Lonigan. Lonigan doesn't even know whose samples they were, so he couldn't have told Marley. I thought he would run them as unknown subjects. I told Cass to mark the bags with a *B* and a *T*. I didn't want Lonigan to know what I was up to.

CHAPTER THIRTY

I find a space next to the copier. Above it, a sign with four figures bent over laughing: "You want it *when*?" Nan has the same sign on her desk. She makes a habit of pointing to it whenever the task—or the individual who asks for it to be done—annoys her.

"You should have given me a call, Megan," Marley says. He's angry and he's right.

Lonigan made out an evidence collection form signed by Cass as giving it to Lonigan and he made Marley sign it. Marley wasn't happy about being forced to sign a form for evidence with no proof it was collected properly. It wasn't an official request from the Sheriff's Department and there was no other record giving him permission to even have it, much less test it.

"What am I supposed to do with this?" he asks, still fuming.

I don't blame him for being angry. That's fine. On the other hand, I don't really care. I only care about the case.

"I'm truly sorry," I say, feebly trying to soothe him. "You're right, Marley. It'll never happen again."

I don't know for sure, but I suspect that's a lie.

My words do little to placate him, but I keep going.

"You're doing so much for me already, I feel bad about asking you to run the new samples against what you have from Leann Truitt, Margie Benton, and Dina Knowles."

I sound thoroughly chastened.

I think.

Marley lets out a little puff of a sigh. "Megan, you only asked if I would see if there was DNA in Truitt's rape kit. That's all."

He's weakening. Good. All I need is one more thing.

"Ronnie said to tell you hello," I say. "She's the one who told me you would help out."

A slight pause on the other end of the line.

"I know what you're doing, Megan."

Maybe I've overdone my act. It's happened a time or two.

"You're trying to fix me and Ronnie up."

I relax. He isn't as smart as he thinks.

"Caught me. She really does think you're cute."

Now all I have to do is convince Ronnie that she thinks Marley is cute. Might not be so hard. Marley is attractive, fit, and not completely geeky. That's rare in a crime lab.

"I'll do it this one time, Megan," he says, "but you need to send a report to me as quick as possible. I can't just run tests on a whim of yours. If I did that, do you know how many people would want me to do it?"

I want to say no. "A gazillion, I imagine. I won't say a word. Promise."

"I'll call you, but don't expect me to drop everything else to do this."

"I don't."

"The samples are marked *B* and *T*. Is that all you have? No names?"

"Not yet, but I'm working on it."

"Okay," he says. "As long as you know where they came from and put it in the report you've just promised me."

"I do."

"Tell Ronnie hello for me."

I smile to myself. "I will."

I hang up and go back to find Clay and Larry sitting back, listening to Ronnie vent about her tough life, and how she always wanted to be a detective, and how the earth cooled, and the dinosaurs evolved, et cetera. I can tell they are trapped when their pained expressions turn to hope as I come back into view.

Ronnie has been at it the entire time I've been on the phone. I don't feel sorry for them. Better them than me.

I interrupt Ronnie's monologue. "That was the crime lab. Marley's doing the comparisons as we speak. And I guess I should tell you that I have two other DNA samples he's going to check against them. By the way, he says hello, Ronnie."

"Oh, that's nice" is all she says.

I'll have to work on her.

Clay leans forward in his chair. "What samples?"

"Oh, no you don't. You said our killer was proud of his work and leaving his mark. You explain that first. Then I'll tell you about the samples. Deal?"

Clay looks from face to face. "Okay. Somewhere near the dump sites he leaves a symbol. A triangle with an eye. Larry's was scratched into the rock beside the body. Mine was scratched onto a log near Dina's body. You don't have one listed in your report."

I didn't put it in my report. I thought it might be nothing. Now I know better.

Larry scoffs. "Hell, we have a lot of little freaks around the islands that believe in all kinds of shit. Voodoo, even. We had a house fire last year. It was an abandoned place. The fire started in the kitchen. I thought it might be homeless, squatters, but then they found the real cause. Some kids were burning a bird's skeleton. I talked to the boys and they saw it on television and were summoning a demon. I gave them demon. Right on their little rears. What I'm getting at is those things could have already been there. They weren't carved into the body, were they? No. It don't mean nothing."

Ronnie speaks up. "I read both of your reports and there's no mention of an all-seeing eye in either of them."

"She's right," I say.

"I guess we all had the same thought: leaks. I wanted to keep something back in case we caught the killer. If he told me about the drawing, I'd know I had the right guy." It's a lie, but it sounds good to me.

Ronnie hands her legal pad to Clay. "Can you draw it for me?"

He does and gives the pad back. It was what Deputy Davis found scratched into the bottom of a rock at Leann's dump site.

Ronnie draws in a breath. "I just remembered: I saw this on the website."

"What website?" I ask.

"Remember the 'Warrior Priestess' shirt Leann's dad was wearing and how strange he talked?"

I did. I thought he was putting it on.

"I looked it up," she goes on. "There's a website. I found this symbol on one of the pages."

I'm thinking Jim Truitt.

Ronnie shoots me an embarrassed look. She didn't tell me about this, and she knows she should have. In her defense, I didn't ask. It was my fault for not looking into it myself. I've been slipping. *Remember this moment, I tell myself. This is another good reason not to work with a partner—or quasi-partner.* I remind myself that I'm only at this meeting to get information. I don't need their help. Or hers. I will use them, however. That's fair game.

My mother taught me that.

Larry scoffs a second time. "Let's not go jumping to conclusions here, little missy. Kids. Vandals. Aspiring taggers. Hell, it's not even a coincidence. Half the religions around here have similar symbols if that's even what it is. This land has always had Native tribes. Lots of superstition around the Salish. Gods of this and that. Some believe in witches up in my section."

"Pagan symbols," Ronnie adds, pulling herself out of the quicksand of her embarrassment. "Wiccan. It's Egyptian, the Eye of Horus. It means protection and health for the royals. It's also a Masonic symbol."

"It's on the back of the dollar bill too," Clay says.

Larry pulls a crumpled bill from his jean's pocket. "I knew I'd seen it somewhere. See? It don't mean nothing."

"I don't think we can read too much into the symbol," Clay says, "except it was found at each of our crime scenes. It must mean something to the killer. I agree with Megan. If we find him, he can tell us what it means."

I don't want to get pulled into this line of thought. And I'm not over the "little missy" comment, either. I still have to eliminate several suspects before I start looking into Native myths or religious sects of every variety that dot the state. Yet, to be safe, I'll have Ronnie keep digging into it. She is the computer wizard. I'll find subjects to interview.

I give them a copy of the pathologist's report. Ronnie made several. She has her uses. They both skim it and I watch them nod as they read.

Larry puts the report down on his lap. "I agree this all seems very similar," he says, "but I still think it could be a copycat. We've had this sort of thing here in Washington and other places before. Remember Robert Berdella, 'the Kansas City Butcher,' 'the Collector'? He looked like Rob Reiner, the actor. They don't all look or act crazy. He did a lot of these things to his kidnapping victims before he murdered them. Maybe this guy's a fan of his."

Clay speaks next, looking at me and Ronnie. "I remember Berdella, of course, but these two are barely old enough to even know who Rob Reiner is, much less Berdella. So you're saying someone is imitating Berdella's murders?"

Larry shrugs a little. "Berdella is dead but books have been written about him. There are a million ways to kill someone. And a good chance someone is using the same methods of killing as someone else without even knowing it."

Clay rocks back in his chair and pauses while he thinks. "Now all we have to do is find a Catholic that believes in witchcraft, kidnaps young men, has anal sex with them, and hates women. Come on, Larry. Why are you trying to make this more difficult than it already is?"

"I'm just throwing out ideas," Larry says. "If you don't look at a case from every angle, you're going to have a hard time in court later. A defense attorney will bring all this shit up and you're going to have to say you didn't even consider it. The jury will think you have something against the scumbag you've arrested."

Clay fixes his steely gaze on me.

"Your turn," he says. "What DNA samples?"

CHAPTER THIRTY-ONE

Make that a frog pinned down to a dissecting board in a high school science class. I can't move. I can't wriggle out of it. The truth is, I made a deal with Clay. I agreed that if he told me about the killer's mark, I'd tell him about the DNA samples I asked Marley to compare. I intended to honor the agreement but not tell him any more than absolutely necessary. "Keep your cards close to your vest" is a motto of mine. In all things. Not just a case. I don't think he particularly needs to know who had obtained the samples for me. I can hear Larry finding legal reasons that a defense attorney would rip the results to shreds. And Larry may be onto something. At the same time, I don't care about taking this to court and putting it in front of a jury, where the killer can sit in his white clothes and white buck shoes, holding a Bible and looking sad and wrongly accused.

He is going to pay for what he's done.

My way.

"I always keep my promises," I lie. "Before our discussion led away from my case, I was going to tell you that I interviewed Leann Truitt's landlord. Her picture was shown around, as you know, and a state patrol officer out on Marrowstone Island identified her."

That is partially true. Actually, Cass identified her, but Lonigan called me about it.

"The landlord is Joe or Joseph Bohleber," I continue. "He rents out fishing cabins for a living."

And blackmails people.

"He was hesitant to tell me the truth about her rental agreement, and flat out lied about knowing the victim's father, Jim Truitt."

Larry puts a big arm down on the desk hard and looks to the side. "Jim Truitt is her dad?"

I nod.

"Well, shit fire and save the matches." He looks at Ronnie and says, "Excuse my language."

I guess he doesn't mind his language around me.

"Jim Truitt has a long reach," he says, "in case you aren't aware of it."

I nod. "Sheriff says the same thing."

Larry pushes back from the desk and makes a motion like *Well, there you go.*

"Am I not supposed to tell you about that interview?" I ask.

"Well, shoot…I mean, there's not much need to," Larry says. "He's a lying sack of…uh, excrement, so anything he tells you will be a lie. But he's connected. Big-time connected. You go messing with Jim Truitt and you might kiss your job goodbye."

Clay says nothing. He doesn't even ask questions, which makes me think he knows Jim Truitt as well. How am I the only one, except for sensitive-eared Ronnie, who doesn't know about this scumbag?

"So I got Truitt and Joe Bohleber's DNA samples."

"What?" Larry comes out of his seat. "You got Truitt to volunteer a DNA sample?" Larry sounds like the idea is utterly ridiculous.

He is right, of course. Truitt didn't actually give the sample voluntarily. He just didn't know he had given it. There's a difference there somewhere.

"It was difficult," I say, "but I obtained one." That much is true. "Got one from Joe Bohleber too. I still need one from Steve Bohleber and Robbie Boyd. Steve should have the same basic DNA as Joe, being a twin."

"Is that what you were talking to Marley about?" Clay asks. "I'll bet he didn't like running all of that DNA." He is looking at me like he is onto what I've actually done. I don't tell them that Marley has no idea who the samples are from.

"Anyway," I press on, "Marley said he'd do the comparisons quickly. Did the DNA from Margie Benton and Dina Knowles get you anywhere?"

I didn't see any mention of either in their reports.

Larry hangs his head. "My samples were contaminated."

"Contaminated?" I ask. I find it hard to imagine a vaginal swab being contaminated in a controlled environment—and there is always a remedy if it is. "Couldn't you just take a new sample?"

"Not contaminated, exactly," he says, like he's confessing something untoward. "My victim led a very active sexual life."

"Mine, too," Clay says quickly, "but we got a good sample."

Larry misreads the disappointed expression on my face as me being peeved by what he's just said.

"Now, don't go thinking I'm a sexist or nothing like that," he says, looking first at me, then at Ronnie. "Hey, anything we say in this room stays in this room. Right?"

I ignore him. I may need some ammunition to use against him someday. I have Ronnie as a witness.

Larry goes on to explain and in doing so shoves his foot deeper in his mouth.

"My victim had maybe as many as twenty 'samples' in her on any given day. She worked at a bar during the evening and was a prostitute on the side. Then she gave up the lower-paying job and quit the bar. DNA would be inconclusive at best."

I assumed that Larry's and Clay's DNA evidence matched. I thought that was the reason they were working the cases together. I was wrong. Maybe the DNA isn't going to be enough to make these cases after all.

It doesn't really matter if everything else leads to the killer.

"I did some digging into Bohleber's and Truitt's past," I say. "Bohleber told me he has a twin brother, Steve. They moved to Marrowstone from Indiana, where they had a farm. I found Indiana criminal records on Steve Bohleber. He did three years for assaulting a policeman. He's on parole now. I checked with his PO and they haven't been able to locate him."

I have their complete attention and I continue.

"Joe Bohleber was a suspect in Indiana for bank fraud and money laundering, but those charges never stuck. Nothing on record here. Neither of the twins ever show employment as farmers. Joe told me they were co-owners of fishing cabins. Leann Truitt lived in one just off Mystery Bay."

Larry jumps in. "They probably have a weed farm on Marrowstone. Maybe your little gal got to snooping around and they killed her to keep her quiet?"

Clay puts up his hand. "Hold on, Larry. Marrowstone Island has had legal cultivation and use laws since 2012. They can grow it in their backyards if they want, and it seems a lot of them do. Why would Bohleber worry about being ratted out?"

I'm sure Bohleber isn't worried about marijuana. I can't prove it yet, but he was into blackmail. Truitt is a different horse altogether. If he is the father of Leann's baby, he has motive to kill or hire someone to kill Leann. Maybe he hired one of the Bobbsey Twins.

"You both said the bodies were hard to get to," I say. "How did you get to them? Who worked the scene?"

Larry lays another picture on the desk. It is a view of the scene from the water. I make out the rail of a boat in the bottom corner of the image.

"Marine Patrol came out," he says. "They took some of our CSIs and worked the scene together. You need names?"

"Not at the moment," I say. "I had Marine Patrol come out also. Captain Martin and a deputy named Floyd. They helped the techs work the area. Marine Patrol recovered the body and brought it around to a boat ramp to get it to the coroner."

"'Marvelous Martin,'" Clay says with a grin.

"Roy took me out on the boat one time during my rotation," Ronnie says.

I'm grateful just then that Larry offers no colorful comment concerning Ronnie's rotation.

"I've read your autopsy reports," I say. "The cause of death for Knowles was strangulation. Benton bled to death. Both had broken necks. Is that right?"

Larry and Clay nod.

"What can you tell me that isn't in the autopsy reports?"

Larry and Clay exchange a look. Larry looks for Clay to take the question.

"The bodies were scrubbed clean," he says. "I mean *scrubbed*. There were some minute abrasions in the skin around the knees, feet, hands, elbows, and butt. We called them scuff marks. Our pathologist used a magnifying glass to examine every inch of skin. We found two carpet fibers embedded in Dina's left elbow. Larry said the same scuff marks were on Margie, but the pathologist didn't find anything of note. He called the pathologist after we talked about the possibility of the killer scrubbing down the areas, and the pathologist said—"

Larry cuts Clay off. "He said he didn't remember. It had been over a year ago, but I remembered so he should have. I don't think he wanted to be embarrassed for missing it."

"Can we get a reexamination of the body, Larry?" I ask.

He shakes his head. "Cremated."

"Same with Dina," Clay adds.

I excuse myself and phone Sheriff Gray in the space over by the copier. It is past quitting time, but I know he'll still answer his cell.

"I was just heading out," he says. "Got something for me?"

I ask him to contact a judge or whomever he needs to talk to and make sure Leann's body isn't released to the family yet.

"I need a specific reason for a court order," he says.

"Carpet fibers," I tell him. "We're looking for carpet fibers."

CHAPTER THIRTY-TWO

I come back to the circle and Larry's rubbing his ample belly.

"Can we get something to eat?" he asks.

"I know you had burgers and fries before you got here," Clay says. "I can still smell them on you." He says this jokingly, but we haven't been working on this for two hours, even.

"How 'bout you gals?" Larry asks. "There's a Thai place next door." He pronounces Thai like "thigh."

Ronnie, who had a salad for lunch with a glass of water, chirps, "I like Thai."

"Well, hell!" Larry says loudly. "Who don't like thigh?"

"I'm allergic to Thai food," I lie. I don't want to eat because I want to get done here and I'm supposed to meet Dan in a couple of hours at Hops Ahoy. "It's right next door, so maybe you could order something. We have to get back to the office."

Clay looks disappointed. He narrows his brow. "What's your hurry? I'm sure Tony won't mind if you both just head to Port Townsend when we're done."

I don't give him a look, but I wonder how he knows we both live in Port Townsend. I didn't know Ronnie lived there until I took her home. Jefferson County is a big place, and the Sheriff's Office is in Port Hadlock.

"Sheriff expects a report on his desk first thing, and he's an early bird."

That's my story and I make a vow to stick to it.

"You've got our reports," Larry says. "I'm starving. I always eat before six because I have stomach issues and acid reflux. If I wait much longer, I won't be able to get to bed until midnight."

I'm glad when Clay steps in.

"Let's get done and I'll buy you dinner, Larry."

I flip through my notes. I want to go and check out the crime scenes for myself, but I don't want to take a boat to San Juan Island. I have the pictures. I need to know who their witnesses are and if they believed them. Their opinions were never in the reports.

"I need to go down your list of people you talked to. Ronnie sent my reports and they are up-to-date. Except for the DNA I got today, and I just told you about that. You've got my crime scene reports."

"I was with Mindy for most of that," Ronnie says.

Clay gives me a questioning look. "Mindy?"

"Mindy Newsom is our best crime tech," Ronnie says. "She's great."

"We could have used her," Larry says. "What's she look like?"

"What?"

"I mean, I might know her," Larry says. "Doesn't she own a flower shop?"

"Yes," I say quickly before moving on.

I am beginning to think Larry is not only lazy, he is a pig. Clay is the real deal. I decide to tell him part of what I suspect about Truitt. But not that I think he's the father of his daughter's baby.

Larry doesn't seem like he can keep that to himself.

I say, "Bohleber said he didn't know Jim Truitt even though Truitt was co-signer for Leann's cabin rental. Joe told me he and his twin brother, Steve, both own the fishing cabin business together, but Steve has nothing to do with it. I talked to Truitt. I thought it was strange that when he found out his daughter had been murdered, he didn't ask any questions about how, when, or where it happened. He didn't ask to see the body. He said he hadn't seen his daughter for two years. But he admitted to paying his daughter's rent since she came home from law school over a year ago. He and Leann had argued about her getting pregnant by Steve Bohleber. Truitt didn't think his daughter should have a baby and ruin her life, but he wanted to make sure the baby got a good home. She wanted to keep the baby. Bohleber, the baby's father, wanted money to convince Leann to give the child up for adoption. If she kept the child, that would mean Truitt would have to put up with Bohleber as family, and as you know, Truitt is very prideful and the Bohlebers are very greedy. He paid Steve Bohleber what he wanted, and the baby was put up for adoption a year ago. He didn't know how to find Steve now because he'd taken off to parts unknown. When we got Jim Truitt's name from Joe Bohleber, Joe called him and said we might be coming to see him."

"I see where you're going with this," Larry says. "You think Jim is the real father of the baby but said it was Steve because he knows the truth. Bank fraud, money laundering. Now blackmail. That's why you got DNA from Jim. Jim may have paid Steve to skip town. He might be paying Joe to keep it all quiet. You think Jim might be the killer?"

Clay says nothing, and I don't want to confirm what Larry has guessed at. Never show your whole hand. I've said too much already.

"I've got four suspects and no witnesses," I say. "No one at the bar where Leann worked could tell me much. They didn't know who she was dating but knew she was seeing guys. Plural. All three of these women had babies. Do you think that means something?"

I do. But I want to see what they suspect.

Clay speaks first. "The baby angle may or may not be important. Unless they all got pregnant by the same killer, I don't see how it would be connected. Only Larry's victim was pregnant when she was murdered."

Larry says what I expect: "You two aren't mothers, but women have babies. It's just a fact of life. All three of them having babies don't mean squat. You're guessing."

Clay and Larry had interviewed policemen who frequented the bars where the victims worked. Margie was found three weeks after she'd been seen last. Dina was missing two weeks before her body was found. Leann was missing a short time, maybe a week or less, according to Cass at the Nordland General Store. She didn't come in for groceries this past Sunday. It fit with the coroner and autopsy report.

"All three of the victims worked at bars," Clay says. "Dina worked at Doc's Marina Grill."

"That's in Port Townsend. I know the place," I say. "My victim worked at the Old Whiskey Mill."

"Not far from where Dina worked," Clay adds. "Bars would be good places for a killer to target victims."

"Margie lived in Crane," Larry says. "But she worked at Front Street Alibi when she worked at something besides on her back."

Clay frowns at him.

"What?" Larry says. "She was a hooker or my name's Father Christmas."

"The Alibi is in Port Angeles," I say.

"Yeah. Sorry for my language, missy."

Missy? That's the second time. I guess I'm counting.

Clay hurries along. "That's only about twenty-five minutes from Port Townsend, where the other two worked. The killer likes them to be found."

Larry takes it from there. "He leaves them naked, or nearly, to humiliate them. Margie was cut open. She had marks around her neck, wrists, and ankles that looked like what your girl had. She had sex recently, but like I said, she was a hooker, so who knows? She'd been missing for at least three weeks."

The pathologist said she'd been dead for less than twenty-four hours.

"Dina had some bruising around the vagina," Clay says, dropping his voice a little. For Ronnie's sake, I think. "It was attributed to a rape, but it could have been abuse. She was promiscuous, so even the rape isn't a given. She had the same injuries as the others. She'd been missing two weeks, more or less. She'd been dead around twenty-four hours when she was found, according to our coroner."

The pattern seems clear, strikingly so. Three weeks missing, two weeks missing, less than a week missing. The killer is on a roll. Speeding up. If he is on a schedule, the next victim is already kidnapped or will be soon.

"Leann was found in a cove near Marrowstone State Park. You know who found her and how. Where were yours found?"

"Dina's body was discovered near Adelma Beach in Discovery Bay," Clay says. "Dispatch received an anonymous call that said they'd spotted the body from the water. We borrowed your Marine Patrol to search the water near the beach."

"Witnesses?" I ask. "Suspects?"

Clay shakes his head. "No suspects. Captain Martin was nearby when the call came out. He confirmed it. She had no family that we could find. Her coworkers said she was flirty with the customers. No one in particular. Neighbors didn't know much about her. She kept to herself. Like both the other victims, she lived near the water. She had a small place just past Haven Boatworks facing Port Townsend Harbor. It's right on the Pacific Northwest Trail along the bay. I don't think Jim Truitt is a possibility on Dina, but the Bohlebers could be a different story. One or both of them maybe have been in the bar and met her."

"Captain Martin had to recover my victim too. That poor guy can't catch a break," Larry adds.

"What do you mean?" I ask.

"His wife drowned about ten years ago. He doted on her. It's a shame for him to have to go through all this, but I guess that's what the Marine Patrol expects. People drown all the time, but murder is something else altogether. I'd hate to be doing his job after what he suffered."

Ronnie's face goes pale. "Did he find his wife?"

"He was with her." Larry looks down at his hands. "They were skinny-dipping. She was six months along."

"She was pregnant?" I ask.

Ronnie goes even more pale. She's chalk now.

"Lost his wife," Larry replies. "Lost the baby. Almost lost his life trying to save her. Damn near lost his job. Became an alcoholic, but don't tell anyone that. He got dried out and they kept him on. He's good at what he does. Hard to replace a guy like that."

I want to ask who worked the drowning case, but I don't. I can find out on my own. Clay gave Larry a strange look when he brought up the drowning, but he says nothing.

CHAPTER THIRTY-THREE

I drop Ronnie at the Sheriff's Office and go home to change clothes. I have just enough time to get to Hops Ahoy. I think about Dan. Detective Osborne reminds me so much of Dan. Not only his looks but his quiet, nonjudgmental manner. I imagine he is easy to talk to like Dan. But he's a cop. It would never work. Not that I have any interest. Going on a date with Dan is hard enough. Dan doesn't pry. He listens but doesn't expect me to tell my life story. I can't, anyway. A cop would keep digging until he drove me crazy.

I flip through the sad contents of my closet. Several possibilities on hangers, all basically the same. Black or blue cotton slacks, white shirts, two blazers, a couple of dresses, and nice jeans for casual. I pick the jeans and one of the white tops. This is definitely a casual event. Not really even a date. A meal and a drink with a friend.

I apply lipstick and eye makeup. I study myself in the mirror over the sink in the bathroom. The top is not right. I change into a button-down long-sleeve shirt. It fits slightly tighter, but I go with it.

I wonder why I suggested Hops Ahoy in the first place. It's a place I go when I'm down. Not for a date. Maybe that's telling.

This isn't a real date, I remind myself.

Funny how I can lie to myself too.

Outside, the yellow cast of the streetlight makes the replacement white top look dingy. I go back inside, change into a new white sleeveless one. It looks good with a blazer, so I can take my gun. I strap on my shoulder holster. Put the blazer on to hide the gun. There's a serial killer on the loose. He targets women in bars.

Who knows? I might get lucky.

I call Dan from the car. I suddenly don't want to go back to Hops Ahoy. I met Dan there last time and stood him up later. Something new is better.

He answers. "Hi. I was just leaving to meet you."

"How would you like to meet at the Pourhouse instead? I know you like live music—*and* they have Scotch." I remember he drinks Scotch.

"Sounds like a plan," he says. "Are you on your way?"

"I'll beat you there." I hang up and within a minute I pull into the parking lot by the Pourhouse. It's more local and not as touristy. I've never been there, but Ronnie was talking about it sometime during one of the long, long drives accompanied by her stream-of-consciousness chatter.

The back patio of the Pourhouse faces Port Townsend Bay and is the venue of the beer garden and live events. It is located between a marine battery shop and a wellness center. One town I traveled through on my way here from Ohio had a little strip like this. Only the bar was located between a gun shop and the city police department.

One-stop shopping, I think. Get a gun, get drunk, get arrested.

I park on the side of the building where I can see the white and blue of the back patio's quartet of umbrellas. I scan for familiar faces. I recognize a couple of city policemen and deputies. Not a problem. This will allay the rumors that I'm a lesbian because I never date.

I don't see Mindy's flower van. I'm a little disappointed that she won't be flying this mission with me. I'm nervous. I find a covered table at the back of the deck, keeping my back to the bay but a view of the bar and the parking lot. There are a few people playing bocce on a court between me and the bay, but I'm not worried about them. A waitress comes to my table with a big howdy smile and takes my order. I want a triple Scotch with a side of water to show the Scotch who's boss. Instead, I order a white wine. I don't want to get drunk until I get home. Alone. Maybe. I don't know what I want. I feel the gun digging into my back and scoot the chair a little forward.

The gun comforts me. It's familiar.

A pair of headlights pulls into a parking space beside my Taurus. The lights go off and Dan gets out of his pickup truck. He starts across the lot, sees me, and waves. I catch the waitress's attention and call her to the table.

I think I will have that Scotch after all.

"Couldn't you find a corner to sit in?" he asks, pulling out a chair and sitting. "I know you like to keep your back to the wall."

"I don't feel threatened by a bocce game."

He laughs. "Fair enough. Should I ask about your day?"

"I should ask why you're in town. Did you bring some carvings?"

"That's part of the reason."

Neither of us knows what to say next. I find myself wishing Mindy were here. Even Ronnie. Strike that. *Not Ronnie.* The waitress brings my Scotch and a shot glass of water.

Dan grins. "I'll have what she's having."

The waitress leaves and Dan turns to me.

"What is that?" he asks. "Scotch with a side of water?"

"I'm introducing the Scotch to the water," I tell him. "I thought they should get to know each other."

We both laugh. I am slightly embarrassed. I normally don't let loose like that with someone who's not a close friend.

Of course, he tops my remark: "When she brings mine, we can let the waters sit by each other, so they don't feel left out. It'll be like a watered-down blind date."

The laughter dies, the drinks come, we sip, stay quiet, sip some more, and I pray the live music will start. The band is tuning up on the platform twenty feet away. The sign is wrong. It isn't *live* music. It's *barely alive* music. The vocalist must be in his late eighties. To give him credit, he can still play a guitar, but he should stop singing.

Please God.

Dan seems to be in a pleasant mood. He's tapping his foot to the music and doesn't seem to notice how off-key the singing is. But that's Dan, I think. Nonjudgmental. Just a nice guy. Unshakable.

"I remember hearing this performer. Do you ever listen to the older groups?"

I don't know what to say. I've never developed a taste for a particular type of music. I can say yes, but then he'll ask me who I like to listen to. I can say no, but then he'll wonder if I hate music. I decide to change the subject.

"So how long are you going to be in town?"

That doesn't come out sounding right, so I quickly rephrase it.

"I mean, when are you going home?"

Crap. Even worse. I'm nervous. Babbling. I sound like Ronnie right now.

"I have to go home in the morning," Dan says. "I have several pieces to finish painting that I've promised to buyers."

I want to ask if he is coming back. I want to see him again. I like being in his company, but I'm sure I'm anything but a good date. I remind myself this isn't a date. So far, I haven't let it become one. I can blame most of my messed-up life on my mother. She never let us stay in one place long enough to make friends, fit in. We were always on the run. Changing identities like some people change shirts. Lying to people. I was always lying to myself to hold on to some sanity.

And now, here is this gorgeous, talented man who likes me enough to reach out and try to keep in touch. Even though I've stood him up more than once. I can say it had happened because of my job, but the truth is I'm afraid of liking anyone that much. If only I could start over from here. But who am I kidding? I am still that girl.

Maybe it's the Scotch, but the singer is starting to sound pretty good. We order food. Wings for Dan. Pizza for me. I must be hungry. There is nothing left to take home. We chat some. Mostly Dan talking about his business and how he plans to expand it.

"One of the reasons I'm in Port Townsend is to scout out some real estate for my business."

"You're going to open a studio?"

He laughs like he's embarrassed, but the man is an artist with a chain saw and paintbrush. No joke. He doesn't answer.

"Would you move here?"

His eyes are asking if I'd like that. I turn my head.

"Not necessarily," he says. "I like working at my place out in Snow Creek. I'm thinking more of a place to sell what I make. Somewhere along the waterfront would be perfect. Of course, it would be seasonal, so I'm taking all that into consideration. And I'd need to hire someone to work the business while I'm busy making things. They'd have to be trustworthy, charming, willing to work long hours."

"Sounds like you've put some thought into this, Dan."

He laughs.

I love his laugh. It lights up his eyes.

"Mindy told me you have another big case." He's learning from me: changing the subject. "Can you talk about it? I won't tell a soul."

I need to confide in someone, if only to organize my thoughts. I feel like I can trust Dan, at least about this. I order another round and we talk. He's easy to talk to and I tell him more than I intend, but he is a good listener. He doesn't tell me how to do my job. I find that surprising in someone, especially in a man. It's their nature to point things out.

When I'm talked out, he sits and thinks and looks out over the blackened waters of the bay.

"Sounds like you have a lot on your plate. I understand why you've been busy. Thank you for agreeing to see me tonight."

"Did you say you have some things for sale in town?"

He gives me the name of a little shop where a few of his carvings are on display.

"A bear, an eagle in flight, and a lighthouse," he says. "The lighthouses go like hotcakes. I'm thinking of doing some diving bell helmets in wood."

He offered me the bear when I was working on the last case in Snow Creek. I didn't take it.

"Where is the bear?" I ask.

"Megan, I'm still holding the one I wanted to give you. I can bring it next time we get together."

Slick. He's setting me up for another date. He's probably succeeded.

"I'll think about it," I say. "The bear, I mean. It looked so real."

Lots of things in my life look real. *I* look real. I can be anything anyone wants me to be. That level of deception is in my DNA. A curse put on me by my biological father. He was a cop. Like me. But a bad cop. I would never be a cop like him. But, like him, I took this job so I can get close to my targets. He did it to kill innocent victims. Me, to kill scumbags like him.

The elderly singer begins again, but my Scotch has melted my dislike. I know I'm getting drunk. I switch to coffee.

"Thanks, Dan."

"For what?"

"For being such a good listener."

"You mean for not telling you how to run your case? Not a problem. I'm a wood carver, not a detective. You don't tell me how to make my carvings."

I look at the time on my phone and he notices.

"I guess we'd better call it a night," he says.

I nod. "I need to get to work early."

I wish I could sit here all night. Not talk. Just look at the stars and the water.

I get up and he walks me to my car, opens the door, and holds it for me. "Good night, Megan."

"Good night, Dan," I say. "I had a nice time."

He leans in and I don't stop him. The kiss is soft and gentle. I've never been kissed like that. He smiles and I kiss him back. Harder this time. Then I pull away and get in my car. He shuts the door.

The kiss has sobered me completely. As I drive home, I can't help but notice my jaw hurts. I just can't stop smiling.

CHAPTER THIRTY-FOUR

It's almost midnight. I drop my purse and keys on the table by the door. I lean back against the door for a beat, close my eyes, replaying the night, the kiss, his smile and laughter. I can't remember having such a relaxed evening.

It was almost normal.

Or what I imagine normal to be.

Even with three cups of coffee, the alcohol is still holding its own. I'm tired but I know I won't sleep for a while. I lock my gun in the gun safe, change into a sweatshirt and shorts, and open my computer to check my email. I'm not expecting one from Hayden, although I've written quite a few to him. Again no answer.

I log out of my personal email and into my Sheriff's account. There are more than a dozen messages. Several are from personnel and training. I've missed diversity training and cultural awareness twice. I don't go because it's four hours of my life I won't get back while I'm stuck in a chair listening to instructions on how to do things that I already know how to do. It's like getting a class on how to tie your shoelaces. I also don't need to qualify with my gun each year. I'm an expert shot with a pistol, rifle, and shotgun. I don't win a prize, just a certificate in my file showing that I complied.

Too wired to go to sleep. That's me at the moment. I decide to listen to the rest of the tape I started last night. I take the box from the top shelf of the closet and put it on the floor by my desk. The player is still loaded with the cassette. I think about getting some wine, a habit I've developed when playing the tapes of my sessions with Dr. Albright. Instead, I go to the kitchen and get a glass of tap water. I need a clear head for the morning. I settle in the chair and hit the "play" button.

The tape picks up in the middle of a sentence.

Me: —spent my whole life thinking I was alone. I had no relatives but Mom and Dad and Hayden. I told my aunt I need to know everything so I can find my mom. And my stepfather's killer.

Dr. A: Go on.

Me: I can tell Aunt Ginger is holding something back. Something big. But I also feel that she cares about me. That's when she tells me that right after my mom had me, a policeman came into the room with flowers. He told Ginger, "Special delivery." Aunt Ginger told him that the other woman in the room, a Ms. Morales, was sleeping. She said the guy was handsome and wearing a uniform. He told her the flowers were for Courtney. My mom. Aunt Ginger thought they might be from their mom and dad, so she took them from the man. He nodded and turned to leave. She said my mom had the rails up on the bed and didn't make a move to take the flowers, so Aunt Ginger took them. He nodded at my mom and left the room.

My mom wouldn't take the flowers, and Aunt Ginger took the card and handed it to her. She said mom started crying and her hand moved to the incubator unit I was in. She told Aunt Ginger, "We need to get the hell out of here." She sounded afraid. Aunt Ginger said she argued with her. She'd just had a baby. They couldn't just leave. But my mom swung her legs over the side of the bed, tore out the tubes in her arms, and let out a whimper. My mom knew that she could do nothing to draw attention to herself. She got dressed and repeated that they had

*to go. Now. My mom was saying, "He can't have her." Aunt
Ginger thought she'd gone a little insane and was going to press
the button for the nurse, but Mom stopped her and handed her
the card. It said, "Congratulation to Us. Bound forever. She's
mine. Always will be. In time, I'll come for her."*

I press "stop."

"I'll come for her. She's mine." I say the words in a whisper.
"Bound forever."

It brings me back to the case I'm working at the moment.
Bound forever. Is that why these women were chained and
collared like a dog? Was some kind of sick ownership at play
here? All three victims were or had been pregnant; two had had
babies and given them up. Yet the first victim, Margie, had the
baby excised from her womb. Pregnancies were an undeniable
connection to the killer.

I drink my water and consider a glass of wine, but only for a
second. I need to keep my focus.

Jim Truitt might have been the father of Leann's child. Could
he also be the father of Margie's and Dina's children? Dina gave
her baby away. Leann gave her child away. But Margie was still
pregnant. Was that something important to the killer? Did he
want to get rid of the baby? Did he want her to keep it? Maybe
he is keeping the fetus as a trophy. Maybe he has a whole shelf
full of jars with fetuses floating in them...

The thought turns my stomach. I start the tape again.

*Me: My aunt tells me everything. She tells me how my mom
and she were certain the man who had brought the flowers was
connected with my mom's rapist. Her tormenter. My father.
They decided that he'd been connected to law enforcement and
that he'd abducted other girls. And that my mom's cleverness
had saved her. But then my mom had me. And he'd found her.*

I can hear the guilt barely hidden in my voice. I was the reason my mother was on the run. I listen as Dr. Albright's soothing voice plays.

Dr. A: Do you feel to blame for any of that, Rylee?

I don't answer for a few seconds. I remember thinking that I knew what Dr. Albright wanted me to say.
She wanted to hear that I wasn't responsible.

Me: I know I'm not.

Dr. A: Exactly. You were a newborn. You made no choices.

Me: But Aunt Ginger said that Mom had considered giving me away. If she had, maybe...

Dr. A: You can't go back and change any of that. You were a newborn.

Me: She almost gave me away. But my aunt said that once I was born and my mom held me, she wasn't going to give me away. She had never even filled out the paperwork. And she wasn't going to let him have me.

I turn off the tape player.
Paperwork. There had to be paperwork filled out for the pregnancies, delivery, adoption, everything. Maybe the paperwork will tell me who the fathers are. The hospitals are a good place to start tomorrow. If I'm lucky, maybe there's even surveillance footage.

As much as I dread playing the tapes of my sessions, Dr. Albright was right in their having a purpose. Clues. I leave the tape in the player, put it in the box, and put the box back in the closet. It's almost one o'clock in the morning. I have to be up at 6:00 and get an early start.

I brush my teeth and coax the tangles out of my hair and on my way to bed stop at the computer. I have to check my email. Compulsive, I know. Personal and work. I've been out of touch for several hours and something might have happened. Not likely, because someone would have called me or found me.

I pull up my personal email account. I scan quickly down the list of emails but all I want to do is lie down and go to sleep thinking about tomorrow. Tomorrow I'm going to track down Boyd myself. I'm going to trade Ronnie to Marley for the DNA results.

A fair trade, I think.

There's nothing in my email that needs to be answered immediately. I go to my work account. One message is from an email address that looks like a marketing scam, but it feels familiar. I hesitate to open it. A chill runs up my spine and I get my gun from the gun safe. My heart pounds in my throat and I check every room, the shower, the closets, the doors, the windows. All secure. I still don't put the gun away. I sit at my desk, gun in hand, and open the email.

The subject line reads: *Hi Rylee!*

The air leaves my lungs just then. I let out a quiet gasp, something that I'd never allow myself in front of another. I see the exclamation point after my name as a kind of dagger. No, a kitchen knife—dipped in blood.

It's him again.

Wallace.

I read:

You are so busy these days. But then, you always were sticking your nose in places it didn't belong. I see you're on the hunt again. And this time you're interfering with Clallam and Kitsap County cases. Good for you. I'm sure you'll find your man. Just hope he doesn't find you first. You're not as clever as you think.

The next line makes my breath catch in my throat and I stand, put my back against a wall, and scan the room.

It says:

I'm in Port Townsend. See you soon. Wallace.

I can hardly breathe. I check the house again. Quickly. Everything is locked but I know from experience that if someone wants in, they will get in. Locks are only as good as the gun that protects them. Kwikset, Schlage, Smith & Wesson.

I pull on a pair of jeans and lay my gun on the desk. He wrote, *I'm sure you'll find your man.* Does he know it's a man? Is he the man I need to find? It's possible. The killings started after I moved here. They are reminiscent of Alex Rader's killings. But he's dead and so is that psycho wife of his. He doesn't have any children but me and Hayden.

Hayden is safely, or at least safe from me, in Afghanistan.

I finally go to bed wearing my jeans and sweatshirt and gun. I don't sleep well. My mind races through questions and plans concerning the case. I will talk to Bohleber tomorrow after I get the DNA results. I will find Boyd and get DNA one way or another. I will track down the children if possible. If the DNA matches Truitt, I'll think about what justice he should get. I don't really peg him as the killer. He's a sneak, a cheat, a coward, an incestuous bastard. Bohleber is a con artist. But you never know what a person will do when threatened.

CHAPTER THIRTY-FIVE

My phone pings and jolts me out of my restless sleep.

I've been having bad dreams—nightmares, actually—about incidents I wish I could just leave in the past. After seeing Leann. Seeing the photos of Benton and Knowles. All of it brings me back to what I did to Marie, who was responsible for Rolland's murder and my mother's kidnapping. When I close my eyes I can still see Marie's body jerking, eyes staring at me from underwater in the koi pond. I thought she'd drowned but she was a tough old bitch.

I was too.

And I didn't give up easily.

I reach over to the nightstand and look at the phone's screen. It shows I have a voicemail from the crime lab. It's two o'clock in the morning. It has to be from Marley Yang. He should be sleeping. It's his way of getting back at me for making him work.

I listen to the voicemail.

"Megan, it's Marley. You and your new partner need to come to the crime lab in the morning first thing. Say 'Thank you, Marley.'"

"Thank you, Marley," I croak out, and it feels like my skull is shattering. I can't wait until the morning. I know he wants to show off in front of Ronnie, but I have to know what he's got. It must be good by the tone in his voice. I hit "call back." Two can play this game. He answers and I can hear a radio playing loudly in the background.

"Hey, Megan. Were you still up? It's two o'clock."

Up and armed. My gun is under my pillow. That explains why my skull is hurting.

"I was working late," I say. "You too, huh?" It's a good lie. Tells him I recognize he's a hard worker and that I am too. A good bonding technique, I think.

"You didn't answer so I left a voicemail."

No shit, Sherlock. "I was so focused, you know?"

"I'm the same way."

Enough with the chitchat. Get to the point.

"Anyway, I have some results for you. You're not going to believe them."

I might if you tell me, I think.

"Try me," I say.

"I found two DNA samples on the slides from Leann Truitt. One is hers and the other belongs to an unknown."

My heart drops.

"Did the DNA database—"

Marley interrupts.

"Yes," he says. "I ran it through the DNA database. I didn't get a name. If you'll wait, I'll give you all my findings."

"Okay. Sorry."

"I didn't run the original tests for the victims from Clallam and Kitsap. The one from Clallam was inconclusive. The body had been cremated so another couldn't be taken. What it gave me didn't mean much. It spit out about a hundred possibilities, but even if we suspected a match with someone, we'd never prove it."

Inconclusive, like Larry said it would be.

"Do you have any good news?" I ask.

"I was saving the best for last," he says. "The Kitsap sample had two DNAs. One was the victim's and the other wasn't in the database, but..."

He lets his words hang in the air.

"But *what*, Marley?"

He hesitates until I want to reach through the phone and slap him upside the head.

"It was a positive match for the unknown DNA collected from Leann Truitt."

I let that sink in and don't realize I'm holding my breath until Marley says, "Did you hear me?"

"Yeah, Marley. Good job. I owe you one." I hope he understands that's a figure of speech. I'd never owe him one for doing his damn job. "I'll send Ronnie in to get the results personally."

"That's great," he says, and then: "I mean, can she give me your report on where you obtained the samples?"

"Yeah." There's no need for a report. Neither Bohleber nor Truitt matched any of the results. "But keep the results on file for 'B' and 'T' for me if you can."

"I guess. I'll put them in the DNA database, but I need a case number to put them under in case someone gets a hit later on."

Crap! I forgot they'd be put in the DNA database and some type of case number had to be associated with the entry. But I guess it's a good thing. Somewhere down the road a detective may get a match with a case they're working. I'd love to see Bohleber or Truitt, or both, snatched up and charged with rape or murder.

"I'll give Ronnie the case number if that's okay." I may just make out an incident report with me as the person reporting. That way, if there's a hit, they'll come directly to me.

"Fine with me," Marley says. "I'll have the results ready for Ronnie in the morning."

I disconnect the call and sit on the edge of my bed. Alex Rader raped all the women he kidnapped. But Alex's DNA would not be in the database because he was a cop. Well, it would be in the DNA database now since I'd left his body to be discovered with evidence of the other kidnappings and rapes he committed. I rescued my mother from those monsters and there's no telling how many future victims were saved.

It's late, or early, and I have to be at work soon to make up some kind of report for Marley. I think it's important that Ronnie visit the crime lab to maintain the good relations I've built with the lab supervisor.

She's useful and I admit to myself that I'm beginning to like her.

CHAPTER THIRTY-SIX

I wake at 6:00 and rush through my morning routine: shower, blow dry, brush my teeth and hair, put on lipstick and eye makeup. Luckily I don't have to select clothes. Several sets of the same thing hang in my closet, so I just grab one set and put it on. I lace up my boots and look for my gun in the lockbox. For a moment I panic: the box is empty. *I put it under my pillow.* I slide it into my shoulder holster. I take my car keys and my purse and I'm on the road. I pull into the parking lot by 6:30. I can do that because I don't have to worry about being stopped or ticketed.

I'm a cop.

Enough said.

I see Sheriff Gray is already in. I also see Ronnie's Smart car.

Nan waylays me when I walk into the office.

"These must have come in last night," she says, handing me a stack of papers. "I got them off the printer this morning. They look important."

She stands there, waiting for me to say something or give her a tip. I take the papers. They're from Marley at the lab.

"Thanks," I say. "Is the sheriff busy?"

Nan looks disappointed that I don't tell her what the lab results are. She's the last person I would tell, with her foghorn mouth.

"Reserve Deputy Marsh is in with him."

She says this like it leaves a bad taste in her mouth. I think it's perhaps because he relied so much on Nan in the past and now

Ronnie is taking her place. Or trying to. I go to his door, knock, and enter. Ronnie's in street clothes today.

"Megan," he says, looking up. "Ronnie was just telling me about your meeting yesterday in Kitsap."

"You have my report," I say. I wonder if Ronnie's account contradicts anything I put in it. Namely, that I had Cass get DNA samples from Bohleber and Truitt.

"And she tells me they have a Rapid DNA machine now."

Ronnie speaks up. "Actually, they've had it for over six months, Tony."

Tony? What the . . . ?

"I saw the DNA results on the printer and put them on your desk," Sheriff Gray says.

So Nan *didn't* find them on the printer. She must have been reading them and made an excuse for looking at them. It's not her job, but it is her MO.

"I have them right here, Sheriff," I say. "I got a call from Marley last night and we went over this briefly. I need Ronnie to go there this morning and talk to Marley. I have some paperwork for him, and he promised to have a more complete report on the DNA comparisons."

"Sure," he says. "I think he's taken quite a shine to our Ronnie here."

Our Ronnie?

I don't tell him I've instigated the infatuation just slightly. Okay, shamelessly. I hate to admit it, but I've taken a liking to her too. She can be frustratingly chatty sometimes, but she apparently kept the surreptitious way I obtained the DNA samples to herself. I appreciate that. It will keep the sheriff from knowing I've violated big-shit Truitt's privacy. What he doesn't know won't hurt him. Even Marley doesn't know who the samples belong to.

"I'm—*we* are finally getting some traction here. Sheriff. The Clallam case is an unknown right now and we can't identify a suspect. The DNA from their case is messed up, so we can't connect it to the other, but we can connect Kitsap's with ours. I was a little surprised that Dr. Andrade didn't put much faith in the rape kit."

"No one's perfect, Megan," he says.

He's directing that comment at me. I know I'm not perfect. I'll be the first one to admit it. But I usually get the job done. If that's as close as I come to being perfect, I'll take it. If anything, I'm probably harder on myself than anyone. Except maybe the anonymous emailer who's sending veiled threats. I've survived this long. Maybe he should rethink things?

"I'm glad you took my advice and left Jim Truitt alone," the sheriff says, and gives me a sideways look.

Ronnie is looking at her lap and her cheeks are turning red.

Well, crap. I take back what I was thinking about her. She spilled her guts. Sold me out. Sheriff Gray was telling me he knew I'd gotten Truitt's DNA on the sly. At least he wasn't giving me a sermon.

"I was up late and have some avenues to pursue," I say. "Ronnie, stop by my desk when you're finished here. I have something for you to take to the lab."

She doesn't look at me but gets up from her chair. "I'm done. I was just saying good morning."

And a lot of other things too. But it is hard to blame her. This is a good case. Not something you get to do at the academy. That's all training. This is real.

I go to my desk, log onto the computer, and pull up a form that she can take to the lab. I only put down what he needs to know to save the DNA samples for me. No names, no locations, no dates, no officer collecting the sample. I don't even put Lonigan in the short report. No sense in dragging him through the mud if this turns into a problem. Ronnie is not mentioned, either, but I play with the idea of attributing it all to her. Throw her under the bus. But I don't.

She stands by my desk. "I'm sorry, Megan." She suddenly looks like an abused animal. Head down, sad expression. If she were a dog, her tail would be between her legs. I don't feel sorry for her a bit. She promised to keep it quiet. A promise is a promise.

Unless it was made by me.

I hit the "print" key and the printer by Nan's desk whirs into life. I rush over and take the paper off the tray before Nan can get it. I save the file in my computer, but I don't make another copy for anyone.

Ronnie takes the report and leaves. I don't expect her back until after lunch. Marley will probably take her somewhere to eat. I remember my aunt Ginger told me how, after I was born, my biological father couldn't resist coming to the hospital to let my mom know he was aware of the birth. Took her flowers. I doubt the killer is the father of all of these babies, but it's possible that he thought some reason up to visit them in the hospital.

I pull out the reports from Kitsap and Clallam Counties and sift through them looking for any mention of a baby, the hospital where the baby was born, birth certificates, anything that will give me a starting place. If I can find the same guy signing in to visit all three of the victims, or even two, I will have a solid lead. If I'm lucky, the hospitals will still have video surveillance tapes. But first I need the names of the hospitals and the dates the victims delivered. In Leann's case I could probably get the information from her father, Jim Truitt, who claimed he knew nothing about her except that she was a disappointment.

I play in my head what I might say to him. What I want to say. *Well, guess what, Jim? She's no longer a disappointment. She's dead. If I find out you killed her, or even had her killed, you're next.*

Thinking of Leann, I wonder when she had her baby and where. I don't find what I'm looking for in Clay's and Larry's files, and I know it's not in mine. I'll have to ask them to see if they ran that down during their investigation.

Then I have a sudden inspiration. Leann was living on Marrowstone Island, and the Nordland General Store is the center of the universe there. Little places like that are gossip central—and gossip, I am convinced, is as good as cash. Maybe Cass will have an idea where Leann gave birth.

I call Cass.

"Nordland," she says.

"Cass, it's Megan."

"Howdy, girl. Did that stuff that I don't know anything about do you any good?"

I remember what I just thought about gossip. I don't want to tell her anymore.

"It's still being looked at," I say. "I'm sure it will help. It will either confirm or eliminate some information."

"Glad to help," she answers. "Hang on a minute."

I hear someone talking in the background and then Cass comes back on in a soft voice. "One of those jerks, probably Joe, told people I was giving away pies. I guess I'll have to put a sign outside that I'm out of free slices of pie."

We both chuckle.

"I don't know how to thank you for this, Cass," I go on. "Please don't mention it to anyone..."

"I'm not an idiot," Cass says in a good-natured way. "I always watch *CSI* and those cop shows. It's exciting to be helping. Even in a small way. Don't you worry. My lips are sealed. Unless you need me for a witness. And then you couldn't shut me up with a shovel. Sample B and sample T got an ass-kicking coming. I hope you get them."

I hope I can trust Cass not to blab to everyone on the island. All that can happen is the sheriff and I get fired for harassment of Jim Truitt, the upstanding citizen, and his spirit guide.

"Cass, I didn't call about the samples. I need to pick your brain."

"Me? Go ahead."

"First of all, you need to keep this to yourself."

"Cross my shriveled heart and whatever," Cass says, once more making me smile. I hope I'm still tough like her when I get older.

"Do you know where Leann had her baby? Or her doctor's name? Anything?"

She doesn't hesitate a beat.

"Honey, the Nordland General Store is known as Gossip Town, and you just happen to be talking to the mayor. I don't gossip myself, you understand, but I've got keen hearing. For instance, I know that Leann went into labor at her cabin and was taken to the hospital in Poulsbo. Sorry, I don't know which one, and I didn't hear the doctor's name." She gives me a date that's close to when this happened.

Poulsbo is in Kitsap County.

Dina Knowles lived and worked and died in Kitsap County.

I thank Cass, end the call, and immediately punch in Clay Osborne's cell number. He's out of breath when he answers.

"Detective Carpenter. Did the DNA already come back?"

"It has. Not how I thought, but it's something, at least. Can you talk?"

I hear traffic and kids laughing, people talking.

"Sure," he says. "I'm out for a run. It helps with stress. Do you run?"

No, I think, *I take my stress straight up with water on the side.*

"I used to when I was in high school," I say. "Not anymore. Not since police academy." We ran five miles a day on most days at the academy. The crazy cadets would run ten miles and then come back for physical training. Push-ups, jumping jacks, sit-ups—all the fun stuff I was never going to miss.

"You should come run with me some time," he says. "Exercise will extend your life."

Not when you have psychos threatening you. But maybe it will help if I have to run. Like, really have to. I'll pass.

"That sounds like a great idea," I lie. "Right now I need some information."

"Shoot."

"Do you know where Dina Knowles had her baby? Doctors? Anything along those lines?"

"Did one of the DNA samples match Dina?"

"In a way," I say. "But that's only part of the reason I'm asking. I'll send you a copy of the lab reports."

"Okay," he says. "Yes, I found out where Dina had her baby. North Kitsap Medical Center."

"Poulsbo, right?"

Another connection. I'm on a roll. This is good.

"That's right," he says. "I can call them if you need anything—records, whatever. I have the doctor's name that delivered the baby and all of that."

I wonder what the chances are that Leann and Dina had the same doctor. It may be risky talking to that doctor until I have to. Who knows what Leann told him? Maybe Jim Truitt paid for the delivery. Maybe they're golf or sailing buddies.

"That would be great, Detective Osborne. I have something in mind. Can you meet me there?" I ask.

"Now?"

"I'm in Port Hadlock." I look at the clock on my computer. "Can you make it in an hour?"

"See you there," he says.

CHAPTER THIRTY-SEVEN

I leave a note on my desk for Ronnie in case she gets back before I do. Not likely. I am in my Taurus, heading south on State Road 19, when my phone buzzes.

It's Captain Marvel.

"Detective, this is Captain Martin."

I imagine him standing on the prow of a boat, one hand on his hip, strong chin jutting forward, cape flowing behind him.

"Yes, sir," I say.

"I went back and scoured the scene again. Didn't find anything. If you need anything from me on this case, just call."

I want to ask why he went back to the scene, but think better of it. It might sound as if I were harping on him doing a good job. He went out of his way and I appreciate it, and yet, at the same time, it bothers me a little.

"Detective?"

"Thank you, Captain. I will let you know."

"How's it going with the case? Any leads yet?"

"Nothing much. Yet."

"I've heard some stories about you. You always get your man."

And I've heard you always get your woman.

"Anyway," he says, "while I've got you on the line, I want to ask you something."

I hope he's not going to ask me out. I mean, I doubt that's what he wants to ask. But if he does, it would crush Ronnie. When she talks about him, she gets this dreamy look in her eyes. I feel a little guilty for pushing her on Marley. And here I am talking to the man she adores.

"What I want to ask, Detective, is if that poor girl had been sexually molested."

His question surprises me. I wasn't expecting him to still be thinking about this case. He must have other things to occupy his time. But then I remember his wife drowned. They had been skinny-dipping. Seeing Leann the way she was might have been a shock to him. I can relate to how things get all mixed up in your mind, how things are triggered.

When I see something red, I associate it with Rolland, dead on the kitchen floor in our place in Port Orchard. A big knife buried in his chest and a pool of blood around him.

"I can't really go into details, Captain."

I can almost hear him wince on the line.

"I understand," he says. "Sorry. I just want to do anything I can to help."

"Captain Martin, I appreciate your effort. I can tell you that a rape kit was turned over to the crime lab."

He goes quiet. I think I've hurt his feelings. Despite my belief that he is an arrogant, swaggering show-off, I feel a little sorry for him.

He finally speaks up. "I heard from a deputy in Clallam that you might have another murder associated with this one."

"Who did you hear that from?" I ask, although I know it was Larry Gray. Captain Marvel had recovered Margie's body. Larry probably couldn't keep it to himself. He has been more of a hindrance than a help so far.

"Just a deputy I know," he says. "Anyway, I hope you catch this guy."

"Thanks, Captain. I will." I'm starting to sound like a boss. Or my mother.

I am sure Nan has read the note I left for Ronnie. It just says that I'll meet her back in the office after lunch. She will be so disappointed. I didn't tell Ronnie where I was going because I didn't want to make a big deal of it. She seems excited to have something important to do.

As I drive south to Poulsbo, I can see thickening clouds far across the bay. Clouds that are heavy, churning. The water is black and roiling as it makes its way to shore.

Yes, I think, a storm is coming.

CHAPTER THIRTY-EIGHT

I circle the hospital parking lot, wondering where people in need of medical assistance are supposed to park. There's nothing. Finally, I see Clay sitting on a Harley. He waves to me to pull into the half space next to him. He's going to get drowned when that storm hits. I meet him at the entrance.

"So what do you expect to find in Dina's records?" he asks as we make our way to the entrance.

I don't answer. Not because I don't want to but because I'm caught off guard.

A policeman, not a security guard, sits at a desk with the receptionist. The sight of a police uniform in a hospital makes me shudder. I can control it. It isn't Alex Rader. Policeman. Serial killer. He is dead. And then the officer looks up and smiles at me. My heart starts thumping. He reminds me of Rader. Same size, same haircut, same smarmy smile.

"What's up, bro?" the officer says to Clay.

He hasn't been smiling at me after all. *Good.*

My pulse starts to normalize.

"Jimmy, this is Detective Carpenter," Clay says. "Jimmy's the friend I talked to about Boyd."

Jimmy gets up and comes around the desk, and he and Clay man hug. A little too long. The look that passes between them is not of the brothers-in-arms type. Ronnie would be devastated to learn that Clay isn't a ladies' man at all.

I don't care.

He is cute but not my type.

"Jimmy Polito." The policeman takes my hand, and despite his hulking size, his handshake is as soft as Ronnie's.

"You're the Jimmy that works at the college?" I say this like I'm not surprised, although I am. Port Townsend has a small police department, and I thought I knew everyone. What's more, it's at least an hour to drive from the campus to here. When does he find time to work as a policeman?

Maybe I never met Jimmy because he's always working off duty somewhere.

"The one and only," Jimmy says, smoothing back his black hair. "Pleased to meet ya."

His accent is different.

He notices me noticing.

"I'm originally from New York," he says. "Manhattan. Little Italy. I got my mother's eyes and my dad's temper." He laughs, and the usually reserved Clay laughs along with him.

"Jimmy worked his way across the U.S.," Clay says. "He was with Kitsap County Sheriff's Office before he became a traitor and went to Port Townsend Police."

"Traitor, huh," Jimmy says, getting into what looks like a boxing stance.

This is like a male mating ritual. I've seen it many times before. But that's not why I'm here, and I haven't got time for another long, long man hug. I need coffee and I'm cranky.

"Since you're here," I ask, "did you get anything on either of the Boyds?"

Jimmy shakes his head. "Neither of them. I had the other security guys and gals keep an eye out. The real Boyd hasn't been seen on campus for a while. His professors said he quit coming to class over a month ago. I checked his dorm. He's in a room by himself. Nothing. No sign of the skinny white Boyd, either. Or the car you described. You want me to keep looking?"

"Can you see if the white Boyd is a student there?" I ask. "Maybe under another name? Maybe show the registrar a picture of him, post a picture in the dorms, see if anyone recognizes him? His picture is on his website."

"I should have thought of that," Jimmy says. "Will do, Detective Carpenter." He gives a little sarcastic salute.

"Megan, please," I say. "And I really appreciate it. You can call me or Clay. I'll give you my cell." Out of business cards, I find a piece of notepaper on his desk and scratch out my name and number. He supposedly has done all this legwork. Clay asked for all this before. I heard him myself. It kind of pisses me off that he hasn't done a damn thing.

"That's just for business, bro," Clay says. "Don't be drunk dialing her."

"Hey, I can't help it if I'm a virile specimen of a man."

They both laugh. I let them have their fun. To be in law enforcement, you can't be offended by every remark or look. It comes with the territory.

"We need to look at some records, Jimmy." Clay becomes the serious, no-nonsense Clay again. "Think you can pull up some past patient records for us?"

Jimmy leads us a few feet further away from the receptionist. "Confidential stuff. I like it." He takes out a notebook. "Give me the names and dates of birth."

I use his notebook and pen and write down all three victims' information from memory. He and Clay exchange a look and Jimmy grins.

"Clay said you were sharp, Megan. Maybe some of those smarts will rub off on his ignorant ass."

Clay stays silent. He's in total Clay mode now. It's good to see he can be both serious and funny. Comes in handy when you're trying to obtain illicit confidential information that you would otherwise need a court order or a warrant to get. I came prepared to lie and/or promise a fake document. This is so much simpler.

"This will take a few minutes," Jimmy says. "The crap-a-teria, and I do mean crap, is down the hall to your left. They have decent coffee and Krispy Kreme donuts, and by the look of you two you're in serious withdrawal."

How can I say no?

Clay and I head down the hall.

"I apologize for Jimmy," he says.

"Nothing to apologize for. He's doing a lot for us. I hope he doesn't get in trouble with the hospital administration." I really don't give a crap. I just want the information without going through a lot of paperwork and maybe ending up getting permission denied.

I looked around the front lobby when we came in and saw no less than three surveillance cameras. Going down the hall now, I turn around and see the cameras could cover the hallway. There are two more here. One in each corner of the cafeteria. Another is behind the counter, pointed at the cash register.

There should be a sign on the register: *Trust no one.*

And an all-seeing eye.

"There's a lot of surveillance cameras," I say as we get our coffee and donuts. "Maybe Jimmy can get us video footage?"

Clay looks somewhat skeptical. Maybe he doesn't want Jimmy to take that kind of risk. Maybe I'll have to find a way to hack into their system. I've done it before—not here, and not for a few years, but I'm pretty sure I can figure it out. If not, I can schmooze someone else at the hospital.

"Forget I asked, Clay. Probably nothing anyway. I'm just crossing *i*'s and dotting *t*'s."

He chuckles at my little joke that was meant to cover a lie. I am getting better at hiding my true thoughts from him because he nods.

"I admire that about you." He takes a bite of a donut and talks with his mouth full. I think he looks disgusting, but I don't say it. I don't show it. "You don't give up. You're like a hound on a scent."

I sip at the coffee while he goes on.

"What do you smell here? What do you expect to find with these records?"

I tell him I'm trying to establish that the victims may have crossed paths. That maybe they had the same doctor. Came to the same hospital.

"Anything that would give us a pattern."

I don't tell him I'm doubly interested in the birth certificates. I don't tell him that I know for a fact that my own birth certificate didn't have a father's name or my own name on it. My mother had thoughts of giving me away. *Like Dina did.* Maybe like Margie would have done. Neither Larry nor Clay have dug that deep. On my birth certificate I was just Infant, another fatherless child. I wanted to see the birth certificates of Leann's and Dina's babies.

I tell him I want to see the exact dates and times of the births. I want to get the names of the doctors that attended and maybe I will find the nurses that were on duty. Someone has to have seen something. If not, I will have at least tried. Clay seems like a seasoned investigator, but it looks like a lot of Dina's investigation fell through the cracks. And Larry...Larry hasn't missed a meal on Margie's behalf. I feel like both victims were deemed losers. They were promiscuous. They were single mothers. So what? Why were they less deserving of a full-on investigation?

My mother and several other sixteen-year-olds were victims. She had lied about being kidnapped before the real thing happened. According to my aunt Ginger, Mom had run off to spend time with a boy. Then she got kidnapped for real, tied up and raped. When she tried to tell the police, they demeaned and then ignored her claim. Even her own parents dismissed her story. A cloud of disbelief and suspicion followed her and made her the perfect target for Rader.

The same seemed to be true for Dina Knowles and Margie Benton. They were dead. They had no one to speak up for them. They couldn't tell their side of the story. That's why I'm here.

It's taking Jimmy longer than expected to access the records. I hope he didn't have to get permission. Or maybe the receptionist hindered him?

In the past, I might have come up with a way to get what I wanted without anyone knowing. But I know someone who can make this easy. I excuse myself, go to the bathroom, and call Sheriff Gray. I ask him to get a court order from his judge friend.

I return to Jimmy and finish my coffee.

Within minutes my phone pings. Sheriff Gray sent a copy of the court order and one to the hospital. Within fifteen more minutes I have the records and the video on a thumb drive.

I have probably burned the Clay Osborne bridge. Clay is unhappy that I went around him, but sorry/not sorry. If I hadn't, I'd have had to go through him. And Jimmy from Little Italy. No problem.

I drive back to Port Hadlock, the rain pelting my windshield and smearing the scenery. I'm pretty sure now that Jimmy didn't look for Robbie Boyd all that hard. He claimed he was getting the hospital records, but when I approached him, he was just chatting up the receptionist.

The last piece in the puzzle is Margie Benton. The hospital had no record of her.

I'm twenty minutes away from the office when the sheriff calls.

"Megan, I've got bad news."

My heart jumps. His tone is uneasy.

"We've located Robbie Boyd."

I'm confused. That's good news.

"And?" I ask.

"He's dead. But that's not all. There's another body."

CHAPTER THIRTY-NINE

The pelting rain slacks off to a fine marine mist when I find Sheriff Gray waiting for me where South Water Street dead-ends. I survey the area as I park and make my way over to him. A spit of land juts out into the water between Port Hadlock and Skunk Island, creating a barrier. Near the tip of this little sandy, rocky stretch, a jetty runs like a pointing finger toward Lower Hadlock Road. This area is technically part of Port Hadlock.

Ronnie is there too.

She's wearing a white button-down shirt, brown slacks, and sensible shoes. She has her leather basket-weave gun belt hitched around her improbably narrow waist. She must have come with the sheriff because I don't see her Smart car nearby. She is focusing a pair of binoculars on one of our Marine Patrol boats heading toward us from the southern tip of Skunk Island. I can make out the form of Captain Marvel posing on the bow.

Actually, he is talking to the sheriff on his cell phone.

"There's no need to fear: Captain Marvel's here," I say when the sheriff disconnects.

"Be nice, Megan," he says. "You and Ronnie are going to need a ride over there."

I don't like boats. I don't even like ferries. A ferry—any boat, for that matter—is like the color red, a trigger. It brings back best-forgotten memories. The Sheriff's Office has two boats, but I don't know the names, nor have I been on one. Ronnie sits on a rock and pulls on rubber boots. I'm wearing my work boots.

Sheriff Gray leans in and says in a low voice, "I loaned her my waders. I didn't want her to get her designer shoes ruined." He gives me a knowing smile.

Not for the first time, I wonder what Ronnie is doing in the sheriff reserves. She obviously has enough money to be going to some Ivy League college or live independently. The clothes I've seen her in over the last couple of days cost more than everything I own. And Smart cars aren't cheap.

The boat makes its way around to the jetty. I grab my phone and a notebook from my car. Ronnie is already on the dock. She looks down at my leather boots but, to her credit, says nothing snarky. Or maybe she thinks I would shove her in the water if she did.

She'd be right about that.

The captain carefully backs the big boat close to the dock. He leaves the wheelhouse and tosses some bumpers over the portside. He throws a mooring rope to Ronnie. She giggles as she catches it and ties it to one of the cleats. She expertly hops aboard, and I ease my way across the open space between the deck and the dock.

Sheriff Gray unties the mooring line and pitches it to me. I miss it but it lands in the boat, so big deal.

Captain Marvel pulls the bumpers back aboard and turns to Ronnie.

"You know your knots, sailor."

He takes a smiling Ronnie's hand and leads her to the cabin. I am left to fend for myself. Perfect. Just perfect.

"You'd better come inside," he says. "This sleek lady has some powerful moves."

I'm not sure if he's talking about the boat or Ronnie. I move along the side of the cabin, grab one of the handholds and plant my feet as best I can. I find myself slung back against the side of the cabin as the twin 150-horsepower engines power up.

I'm all but certain he's just showing off.

As we get closer to the scene, I can see white-clad Crime Scene techs. The captain drops anchor and lowers a rubber raft over the side. He hangs a ladder on the railing. Ronnie and I are able to make our way into the raft. A pair of plastic oars are in the raft, but Ronnie has picked up a coil of rope that is tied to the front of the raft. She yells for one of the techs and then tosses the line to him. The tech pulls us up onto the beach. Ronnie is off the raft first and comes back with a heavy rock and places it on the coiled rope.

"There," she says. "Now it won't float away."

She makes it so easy for me to hate her. On the other hand, I love having someone around who knows how to do this kind of stuff.

The Crime Scene tech says the coroner is stuck on an arson with fatality case in another part of the county and they'll remove the body after processing the scene.

"We're just starting," he says, motioning around with a wave of his arm. "There's no need to string caution tape. Skunk is uninhabited."

I look around. Large basalt boulders form a barrier on the southern tip of the little island; the rest is forest and beaches. The tide might have washed away any footprints.

"Hey, Detective Carpenter."

It's one of the techs coming out of the tall, weather matted brush inland.

"You might want to see this."

I weave my way through the rocks that litter the beach. The tech yells for me to move to my left and come straight at him. I take two steps to my left and walk into the brush. It's higher than my waist, and blackberry brambles pull at my jacket. I'm grateful for the heavy work pants. I stop, button my jacket, and hold my arms up to keep them out of the worst of it. As I approach a wooded area, there is a shallow incline where the brush thins out. The tech leads me up into the trees several yards and stops.

My eyes follow his gaze.

I see it immediately.

The body has its back to us and is turning with the breeze to face us. Boyd is wearing the same tattered clothes. One scuffed tan army boot is off, and a dingy sock shows beneath the cuff of faded jeans. His head is tilted far to the left and down, neck stretched from the weight, hanging from a length of yellow nylon climbing rope. Long, curly, greasy black hair hangs over the left side of his face. His tongue looks like a black stopper has been corkscrewed into his mouth.

It isn't the real Robbie Boyd, but it is the man who identified himself as such.

The tech looks at me, then back at the body.

"There's something in his hand," he says.

I squint a little. In the right hand, a piece of white, red, and black cloth is just barely visible.

I look back the way we came and can see a narrow path in the brush where someone trampled parts of it down from the body to the beach. I scan the body once more. The rope was thrown over a low-hanging limb about ten feet off the ground, then tied around the trunk of the tree. I can't see the knot at the neck with the head canted, but I know it's there.

"Rock-climbing rope," I say.

The tech nods.

I work my way back to the beach, where another tech is chatting up Ronnie. They are both smiling, and the tech has a notebook out and is writing something down.

I approach and the tech suddenly becomes busy and Ronnie looks away.

"Who found her?" I ask.

Even from this distance I can see the victim is a younger woman in the age range of the other victims, maybe a little younger. The body is lying faceup, legs spread wide, arms stretched out to each side, with the back of the head in a notch between two big rocks, making the face clearly visible. A redhead.

Just like the others.

Blood has run down the inside of the legs, and her crotch is covered in it. There are large bruises along the side of one leg and binding marks on the wrists and ankles and a wider mark around the neck.

"Joey said Roy found her," Ronnie says.

"Captain Martin?" I ask.

She nods.

"And Joey is?"

"Sorry. Deputy Joe Fischer."

The tech is crouching by the body and raises a hand without turning around.

"That's me," he says, getting up and coming over to us. "Captain Martin said he was patrolling this bay and spotted her. He called and here we are. My partner found the hanging man."

I don't care for his attitude.

"Good job," I say.

This body is different from the others in that she's completely nude. Her eyes, however, are open just like the others' were.

I move toward the body.

"Just don't touch her," he says.

Ronnie snaps on latex gloves.

"Can I go with you, Megan?" she asks.

"Stay behind me," I say, "and don't trip and fall on the body in those clunky big boots."

"I promise."

The tech points to other tracks in the sand where he made his approach. We will stay in his footsteps.

The sun glints off of something metal or glass halfway buried in the sand. I turn to the tech. "Something's in the ground there."

Joey plants a marker flag in the sand beside the item.

I continue and stop two feet from the body. There's deep bruising on the chest, ribs, and stomach. I squat down for a better look. Her knees are scuffed. I can't see the palms of her hands, but the knuckles are definitely rubbed raw and scabbed over. There are bruises on her shins, and the ribs have deep purple and yellow bruises the size of a fist or a boot. Her red hair has been spread out around her head like a fan. It looks to have been done on purpose. Her blue eyes stare up into nothingness. Her lips are slightly parted but not split like the other victims' lips. In fact, her face is unscathed by injury.

The deputy in the woods yells down to us.

"Detective, you might want to come back up here."

I make sure Ronnie moves back out of the scene with me before I return up the trail.

"I found a purse over there by that downed tree," he says. "Some clothing is a few feet away. A dress and bra, by the looks of it. I took pictures of the purse if you want me to collect it while you're here."

"That would be perfect," I tell him. "And check around here to see if you find any kind of symbol, will you?"

He gives me a questioning look.

"The other cases I'm working," I say. "A symbol, about the size of your palm, was scraped or carved into a rock or a tree trunk."

While the tech goes to get the purse, I examine the tree and the body. The tree is a young alder, maybe a foot in diameter. The rope is draped over a limb and Boyd's toes are just touching the ground. Of course, his neck is stretched a few inches. I try to picture him coming here and doing that to himself.

It doesn't feel right.

If I were going to hang myself, I would tie the rope to the trunk and then throw the line over the limb. Then I would stand on something, tie the rope around my neck, and kick the stand away. There is nothing to stand on here. I'll have to wait for the pathologist's report.

"Can you get a picture of the limb where the rope is touching?"

The tech agrees. "You want to see if there are any burn marks," he says. "Like the body was hoisted up and then tied off."

"What's your name?"

"Bart, Detective Carpenter. Deputy Bart Johnson. You spoke at the academy last year and I was in your homicide class."

I remember being forced to do the class by Sheriff Gray. He usually did those types of things, but he was busy that day. Probably playing Candy Crush on his computer.

"Bart, do you think you can get that picture for me before I leave?"

"I can get it right now," he says, unzipping his Tyvek suit down to his waist. He reaches inside and pulls out a long, narrow rod.

"It's for taking selfies with a cell phone," he says. "I keep one just in case I have to look on top of things I can't reach."

Finally, I think. *A good use for those insufferable selfie sticks.*

He expands the rod to thirty inches. He reaches back inside his coveralls and pulls out his cell phone. He walks around the tree, getting different angles, and shows me the video.

"Stop here," I say.

He does.

"What's that look like to you?"

The video is of the backside of the tree trunk. He expands the picture to zoom in.

"There's your symbol, ma'am."

The all-seeing eye.

It's here.

I have him send the video to my phone. I open it and can't tell if the rope rubbed the bark significantly or not.

"When you get the body down, can you take more pictures of the limb and the knots? And of that symbol?"

"I'll send everything to you, ma'am."

This tech isn't any older than I am, but he makes me feel old.

"Ma'am" is like "marm," as in "schoolmarm," a prim and prudish spinster.

I return to the beach. The boat is standing by, and Ronnie has found another big rock to perch on and watch as Crime Scene does their thing.

"Joey," I say to the tech, "when Bart gets the body down, can you check the dead man's clothing for a knife?"

"Yes, ma'am."

I want to tell him to stop calling me "ma'am," but my phone rings.

It's Sheriff Gray.

"Is it your guy? Boyd?"

"Yeah," I say. "He's hanging in a tree."

"Murder or suicide?"

Yet to be determined, but I say what I think.

"It looks like he hanged himself," I reply, with a perceptible touch of sarcasm.

So far, all of the victims have been posed carefully. The killer is telling a story. If Boyd was the killer and committed suicide, the story ends here.

If not, I'll have to end this story.

"But you don't believe it's suicide?"

"They found a purse up here near Boyd's body. And some women's clothing."

"But you think someone is setting Boyd up as the killer?"

"Too early to tell," I say. "Hopefully, there will be some identification for both of them."

Just then, Bart comes toward me with his phone.

"The cloth," he says, looking uncertain.

"What about it?"

"It's a note," he says holding out his phone.
I look down and I feel the sand slipping under my feet.
In block letters:

I'M SORRY MEGAN

CHAPTER FORTY

I'm thinking of the message left for me at the crime scene. I wonder if someone has followed me from my past, or if this is a new admirer. I look over at Ronnie. Her mouth is moving, and I do my best to shake off my anger and worry and listen to her as we drive back to the office.

"Vitruvian Woman," Ronnie says.

For the last few miles she has complained about the way her parents treat her and how they don't want her to be in law enforcement.

Right now, I'm agreeing with them.

"You know?" she asks me.

I don't.

"Vitruvian Man," she goes on. "Leonardo's famous drawing of the human body. A male figure in a circle with his arms out to the sides, legs spread. He believed it showed the divine connection between the human body and the universe. The perfect man. You've seen it. I know you have. Only this one is a woman. Her legs and arms spread. Posed. Just like a drawing."

I think about it. Maybe she's onto something?

"Look it up when we get back," I say.

She takes out her ever-present cell phone and begins punching, tapping, and sliding her finger across the poor abused screen.

"Here it is. See?"

She holds the screen where I can see without taking my eyes too much off the road. I've seen the drawing many times.

"What do you think it means?" I ask.

Ronnie shrugs a little. "It's a woman instead of a man. If he's substituting the woman for a man, it must be important. Maybe mother issues? I've heard of several serial killers that had mother issues. The perfect woman. Only she's dead."

The perfect woman is dead.

"Think about it some more and see what you come up with," I tell her.

I have other things on my mind at the moment. For example, the piece of cloth Boyd was clutching in his dead hand was a piece of the skirt that was found near his body. A Sharpie pen was found in the back pocket of his jeans. The pen and the piece of cloth were covered in blood.

My name.

Since Boyd wasn't bleeding, I assume the blood was from the female victim.

Vitruvian Woman.

In addition, there was a Washington State driver's license in the purse that identified her as Karynn Eades. Karynn with a *y* and two *n*'s. I switch my thoughts to the cloth in Boyd's hand. Boyd's hands were bloody, but he had no cuts.

Sheriff Gray, Ronnie, Captain Marvel, Joey, and the other crime scene guy, Bart, were convinced it was a suicide note. I really can't be sure. Their reasoning was that Boyd knew I had figured out he was the murderer. He took one more life before ending his own. It made sense, and that was what pissed me off most. Boyd had disappeared after that day at the cove on Marrowstone.

I'd given him my name at the scene.

And it was me who let him go. If this was a suicide, it was my fault Karynn with two *n*'s was dead.

I don't want to believe he's the killer.

I play back the other details from the scene.

The clothes were the right size for the victim. No shoes were found. The bra was rolled up with the skirt. The skirt was missing a piece of fabric, the size of the note. The glinting item I spotted buried in the sand near her body turned out to be a spent .45-caliber shell casing. Crime scene techs used a metal detector and found several other pistol and rifle shell casings of various calibers. Captain Martin says he's heard shots fired in the bay in the past and suggested the shell casings were probably left over from the Fourth of July or New Year's.

Ronnie is silent until we reach the office and pull in. I shut off the ignition.

"What do we do now?" she asks. "Boyd is dead, and he practically admitted to the killings. At least to Karynn's, and he was right there with her body."

I don't say anything. I'm thinking. I get out of the car and head inside with Ronnie following behind. I almost make it to my desk when Nan hands me a pink message slip.

"Detective Osborne called," she says. "He said to call him back as soon as you can."

He has my phone number. He could have called direct and not gone through nosy Nan.

"He said he didn't want to disturb you at the scene," she says with a frown, as if she has read my mind. She stands there.

If you're waiting for a tip, here's a tip: Stop being so nosy.

"Thanks, Nan," I say, and force myself to smile.

"It's my job," she says, and briskly walks away.

I might have hurt her feelings. I don't care.

Ronnie pulls up a chair and opens her mouth in preparation for another barrage of insight or questions. I phone Clay. I will call Larry next out of politeness. I don't expect Larry to do much of anything. I guess Clay can call Jimmy from Little Italy and tell him to call off his search.

"Megan," Clay says, answering. I hear loud traffic in the background and the growl of an engine. He's on his Harley. "I hear you found Boyd."

"Skunk Island."

"Appropriate place to hang himself."

Who have you been talking to?

"That's the general consensus."

The line goes silent, then he says, "But you don't think so."

"I just want to be sure," I say. "Wait for all the evidence."

"That's the smart thing to do. But from what I hear, he was twenty feet away from another victim's body."

Her name is Karynn. I hate how a living person is reduced to a thing, a victim, when he or she is murdered.

"The bodies are on their way to Dr. Andrade," I say.

"She one of ours?"

"I think so."

Clay chimes in with a singsong voice. "I know. I know. You want to wait for all the evidence."

"When Dr. Andrade gives me a time for the autopsy, I'll give you a call if you want."

I hope he says no. I don't want to throw up in front of him. Even if he's not interested in women.

"That'd be good," he says. "Do you want me to call my friend Jimmy?"

"That's part of the reason I called you back. I'd like to look at Boyd's dorm room."

"What are you looking for?" he asks.

"Just turning over every rock. Will you clear it? I don't have a warrant, but the guy's dead. There won't be a trial."

"I'll call Jimmy as soon as we hang up. But you remember he stole the identity of the real Robert Boyd and he's missing. We have to assume he's alive. Might even be there."

I hang up.

"Are we going to the college?" Ronnie asks.

"Not we. Me. I need you to stay here and do the computer searches."

She looks like a disappointed child. She'll get over it. I actually have a little faith in her.

CHAPTER FORTY-ONE

I park in a space marked for Campus Security. I'll probably get a ticket, but they'll never take me alive. True to his word, Clay called me right back. Jimmy gave me his blessing and called ahead to the chief of security. She'll meet me at her office and accompany me to Boyd's dorm room. Jimmy has finally come through with something.

My phone pings with a text from Dan.

Dan: Hey you. Had a great time.

Me: Me too.

Dan: Let's do it again.

I don't know what to say. I want to see him again, but I don't know how to fit something good into my life. Without ruining it, that is. I take the easy way out. I send Dan the "thumbs up" emoji and tell him that I'll call him later.

"On the case."

Now he gives me the "thumbs up."

There is a knock on my passenger-side window and all I can see is a uniform and gun belt. I put down my phone and roll down the window, expecting to be told I can't park here. A woman in her thirties squats even with the window.

"Detective Carpenter?"

"That's me."

"I'm the one you're supposed to meet," she says. "Come with me."

I exit the Taurus and meet her on the sidewalk. I was wrong in my assessment of her age. She is easily in her late forties. Tall, thin, athletic looking, with short-cropped black hair, no makeup, dark blue uniform, and three silver stars on each collar. Fine lines around her eyes indicate a tanning bed or years of hard living.

Not sure which.

"Chief Holmes," she says, not offering a hand. "Jimmy said you wanted to see Robert Boyd's quarters."

Quarters. Not room or dorm room. She's ex-military.

"Ex-Army?" I guess.

"Navy," she says with a hint of a smile. "Chief petty officer. Submarine duty." She walks away. I suppose I should follow.

"I appreciate this."

"Don't thank me. Thank Jimmy." Her pace is much quicker than mine and I have to jog to keep up. I don't like to jog unless I'm chasing someone or running away. She notices and slows.

"Sorry. Old habits."

"Not a problem," I say. "Did you know Boyd?"

"I didn't know him, but I was keeping an eye on his activities on campus."

I wait for her to expand on what she meant.

"He was a source for fake IDs. He was a source for illegal drugs. He shared a room with another student. Neither of them ever made it to any classes, but they seemed to keep their grades up. I suspect someone was taking exams for them. Or they were hacking the school computer system, entering grades."

I knew how to do that. In fact, I've done it. It isn't difficult if you have one of the employees' passwords.

"Who was his roommate?" I ask.

"Qassim Hadir," she says. "Came here from Syria. Jimmy told me he has a Washington driver's license in the name of Robert Aloysius Boyd. I'm not sure which of these two made the IDs."

Clay told me that Robbie Boyd had stolen the identity of his roommate, who was a black male. Now Chief Holmes tells me the other guy's name is Qassim Hadir. I guess he could pass for a black male.

"How do you know Qassim Hadir is his real name?"

She shakes her head. "That's the thing: I don't. Both of these guys check out if you don't look further than their applications to school. None of the jobs check out. None of the references check out. I had a friend run Boyd through Social Security with the number he'd provided. That Robert Boyd died nine years ago at the age of sixteen. Using a dead guy's information—can you believe that?"

I can.

And, yes, I'd have done the same thing, but for a different reason. Survival. And who's to say that's not what these two were up to. One of them *was* dead. Hanged. Maybe set up for several murders. The other was missing if Jimmy could be believed. It was ironic. Or was it? What if the killer used Boyd to send us in a different direction? Boyd and Qassim could change identities like some people change underwear. Boyd could have just disappeared too. Like Qassim.

But he didn't.

I had the feeling someone else was pulling the strings on these two.

"I can believe anything," I say.

The two-story apartment building has five units up, five down. It's wood framed with paint that's a faded and chipped battleship gray. Black iron railings and concrete stairs complete the picture.

From the outside, I check out Boyd's room upstairs. Cheap white plastic chairs are on each level, facing out toward the bay. One of the balconies, Boyd's I think, has a large wooden spool for a plant table. On top, an ashtray and a trio of empty beer cans.

Chief Holmes uses a master key to unlock the door. I make a mental note to collect the beer cans if I don't find anything more useful inside. I already had Boyd's body, hence his DNA, but if someone hired him, it's possible the real killer left something behind.

The chief swings opens the door and the smell hits us. Hard. Like a semitruck of stench.

CHAPTER FORTY-TWO

The Kitsap County Sheriff's Office is out in force. Clay is there, wearing his stern, all-business face, along with two other detectives going door-to-door, talking to any dorm resident who might be home.

Not many are.

Most everyone is at some kind of protest on the other side of campus where bulldozers are threatening a tiny grove of trees. A serial killer is on the loose, but they wouldn't know that or even care if it didn't interrupt a good party or a protest.

"Did you have a warrant to enter?" Clay asks me.

Chief Holmes saves me an explanation.

"She came to check on the welfare of Boyd's roommate. I knocked and didn't get an answer. I smelled something disturbing and opened the door with my master key. I knew the smell immediately and entered to ensure there wasn't someone else inside injured."

Clay rubs the back of his neck and grins.

"Textbook explanation, Chief."

He looks at me. "Is that your story as well?"

"Yes," I tell him. "I also entered. We touched nothing and came right back out and called you."

That part wasn't true, but the chief didn't even flinch. I was starting to like the Navy way—or at least her version of it.

Chief Holmes speaks up. "The name the guy gave when he became a student was Qassim Hadir." She fills him in on how the Social Security number came back to a guy dead for nine years.

"I'll run his fingerprints through AFIS and locally," Clay says. "You should have fingerprints from the body this morning. If you run those, can you let me know if you get a hit? I'll do the same."

I nod.

"Well, looks like you don't need me or my people here any longer," Chief Holmes says. "We'll get back to policing the campus. Keep me in the loop on this one, Clay."

It wasn't a request. Someone had been killed on her campus.

"Looked like his neck was broken," she says.

He nods.

Chief Holmes gets on her radio and tells her people to go back to their jobs. I catch up with her as she leaves the front walk of the apartments.

"I appreciate what you did back there."

"I didn't do anything."

"I want to catch this guy."

"I know you do. Good luck. He'd better not come back on my campus."

I return to the apartment, small space with a combination living room and kitchen. The living room couch has been made into a pull-out bed. It looks like it hasn't been slept in and is cluttered with dirty clothes, magazines, and snack wrappers. I get on the floor and look under the couch, in the kitchen cabinets, in the oven, in the refrigerator. Adhering to the front of the refrigerator with a magnet is a poster. It's a crude drawing of a pig. The eyes are crosses and the tongue is hanging out. Next to the pig is an even cruder drawing of a handgun with flames coming from the barrel. Under the drawing, someone has written in rough letters, "SORRY PIG." I fold this up and stick it under my blazer in my waistband. The residents of the unit weren't very literate and there is nothing else around that I can compare with the note found in Boyd's hand.

I study the body lying on its stomach on the bedroom floor. It's a black male, twenties, short, chubby, long arms. Three things strike me. One, he has tattoos on the backs of both hands. Each tat is of an eyeball. Two, his head is almost turned around facing me. Three, he has been posed in the same manner as Karynn Eades.

Vitruvian Man.

Nothing is out of place. The apartment is a mess but not any more than you would expect with two younger men living there. I hear a siren. I go outside to wait with the chief. I don't need photos of what I saw inside.

I have it all stored in my head.

Chief Holmes returns and I ask her to dig up any records she can find on Boyd and the dead guy. She promises I'll have them before the end of the day.

A beat later a uniformed Kitsap County deputy climbs up the stairs with Detective Clay Osborne.

Now Clay is inside the apartment while I sit on the top step, waiting. Trying to stay out of the way of the crime scene techs.

"What a mess," he says.

Clay has come up silently behind me. I hate that.

"At least we found both of the Boyds," I say.

"What do you think is going on, Megan?"

"You tell me."

"I don't want to jump to conclusions."

"Me neither."

It was a stalemate.

"You first," I say. "Anything you say can't and won't be held against you in a poll of public opinion."

Clay grins. "Okay. I'll go first. Here's what it looks like. The key words here are 'looks like.' An alleged fourth victim of the killer is found on the rocks on Skunk Island. She's got a broken neck and is laid out in a cross, like this guy in here. Not far away the Robbie Boyd you were looking for is found hanging in a tree. He has a piece of cloth in his hand with 'Sorry Megan' or something like that written on it. Some clothes and a purse are found nearby with the victim's driver's license."

I remain quiet and don't give anything away as his eyes search mine.

"So it looks like the white Boyd broke the black Boyd's neck and posed him on the floor. He then took the latest victim, Karynn, to Skunk Island. Her neck may have been broken before she was taken there. White Boyd feels like the jig is up and decides to off himself. He writes you a confession note, throws a rope over a limb, and hangs himself."

Hearing Clay say it out loud convinces me the killer had set this all up. Four women sexually assaulted, murdered, dumped. And now two guys, criminals, die to clean up after him.

I have another question. But I hold my tongue. How did Boyd get Karynn's body to Skunk Island? We've never found Boyd's junk car. There is no way to get to Skunk Island except by boat. There was no boat found abandoned on the island.

"That's it?" Clay asks.

"I guess so."

"You're going to keep digging, aren't you?"

"Aren't *you*?"

He looks at his feet. "Who's going to tell Larry Gray about all this?"

I meant to call Larry. I forgot.

"He's your friend and you already have a working relationship," I say.

Clay pushes back. "He's related to your boss."

Another stalemate. Clay just doesn't want to listen to Larry whine about how he wasn't brought in on finding Boyd's body. He'll want to wrap his case up and get back to important things like eating or making sexist remarks. He is a stark contrast to Sheriff Gray, his second cousin twice removed on his mother's side. Whatever. I told the sheriff about Larry being one of the detectives on the cases and he just frowned.

"I'll call Larry," I finally say. "I was going to anyway, but this came up."

Clay goes back inside the apartment and I return to my car. It's still where I parked it. No parking ticket. I get in and start driving back to Port Hadlock and the Jefferson County Sheriff's Office. A lot of things are running around in my skull, always ending with *How did Clay hear about Boyd's body being found?*

Probable answer: the police grapevine.

A cop talked to a dispatcher and that information was passed on to NASA and broadcast from a satellite. Another possibility: there is a collective intelligence, like an ant colony.

I have an ulterior motive for contacting Larry. The DNA of my initial suspects, Jim Truitt and Steve Bohleber, didn't match anything including the unknown matched samples collected from Dina Knowles and Leann Truitt. Margie Benton's DNA sample was contaminated and couldn't be matched to anything. None of the DNA was in the database kept by the FBI.

I have four female victims and DNA has been collected from all four. This person has killed at least four people—maybe more if the Boyds are victims. A killer that prolific should have a record of some kind. Yet there is nothing in the DNA database. So, whose DNA wouldn't be in the FBI's database, which is the most comprehensive on the planet? There are a couple of possibilities. People who never committed a felony offense. People who are exempt, like government workers, politicians, law enforcement…

I feel a chill. Shades of Alex Rader cross my mind. He was a cop. He was a kidnapper. A torturer. A murderer. And, of course, he's dead. Yet, even when he was alive, his DNA would not have been in the FBI database.

CHAPTER FORTY-THREE

I get the coroner's phone number for Kitsap County. Dr. Wilson has come to the campus dorm and had the body taken to the morgue in Bremerton, where he will perform the autopsy. He promised to call me with the results. I decide not to bother driving back to the Sheriff's Office in Port Hadlock. The sheriff and Ronnie would already be gone by the time I arrived.

As I drive home, I call our own pathologist, Dr. Andrade. His assistant answers. They received the two bodies from Skunk Island, but the doctor hasn't given her a time for the autopsies. She asks me not to bring them more work. *Very funny.* She advises me that she will contact me when a time and date has been set. I remind her this is now a serial killer investigation and ask that she please pass that on to Dr. Andrade. Time is important. The call goes dead in my hand. I call her back. When she answers, I tell her to call Dr. Andrade and have him call me or I will find the doctor and make him available. I tell her it's not up to her to screen emergency calls and then I hang up on her.

That felt good.

I park in front of my house. It isn't really *mine*, but I've come to think of it that way. I've been here longer than I've lived anywhere. That's the opposite of my life growing up. We never stayed in one place very long. My mom would have me or Hayden pick a city name out of a bowl at random and that was where we would move to next. Randomness would make us safe. If we didn't know where we were going, no one else would, either.

Even with the threatening emails from "Wallace," I see no reason to move. This is home. Let him come. Yes, I'm afraid. Sometimes fear makes you brave.

I put my purse and keys on the table, go to the bedroom, and flop across the mattress. My brain is tired. I can't keep all of this straight. I get up, find a notepad and a pencil, and begin a chart. Victims, witnesses, evidence, counties involved, hospitals, DNA, locations the bodies were dumped, places of employment, where they resided, what they drove, and on and on.

I tear that sheet off and try again.

The locations of the dump sites are similar in that they are all near the water. The victims also lived near the water. The women worked in bars. Two of the women had given children up for adoption and one was pregnant. Did this have to do with the children? What were the odds that all of them would have had babies? The only one who doesn't fit the profile is Karynn Eades, but I haven't run down much information yet. I was sure that Boyd's roommate would be my best lead. I was fairly sure Boyd wasn't the killer. I feel he was involved somehow. Now Boyd's roomie is dead. *Murdered.* His neck was broken just like Karynn Eades and the other victims.

I need more. Marley can get the DNA done in a few hours, but he needs the samples to run and I need to convince him to do it. I pick the phone up to call Dr. Andrade and see it's late. He hasn't returned my call. I call Dispatch, get his home phone number, and call it. A woman answers.

"Is this Mrs. Andrade?"

"Yes," she says. "Who's calling?"

"Megan Carpenter, Mrs. Andrade. I'm a detective with Jefferson County."

"Oh, *that* Megan?"

"I guess so, Mrs. Andrade. Is your husband there?"

"Detective, he is having his dinner. Late as usual. Can you call him at work tomorrow?"

I hear a gruff voice in the background and then Dr. Andrade is on the phone.

"Megan, I was going to call you, but I heard you were over in Kitsap finding more dead bodies. You're like the angel of death."

"I was trying to find a witness and—"

"You want to know if I sent the Eades rape kit to the crime lab. The answer is yes. I knew you'd want it rushed through. I also had buccal swabbings done on the male, Boyd. All of that is with the lab. Good luck."

He hangs up.

I'm putting the phone down when it rings in my hand.

"I thought you'd want to know that I'll do the autopsies in the morning," he says. "Eight o'clock."

"I'm sorry for calling you at home—"

The line goes dead again.

I have what I want. I don't really need to attend the autopsies to know what he'll find. I just needed the samples sent to the lab. Now I have to get Marley to work his magic again. If the DNA from Boyd matches Leann's and Dina's unknown sperm donor, I will have my killer. If it doesn't, I have proof the killer is still out there.

I make another call.

"Ronnie Marsh," she answers. She sounds distracted. I hope she's not on a date, because I need her to do something.

"Are you busy?" I ask.

"I'm going over the records from that thumb drive you gave me."

"You're still at work?" I look at the time.

"I think I found something. Leann Truitt and Dina Knowles both had their babies at Kitsap Medical Center, but there isn't a father's name on the birth certificates. The babies were put up for adoption. I don't have any way of getting the name of the couples that adopted the babies. The delivery doctors were different for them both. But guess what?"

I wish she wouldn't do that.

"What?" I ask.

"I found the dates they delivered and checked that with the video surveillance tapes. I've been going through them but there are several cameras and I don't know what I'm looking for."

I'd forgotten to ask which camera went with which floor or unit. *Crap!*

"Good work. You really didn't have to stay so late."

"It's okay, Megan. I want to catch this guy."

She means it, and I feel a little guilty about asking her to work even later.

"Thanks for everything," I finally say. "I should have asked for the camera numbers for the floors we need to monitor."

I said "we."

It passes through my mind just then how helpful it is to have a partner. Not that she is a partner. I mean, Ronnie's a reserve deputy. Chances are she'll go to corrections or some office job. She's too skilled at computer work to be sitting in a patrol car or writing tickets.

"You can let that go for tonight and I'll call the hospital to see what camera numbers we need. We can look at it together tomorrow. I can use your eyes on this one."

"Really?" she asks.

She sounds so happy just then. I don't know if it's because she thinks she is going home or because she gets to work with me on the videos.

"I want you to do me a big favor tonight."

"Whatever you need, just ask me."

She doesn't balk.

I give her Marley's work number and personal cell number and tell her to set up a meeting.

"Dr. Andrade assured me the rape kit and a DNA sample from Boyd are at the lab," I continue. "I know it will take a couple of hours. Do you mind babysitting Marley until he gets a result?"

"You want him to compare Boyd with the unknowns from Dina Knowles and Leann Truitt. Then you want to know if he sexually assaulted Karynn. I watched the techs taking swabbings from her body, so there should be several samples from both of them. It may take overnight to get the results."

She's right, of course.

I give more instructions.

"Ask Marley to do Boyd first and see if his DNA matches the unknowns. I hate to ask you to do this, so you can decline."

I don't hate asking, but I know there is value in pretending so.

"I'll see what Marley says, Megan. I don't know that much about the DNA machine. Do you want me to call you if it's real late?"

"No time is too late," I say.

"Oh, I forgot. I ran Karynn through the system. She's clean. No record. No tickets, even. I put together a list of links to her social media, family, friends, and addresses."

"Send it to my department email. I'm at home and I'll go through it here. I may call some of the people listed and see if they can talk to me tonight. Tomorrow we're taking a road trip."

"Where are we going?"

"I'll tell you then. Thanks for helping with this. Tell Marley I said thank you. And don't spend the night there. Marley can call you or me with the results. You'll need some rest for what we're doing tomorrow. Try to be in the office around eight if you can?"

"I'll be there."

I end the call and pull up my work email. Ronnie has already sent her list. She also included the hospital video. It's a massive file. I will be glad to have help going through it. Maybe it will be a waste of time. But I trust my gut.

CHAPTER FORTY-FOUR

I spend the night reading Ronnie's list of people that we need to interview for Karynn's murder and finding anything and everything I can about Margie Benton. I hate to admit Larry Gray was right about any of this, but Margie Benton did not exist. No police record. Nothing on social media. Nothing in the news. Ever.

I phone Clallam County and ask the weary dispatcher to check her address for previous runs. There were only two police calls for service to that address or near it. Neither involved Margie. One was a drunk on the street and the other was a report of someone peeping in windows. The dispatcher tells me the deputies said there was no one there when they arrived both times.

"Calls were determined to be a hoax," she says. "Kids maybe thought it was funny to cause a commotion and were just giving random addresses."

Margie's landlord's name was in Larry's report, but according to Ronnie the landlord is now deceased. Her little house is being rented by an elderly couple. According to Larry he talked to them. I'll go back and do it again. I decide not to call Larry and tell him about the new victim until I am finished reinvestigating Margie Benton's murder.

I suddenly think about Karynn Eades. She wasn't a name I requested from the hospital records. I'll have to get another court order and I don't want to take the time. At the rate the killer is working, he'll probably hit again.

I call Clay.

"Detective Carpenter," he says. "What can I do for you at this time of night?"

I look at the clock. Normal people are sound asleep. Clay doesn't sound like he was asleep. "I just wanted to say again how sorry I am I went around you at the hospital. I just really needed that stuff and I'm a little freaked by this guy. You know?"

I hear a sigh. "All is forgiven. You need to remember, we're on the same team. I take it you always work alone."

"That's right," I say.

"If you're a loner, you do things in a pattern. You know how you want to do something and then you do it. If something gets in your way, you work around it."

He's right.

"I understand," he says. "Really I do. I'm the same way. I always work alone. Then I worked with Larry for a short time and that convinced me that I was better off working alone."

I laugh. "He's a ball of fire," I say.

"Yeah. He is that. So did you just call to apologize, or do you need another favor?"

This guy is good, I think.

"Since you asked so nicely, I do need something. Don't get mad, but I need to see if the hospital has records for Karynn Eades. That's 'Karynn' with a *y* and two *n*'s."

"What, no court order this time?"

He sounds ticked off. I don't blame him, but he'll get over it.

"No court order," I say. "Just a request from one team member to another."

He's quiet. I wait.

"Can you text me her information? I'll get the records for you, but you'll owe me."

I want to tell him I don't owe him anything for doing his job. I'm solving his cases too.

"I understand."

He is true to his word. Five minutes later I have a record attached to a text:

"Karynn Eades delivered a baby boy six months ago. Given up for adoption. Father unknown. She was on public assistance."

I pull up the hospital record on my computer. It lists no workplace. The address is the same one I found on her driver's license. No next of kin is listed. She's as invisible as the others.

Except for Leann Truitt. Born to a wealthy family. She is three for three on the profile-o-meter. Matches the description, worked in a bar, had a baby that she'd given up. The only differences are that Margie was still pregnant, so she hadn't given up the child. Yet. And Leann had family that can be contacted.

I don't need Marley's report to know that Boyd's DNA won't match any of the victims. My killer is still out there.

I fall into bed hoping that I'll get a solid three hours of sleep. Such hope evaporates as my mind refuses to push away the anxiety that the emails have caused. I think about the people I've hurt in my life, either intentionally as part of some greater cause, or by being unable to show the kind of love that I know is inside of me. Someone out there knows my weaknesses. He knows my story. He knows that I'm a fighter.

And when I meet him, I intend to prove that I have never had time for, or trust in, the word "sorry."

CHAPTER FORTY-FIVE

Sheriff Gray is standing by my desk the next morning, talking to his second cousin, Larry, who is slouched in my chair.

I'll need Clorox wipes.

Larry stands and gives a theatrical bow. He's added an extra squirt of oil on his hair and I'm all but certain he's flammable.

"There's the little lady now," he says.

"I was going to call you last night."

"Don't you worry your little head about it. Tony's been filling me in. You've been busy, Missy."

Missy?

Sheriff Gray steps in before I can say anything. "I guess she's got this thing about cleared up. Reserve Deputy Marsh is going by the crime lab to get the DNA results from the Skunk Island deaths."

Larry sits on the edge of my desk and slaps a big hand down on a big thigh. "All wrapped up in a neat little package. Boyd's the guy. I guess his roommate out at the college found him out and Boyd killed him too."

"Yeah," I say. If that helps Larry sleep at night I won't argue. "Detective Gray, I need to ask you something."

"You can call me Larry," he says, quickly adding, "In fact, I insist. You just cleared my biggest case."

"Thank you, Larry," I say.

And you have no idea what's going on.

"I want to tie up any loose ends," I say, "you know, just to cover our tail ends."

His face grows serious and he huffs out a breath.

"I know all about that, kiddo," he tells me. "I been through that wringer. Some attorney wants to make a name for herself and drags a cop through the mud."

Just then I guess that some lawyer had the unfortunate luck of being a woman and took exception to one of his poor investigations.

"I'm going to go ask some questions about Margie if you don't mind. You know. Talk to her last employer, see if I can find friends, that kind of stuff."

I say all of that with very little enthusiasm, as if it's a bottom-of-the-barrel endeavor but someone has to do it.

"I'll escort you myself," he says. "Bring that little gal partner of yours along and I'll treat you to a breakfast that's to die for."

"That's not necessary, Larry. Just covering some bases."

"All righty. But you call any old time and the offer's still on the table," he says with a wink.

My skin crawls.

"Thank you, Larry," I say. "I will."

I will never.

Larry stands and thumps Sheriff Gray on the shoulder with a serious look on his face. "You remember to call me now, cuz. It's been too long and we're family."

"I'll do that, Larry."

Sheriff Gray isn't going to call him. I can tell by the way he's biting his lower lip. He always does that when he is about to tell you something he doesn't think you'll like. I get the feeling that he's been avoiding Larry for a while.

Larry pulls me in for a hug and I barely hold back a scream.

"See you later." He waves at Nan and leaves the office.

Sheriff Gray lets out a breath. "I thought he'd never leave."

I give him a look. "Second cousin on your mother's side, right?"

He shakes his head. "I don't claim him. My mother didn't like him, neither. Hell, I don't think his own mother claimed him."

He motions for me to follow him into his office. He sits in the chair from hell, wiping tears from his face. "Shut the door."

The door squeals as I shut it.

His expression is dead serious. "Boyd didn't do it, did he?"

I shake my head.

"Take a seat."

"Before you tell me no, I'm just going to talk to a few people about Margie Benton."

Sheriff Gray holds his hand up, palm out. "I understand. You've got to do his work for him. You do whatever you have to do to get this guy. We've had enough killings."

"I want to take Ronnie with me."

"Seriously?"

"I think she has promise," I say. "And don't you dare tell her I said that."

He gives me the go-ahead and I leave the office.

My phone rings. It's Ronnie.

"Marley must have slept in the lab," she says. "Poor guy. I'm on my way to pick up breakfast and coffee for him. Do you want me to bring you something when I come in?"

"He worked all night?" I ask.

"He did. He said he's got something for us, but he wouldn't say what it was until I bring him some coffee. You know, he's kind of cute. Kind of nerdy cute."

God, what have I done?

"He's one of a kind."

"So you don't want anything?"

"I'm fine. Just get back as soon as you can. I talked to Detective Gray and the sheriff and we're good to go. We'll get coffee on the road."

I hang up and have a bad feeling. What if Marley has matched Boyd's DNA to the others? I know I should be glad if that's the case. The killer's dead. The cases are solved. But my gut isn't happy.

I don't want him to be the guy. I want to be the one who catches him. Ends him.

In any case, I'm still planning on running the Benton case down. There is so much Larry has left out. So much he didn't do. So much he hasn't bothered to investigate.

My phone rings again. I'm popular this morning.

I answer.

"Megan, it's Clay. I guess you called Larry last night. He called a while ago and didn't seem surprised about Boyd. Are you satisfied with the results now?"

"Larry was here this morning talking to the sheriff. He's satisfied, so I'm satisfied."

The line is quiet for so long, I think he's gone. His voice comes back sounding incredulous. "I know you don't mean that."

"Yes," I say. "I do. I'm done. Case closed."

"Really."

"Well, I mean, I still have to finish some things up and write my reports, but yes."

"What *things* do you have to finish up?"

I shouldn't have said that.

"The video from the hospital," I tell him. "I still haven't looked through it. I'm crossing my *i*'s and—"

"Dotting your *t*'s," he finishes. "Do you want some help looking through all of that? Probably a ton of video to review. You can bring it here to the office. Or I can come there."

"I thought you were done with this?" I ask.

"I'm satisfied. Larry's satisfied. If you're not, then I'll pitch in. We're a team, remember?"

Team.

Right.

"I'm going to Ronnie's tonight and we're going to run through it," I lie. "Have some wine. Pizza. Make a night of it. I appreciate the offer, but I've got this. Like you said, I'm the only holdout."

I'll have to listen to Ronnie's chatter all evening, but I'm used to it already. Maybe Mindy would like to come too. A girl's night while looking for a murderer. My kind of an evening.

"You're sure?" he asks.

"Sure as sure. Besides, you have to keep Jimmy in line."

"He's a character, but he's okay. He said to tell you he forgives you for going over his head too."

I really don't care.

"That's great," I say. "He's a nice guy."

"Well, if you're sure you don't want an extra pair of eyes, I'll leave you two to it. It was good working with you, Megan."

"You too, Clay." The call ends and I think I'll miss him. Clay reminds me of me a little. And he's easy to talk to when I don't have to lie to him.

I have a strange feeling and I can't quite put my finger on what it is. It will come to me if it's important. I log onto the computer and bring up my personal email. No email from Hayden. I log onto my work email and freeze.

Wallace.

I hear congratulations are in order. You got your man. Kind of, anyway. But in a way he got away, didn't he? Are you disappointed you didn't get to finish him?

He doesn't call me Rylee this time. No need. He knows who I was. Knows who I am now. He's messing with my head. Letting me know he is still close. Congratulating me and trying to tell me I am a killer in the same breath. The email came in around the same time I was on Skunk Island. That wasn't on the news until several hours later. Where was he getting his information?

Not for the first time the thought that someone close to law enforcement was giving information to him crept into my mind.

CHAPTER FORTY-SIX

"Where to first?" Ronnie asks.

We're sitting in my car and I'm debating if I should take her with me. I could have her take the video home and go through it. That would be a better use of her time and skills. But she's like a kitten. If you feed it, it'll follow you home. I'll let her work all of this with me. I feel like I should at least let her do this. If it turns up nothing, that will be a good lesson too. Investigations are a lot of legwork with little reward sometimes.

"First tell me what Marley had for us."

"He didn't get a match with Boyd on any of the cases."

Hallelujah.

"What did he get?"

"He said the rape kit on Karynn Eades was a match with Dina Knowles and Leann Truitt's unknown DNA. We have a connection between three of the murders now."

I drive out of the Sheriff's Office parking lot and head north.

"Adelma Beach is our first stop. We're going right past there on our way to Crane, where Margie's last known address was. I want to get a look at the area where Dina was dumped. Have you got the pictures?"

Ronnie pulls out three photos that provide the best view of the scene. They were taken from three angles away from the body.

"We won't need them if you want to know the exact location of her body," she says. "I have the GPS coordinates."

She can use her magic phone and get us right to the spot. It would be nice to see this symbol that Clay said was carved into a fallen tree trunk.

"I don't suppose you have all the addresses for Dina and Margie?"

"Of course," she says. "I put them in last night while I was waiting for Marley."

The way she says his name told me there might be romance on the horizon.

"You like him, don't you?"

I don't know why I asked. Yes I do. I need her to keep a connection with him. He wasn't my type, and although I'd do most anything to get information, I don't want to go out with Marley.

"He kissed me last night," she says suddenly, and gives me a worried look. "That won't get me fired, will it?"

I laugh out loud, and she sits back with a pouty look plastered on her face.

"If that would get you fired, we'd lose half of the department."

"But Marley said to keep it between us. I probably shouldn't have told you."

"No. You should have told me. I'll keep your secret until you're ready to tell."

She smiles. "You're a good friend, Megan."

Yeah. Then why do I feel like such a bitch for pushing them together for my own totally selfish reasons? But who knows, maybe they would have gotten together anyway. Marley? I can't believe he'll want to keep Ronnie a secret. He isn't a bad-looking guy, but I can't see him scoring with a beauty like Ronnie.

"I've got directions to Dina's scene."

She touches the phone and a disembodied female voice starts giving turn-by-turn directions. I turn at Four Corners Road and soon we're at Adelma Beach, driving along South Discovery Road at Discovery Bay. Much of the bay shoreline is seeded with everything from log cabins to multimillion-dollar estates. The GPS leads us to a deserted stretch that's so rocky, it doesn't qualify for a beach. We make our way on foot to the coordinates, trying not to break an ankle.

The phone announces we've arrived.

I'm standing in a sandy area no bigger than my bedroom. The tree trunk is easy to find. It's three feet in diameter and twenty feet in length. It was carried by high tide onto this little section of beach and its thick roots are buried in the sand and act as an anchor. The far end of the trunk disappears into the water. I climb over it and find the carving. It's been gouged into the wood with a sharp blade and is the size of the mouth of a coffee mug.

The all-seeing eye.

Ronnie snaps a close-up of it with her phone. I climb back across and look out into the bay. She says what I'm thinking.

"The body couldn't have been here very long. If the tide could bring this monster in, a body would have been pulled out when the tide went out."

"Good thinking," I say.

I look at the pictures. Dina's body was on this side of the trunk. Spread out in the same way as the other bodies, about five feet from where the roots stretched out. I don't see any drag marks in the picture. I drag a boot across the moist sand.

"She was dumped here after high tide," I say. "She had to have been found within hours. The coroner estimated she'd been dead for no less than twenty-four hours."

"So where was she killed?" Ronnie asks. "Where was she being kept before he dumped her here?"

"Clay said she had very faint scuffs or scrape marks on the skin of her knees and elbows. I didn't see anything in the autopsy report about carpet fibers, did you?"

Ronnie shakes her head.

We clambered over a hundred feet of sharp rocks to get here. I wonder if the body was recovered by boat.

"Did the report say how the body was recovered?"

Ronnie looks back the way we came.

"I doubt they carried her out. Roy was the one who spotted her." She started nodding her head. "I know what you're thinking. Roy loaded her on his boat. He pilots the *Integrity*. It has a rough deck. That could have caused the scuff marks."

My job is safe. That wasn't what I was thinking at all. That wasn't even a possibility. The marks were only on her knees and elbows. Unless she crawled around on the deck, it couldn't happen. But it could have happened if she was confined in the trunk of a vehicle while she was alive. Or in a house with carpeting.

"Where were the scuff marks?" I ask. School is in.

She thinks only a moment, to her credit. "It couldn't have been on the *Integrity*. The marks were made while she was alive. Carpeting. There's no carpeting on any of our boats."

"Where do you find carpeting?" I ask.

"A house." She snapped her fingers. "And the trunk of a car. But she would have had to have been alive to get the marks. Maybe it was when she was kidnapped? She was transported in the trunk of a car."

"My guess is that the marks came from carpeting in a room where she was being held," I say. "It was a carpeted room, so probably not a basement or a toolshed. I know that doesn't limit the location much."

"But if we get a suspect, we know what areas to search for evidence," Ronnie says.

This girl is quick on the uptake. But she won't be sticking around after the case is finished. She's on rotation and only has today left. Then on to somewhere, maybe Records or Dispatch or riding with a sworn deputy on patrol.

"Pull up the next location," I tell her. "Crane isn't far away."

"Are Clay and Larry going to join us?"

"They're busy," I lie. I don't want anyone going to our possible witnesses before we do. It can be hazardous for their health. For example, Qassim Hadir. We started looking for Boyd and his roommate, and they both ended up dead before we found them.

CHAPTER FORTY-SEVEN

I follow State Route 20 and turn north onto SR-101. Ronnie's GPS leads us to Crane, a small unincorporated town of about a dozen households. I thought we were lost twice before we found a row of houses with a view of the water. Margie's home was a neat little bungalow with a handicap access ramp and lots and lots of yard gnomes and potted plants.

The man who answers the door looks to be in his nineties. A woman in a wheelchair behind him is older, or maybe I think so because of the wispy white hair that barely hides her scalp. They are Mr. and Mrs. Ivy. They didn't know Margie Benton—had never heard of her—and the neighbors on both sides of them had only been there for a couple of months. The Ivys, like most of the elderly I've encountered on this job, invite us in for coffee and maybe to stay and talk for a few hours. I decline the invitation.

"Let's go to the Alibi and see if anyone there remembers her," I tell Ronnie. "No point in talking to the neighbors."

We're in Port Angeles in fifteen minutes by skirting SR-101 and sticking to backroads. It's almost noon. Our choices for food are McDonald's, Wendy's, or the Asian buffet. I drive past the Port Angeles U.S. Border Patrol building and turn in at Wendy's. We eat in the car. Ronnie has pulled up a map of Port Angeles.

"Where did you go to college?" I ask to be polite.

"Washington State University. My dad wanted me to be a lawyer and join his practice."

"But you went into law enforcement. Why?"

"I couldn't represent someone that I believed to be guilty."

It's a straight answer. I had her pegged for one of those rich kids that tried too hard to show that they weren't entitled or privileged. Her wardrobe screams privilege. I can't afford her footwear. But, like her, I'm not in this job for the money. I'm in it to find and end the assholes who prey on other people. The killers. The rapists. Kidnappers. Like her, I could never represent anyone like that. Unlike her, I don't want to arrest them. I want them gone permanently.

"How about you, Megan?"

I don't answer.

"Let's see what we can find at the bar."

The Front Street Alibi is located between Baskin-Robbins and the Wok. Parking is on the side. It's just after noon and the lot is almost full. A karaoke stage is in the back, the bar and kitchen are to my left, seating is to the right. A sign over the bar says, "Happy Hour All Day." That's why there were no parking spaces left. The place is full, and everyone is drinking and talking loudly.

There are two bartenders behind the bar. One is a male who looks to be underage. The other, a female, is in her forties or fifties with a beer belly peeking below her midriff peasant blouse.

The woman asks, "What you having?"

I show her my badge. Ronnie, thankfully, has worn civvies today. She takes out her reserve deputy badge case and shows it to the bartender.

"What are you having?" the woman asks again. "Lots of badges come in here. Most of 'em this time of day. Drinks are on the house for cops."

"We're not here for a drink," I say. "I'm looking for someone."

"Ain't we all, honey," she says.

Ronnie pulls out the picture we found in Larry's file on Margie Benton.

"Do you know her?" I ask.

She barely glances at the photo and then back to me. "What do you want with Marge?"

"So you do know her?"

"Yeah. I *knew* her. She's dead. What's Jefferson County want her for?"

"You knew her when she worked here?"

She nods and swipes at the bar with a clean white towel. "She's been dead going on two years now. What's this about?"

"I'm looking for the bastard who killed her," I say.

She stops wiping the bar top, looks me in the eyes, and stretches her words out, "'Bout goddamn time."

The bartender's name is Missy Johnson. Not surprisingly, she knows Detective Larry Gray. She knows him very well. Missy confided in us that she knows Larry is married, but he's a smooth talker. She tells us she met Larry after Margie was found murdered and he came around asking questions. He had been an infrequent customer before that, but he became a regular. At least three nights a week until closing, and then he was a regular at her place.

"Don't get me wrong," she says. "Larry's a great guy. But I don't think he cares about his job. Not even a little. He's just riding out his time to retirement."

"What do you know about Margie's murder?"

She looks around the bar, then back at me. "I'll tell you what I told him, and that was a while back, so stay with me."

Margie used to tend bar with Missy. They were great friends. Margie was well-liked. Maybe a little too much. She had a regular following, but then, that's not unusual for a bartender. Except Margie got pregnant by one of her customers about three years back, had the baby at home, and gave it up for adoption. The adoption was kind of under the table. According to Missy, Margie needed money and she didn't need a kid. She said they disagreed on that, but they stayed friends until Margie got knocked up again.

"She was pregnant when she was killed. But you already know that. I think she was maybe four or five months along. She didn't know whose it was or even when she got pregnant. We really had a falling-out when she told me she was going to give that one away too. She already had a young couple interested. She was a bitch; not to speak ill of the dead. She didn't mind giving the baby up. She was only sorry that she wasn't getting more money."

Now I knew why Larry hadn't worked any harder on the murder.

He figured Margie wasn't worth the effort. The idea made me sick. She wasn't just a hooker, as Larry called her. She was a baby factory.

"Do you know of any regular who had a problem with Margie?"

She shakes her head. "Someone who might kill her? Nah. Everyone liked her, like I said. I don't think anyone knew about her selling babies, though, except me and maybe Roy Martin."

Ronnie grips my arm. I'm startled.

"Roy Martin with the Jefferson County Sheriff's Office?" I ask.

Ronnie eases her grip, and we exchange a brief glance.

"Yeah," she says. "Boat captain or something. He was in here all the time up until after Margie was gone. I asked Larry one time; I said, 'Larry, how come that good-looking Martin don't come in here anymore?' He tells me that Martin was the one that found Margie's body. It got to him pretty good, I guess."

Ronnie probably can't imagine her hero hanging around a bar like this in another county.

"Did Roy know Margie?" I ask.

"Yeah," she says. "Like I said, he was in here all the time. He was one of Margie's regulars. I don't think he was sweet on her or anything, but she always waited on him. He's a real jokester. Kept us all laughing."

Superhero. Stand-up comedian. Boat captain. Roy is a deep man.

"Do you have an idea who might have done this?" I ask.

Missy goes back to wiping the bar. She lowers her voice.

"Don't get mad," she says. "I don't know anything for sure."

"But...?"

"I think it was a cop. I know you all get a bad rap lately, and I don't mean no disrespect, but that's what I think."

I question her in more detail, but she really doesn't know who. Just cops in general. She thinks that based on a few things. Like the fact that Margie's flings were almost always with cops. Margie hinted that her first baby was adopted by a cop family, but would never say who. Margie laughed about being pregnant a second time and claimed the cops were keeping her in business. She never said who the father might be. Missy didn't think Margie knew for certain. And she figured that if Margie was with that many married cops, she would have a lot of dirt on some of them. Margie was greedy enough to sell her own kids. Was she capable of blackmail too?

CHAPTER FORTY-EIGHT

We sit quietly in the Taurus, digesting what we've just been told. It fits my theory. It doesn't prove anything, but my gut is telling me to pursue it. Missy refused to name any of the cops who frequented the bar. She said Margie flirted with all of them because they were good tippers.

I believe one of them is also a killer.

Ronnie is upset.

"So Detective Gray lied to us," she says.

"Everybody lies," I say.

Even me.

For me, it's survival. For Larry, it's for personal gain. He doesn't want his affair to be known. He didn't want us to talk to Missy Johnson. I'm not concerned with his lying. I'm wondering if he messed with the DNA. Was he having an affair with Margie? Who better to mess the case up than the detective working it? He had access to all the evidence, records, and reports, and he knew who was interested and if the case had any chance of being solved. He'd tried to dissuade me from the get-go.

He said the symbol found at the scenes meant nothing. And why was he with the sheriff this morning? He and Tony hadn't talked for years. Didn't even like each other. Was he there gathering intel? Plus he offered to come with me this morning. Was it to make sure I didn't find Missy? And he claimed Margie hadn't worked at the bar for many years and said she worked the streets as a hooker.

Missy Johnson said Margie worked the bar right up to her death. She didn't know anything about Margie being a prostitute.

I feel slightly queasy, and it has nothing to do with lunch at Wendy's. If Larry turns out to be the killer, how will I tell the sheriff? And even if it wasn't Larry, this is a scandal that will stain everyone.

I have to tell the sheriff.

I start the car and head back to Port Townsend to Doc's Marina Grill, where Dina worked. She'd given up a baby for adoption before she was murdered. But she'd done it through the hospital. There was no financial gain on her part. And there was no father listed. Did she know who the father was? Was she also seeing a cop? Was Doc's a cop hangout like the Alibi?

"Megan?" Ronnie asks.

I've been deep in thought, driving on autopilot. I look at her.

"Do you think it's a cop?"

Yes, I think.

"I'm not convinced yet," I tell her. "But I guess it's possible."

"When we go through the hospital video, we need to keep that in mind."

She's right. We'll do it tonight. I told Clay we were doing that at Ronnie's place. He offered to come over and help. I add paranoia to the queasy feeling roiling inside me.

"Roy was sweet on Margie. You don't think…"

I keep my eyes on the road.

"Everyone is a suspect until they aren't," I say. "We'll keep everyone in mind for now. Okay?"

Captain Marvel is a suspect now. He knew Margie Benton, possibly intimately, and never offered that information to me. He found the bodies but maybe he had dumped them as well. If he was the killer, he covered his tracks nicely. He was at every crime scene, but his Marine Patrol duties could account for that.

And then there is Clay and his boy buddy, Jimmy from Little Italy. I can imagine Jimmy as Clay's murder sidekick. Jimmy is always clowning while Clay is more serious. Jimmy was flirty when we first met, but it was playful. Then there was the way that those two looked at each other. The way they were together. All of the victims had been raped. Those two just didn't fit. And Clay was helpful only because I had asked for his help. He didn't inject himself into my investigation.

"What do you think about the symbols at the scene and the way the bodies are being posed?" I ask Ronnie.

"Distraction," she says right away. "Or maybe it has some psychological meaning to the killer like we talked about. I read that serial killers have a signature. That might be what's going on with this guy. And there is no jewelry on the bodies. We know that Leann was getting dressed to go out. Can you imagine going on an important date and not wearing a necklace or something?"

Actually, I *can* imagine it. I barely put on makeup when I had my date with Dan.

We're in Port Townsend. I turn down the street and head for Doc's Marina Grill on Hudson Street. The street is lined with campers and motor homes and picnic benches. The view of the bay is spectacular. I've eaten at Doc's a few times and the benches remind me of times when I took Hayden down to the bay and we sat on a bench like these, watching a seagull fight with a smaller shorebird over a French fry.

My heart aches for my little brother. I wonder how he is. If he ever thinks about me.

"They look busy," Ronnie says as I see a truck pulling away from the curb. I take the spot.

"Clay has the names of Dina's manager and the owner in the file," I say.

Ronnie already has the names written down, of course.

"We're going to just do like we did in Port Angeles. Let someone come to us and see if they recognize a picture."

"You don't trust Detective Osborne?" she asks.

"It's not a matter of trust," I tell Ronnie. "If we cover the exact same ground he did, we'll get the same answers." *Or not.* "I want to see if there's anyone he should have talked to."

That's a nice way of saying I want to see if he's been hiding something from us like Larry did.

Instead of going in the front door, we go to the back where I know there is a fenced seating area. We stop a waitress and I show her my badge. Ronnie pulls the picture of Dina Knowles out and shows it to her.

"This is my first week," she says, shaking her head. "I've never seen that girl."

She directs us to the manager inside.

I ask, "Is there another waitress that's been here a year or so? I don't want to disturb your manager."

She says to wait and goes inside. A short, squat woman of about forty comes out wiping her hands on a short apron.

"Can I help you?"

I identify myself, and Ronnie shows her the photograph.

"Dina," she says. "She's dead."

"I know. That's why we're here."

"I thought that Clay was investigating her murder," she asks.

"We're a team," I said. Clay's words, not mine.

"What do you need to know? We're pretty busy right now, so I can't talk but a second."

"I just need a few minutes. Did you give a statement to Detective Osborne?" If she did, Clay didn't mention her in his file.

"You don't have it?"

She's the kind of person who answers a question with a question. I dislike that very much. I do that when I don't want to answer a question.

I look at her name tag. "Bonnie, I need to ask some questions. If you don't want to talk here, we can do it back at our office in Port Hadlock."

She looks uncertain. I don't have the authority to take her to Port Hadlock, but she doesn't know that.

She decides to play it safe. "She was a good kid. Kind of messed up, but who isn't these days?"

"What do you mean 'messed up'?" Ronnie asks.

Bonnie leads us to the corner of the deck where no one is close and lowers her voice.

"I actually did talk to the detective, but he only asked my name and when I was off work. He never tried to find me, so I thought this was all over."

We wait. Ronnie doesn't ask a question. She has picked up one of my tricks.

"I don't want to speak ill of the dead." She looks from one of us to the other and realizes we are going to keep at her. "Okay. I guess it doesn't matter anyway. I heard from one of the other girls that Dina had been stealing."

"Explain, please," I say.

"She was taking down credit card numbers," Bonnie says, keeping her eyes on us. "I'm sure she was running the credit card twice and pocketing the money. I liked her, but that's a big no-no in this business. Customers don't always complain, but they don't come back. That's for sure."

"That's not what you're worried about, though, is it?" I ask.

Sometimes it helps to push.

She closes her mouth, a true sign that she's afraid she'll let something slip.

"You're going to find out anyway," she finally says. "I heard that the manager told Clay about some other times she'd done it. Timmy—that's the manager—warned her a couple of times but felt sorry for her because she'd just had a baby. Then we found out that she gave the baby up. That didn't sit so good with most of us, especially the manager. Very religious. Dina didn't steal again that I know of, but I know the manager talked to some cop about it."

"Do you know who the cop was?"

"No," she says. "Then that detective came in and we found out she'd been killed. We were all feeling guilty about the way we'd been treating her. I didn't want to talk about Dina, so I took off early. I should have told the detective what I knew, but what good would it do? She was dead."

"You sure you don't know who the cop was?" I ask. "The one the manager talked to about her stealing?"

"He's not in here much unless he's at the bar. Good-looking guy. I mean, movie star handsome, if you can believe that. I knew he was a cop only because they always give him his meals and drinks for free."

CHAPTER FORTY-NINE

Ronnie is quiet in the car as I drive back to the Sheriff's Office. It feels strange, as her incessant prattling has become background noise that I've become accustomed to. But now she's thinking. That's good. She's putting together the pieces.

A lot of pieces.

She's also wondering whether or not this is the job for her.

We talked to the manager, another waitress, and a bartender. They all verified what Bonnie had disclosed. It all fit now. I am sure if we got a DNA sample it would match all the victims but Margie. I am sure Larry screwed up the DNA on that one, but I don't know how he could have gotten his hands on it. Normally those things are collected by Crime Scene, the coroner, or a pathologist. Larry might have had friends who helped him out. Especially if he convinced them that Margie had gotten what she deserved. Larry couldn't be the only cop who felt like the end justified the means. I wasn't one to talk. I hadn't planned on taking the killer alive. But at least I was doing it for a better reason than to cover up an affair.

The cop whom Timmy, the manager, had talked to was Captain Marvel. I didn't know exactly what his reason would have been for killing these women. For torturing them. Was it trauma from the death of his wife and baby? PTSD? I didn't know his past. I wondered if there were more victims than we knew about.

Ronnie is quietly holding her phone. Not flipping screens like crazy. We pull into the Sheriff's Office parking lot next to her Smart car. I can see she is crushed. She gave up a more lucrative life to take a job in law enforcement. Right about now she's questioning that decision and, worse, she's thinking maybe her father was right all along.

I turn off the engine.

"Ronnie, there's bad in every job. Bad on the streets. Bad in every home. It's just when it's close to you, like a family member or a coworker or a best friend, that you don't see it. Maybe you ignore it. Maybe the bad is good at hiding among us?"

I'm an expert at being deceived. My mother, my father, my aunt. But I'm on the lookout all the time. Ronnie still has some innocence. She'll lose that if she stays in this job long enough. She'll look for the bad before she lets her guard down and trusts anyone. Even a little.

She doesn't respond or look at me. Then she lets out a sigh. A big sigh.

"I guess so. I need to write a report." She opens the car door and I reach across and stop her.

"We can do that tomorrow. We still have no real evidence. I don't want to tell the sheriff our suspects are cops. I sure as hell don't want Nan to hear what we've found. Why don't you go home, and we'll start again in the morning if you're up to it?"

"I want to finish this." She's lost the hurt look.

"I've got an idea." I'll probably hate myself for doing this. "Follow me to The Tides. We'll have a stiff drink before we go home. Try not to think about this tonight."

Like I wouldn't.

She smiles tentatively. "I've got a better idea," she says. "You follow me to my place, and we'll have several drinks. I've got room for a guest and we can go through that hospital video—maybe come up with a plan for getting the evidence. I don't want to work with a killer. I don't want him getting away with this. I want to end this."

"You're on," I say.

I follow Ronnie's improbably little car to the Big Red Barn and park on the street while she finds a spot in a short gravel driveway. We walk across the footbridge and I can't help but wonder what it would be like to live in a place like this.

"I had to pour you on your bed the last time I was here," I say.

She laughs. Some color is coming back into her cheeks. I hope someone won't have to carry me into the office tomorrow. She opens the front door without a key. That's a demerit.

She sees me frown slightly.

"Nothing ever happens here. My neighbors are great and there's never been a problem before."

"I can't tell you how to live, but you do remember what we're working on? Who we suspect?"

"Oops. I'll start locking up. I just don't want to get paranoid."

Better paranoid than dead, I think. *Scotch eases paranoia a bit, but it does nothing if you're dead.* I don't tell her this. She is, after all, providing the drinks.

"Let me give you the tour."

I don't tell her I took the tour while she was passed out.

She shows me the two most important places in any house: where the bathroom is and where the liquor is kept. She points to the door leading out onto the deck. "Go on out and have a seat. I'll get the drinks. Scotch with some ice, right?" I nod and she leaves.

I sit in one of the Adirondack chairs and look at the magnificent view of the Port Townsend Bay.

Hayden comes to my mind and I feel ice form in the pit of my stomach. I can't shake the feeling there is something wrong. I wonder for the umpteenth time if he's okay. Maybe he's been in a battle. Or an IED has blown him up. I don't even know if he listed me as his next of kin. How would they know to notify me? I'd made myself hard to find. At least, by normal standards. Yet my stalker has found me.

The last time I stood out here, Ronnie was unconscious on her bed. I looked out over the bay and made a promise to Hayden. When this was over—when I took care of my stalker—I would get us a place like this. Two bedrooms. Two bathrooms, because he is probably still a slob. We'll be a family once more. I'll never do anything to push him away again. I'd try to live like a normal person and put the past behind me. Dr. Albright is convinced I can do it. I just have to convince myself. Switching gears to normal scares me more than killers.

Ronnie returns, hands me a drink, and takes a seat.

"Did you ever wonder why it is we chose this kind of work?" she asks.

I sip and ice rattles in my glass. "No. I'm driven to do what I do."

"Well," she says, a little too quickly, "I am too. But where do you think it comes from?"

I give Ronnie a look, then a smile.

"A good place, Ronnie. It comes from inside."

She nods and we drink. The sun will set in an hour and I want to stay right here and watch it, but the case calls to me. I don't want to talk about the elephant in the room, Captain Marvel, and Ronnie doesn't bring him up. I could get used to her. Not for long periods. Not like a friend.

A coworker that I didn't hate would be okay.

We sit quietly like two old friends, comfortable with silence, watching the water, interrupted only by the refreshing of our drinks until the sun goes down. I stand and say, "Want to watch a movie?" I don't look forward to viewing hours of videotape of people wandering up and down hallways and in and out of doors. It needs to be done. It might turn up the needle in the haystack I'm looking for.

We are looking for.

We go back inside, and I put my duty weapon on the kitchen counter next to Ronnie's. It has been pressing into my side and

I'll probably be bruised. We get another drink and I sit on the giant leather couch. Ronnie puts the thumb drive in a port on her big-screen television and sits on the other end with the remote. She fires up the TV and the screen splits into four views. Each is a different camera and they rotate every four seconds. Each quadrant has the date and time in the upper left corner with the camera number. One is of the emergency door from inside looking out. Another is the front entrance from the receptionist desk. Others show hallways and elevators.

The view we want is of the labor and delivery hallway and the nursery, but they aren't marked as such.

"I called the hospital and talked to the switchboard operator," Ronnie says. "She has these cameras in her office. She said the elevators on the first and second floors would cover anyone going to or coming from labor and delivery and the nursery on the second floor. And she gave me the camera numbers to watch."

"Good job." I'm not excited about doing this now that Captain Marvel is the main suspect. I don't think the babies were involved except for the fact they were given up by their mothers. He probably wasn't the father. We may never know who the fathers were. Larry would be more likely than Clay. He lied a lot. This might turn into a drinking session of disappointment, but investigations are like that. If something doesn't work out, you don't just give up. Television has promoted the false idea that if a murder isn't solved in the first twenty-four hours, it's not likely ever to be solved. That's bullshit. If I ever gave up that easy, I might as well quit.

We sit back on her comfortable leather couch and I'm almost hypnotized by the camera's changing vantage point every few seconds. This could give some people seizures. But the time flies by, and when I look at the time on my phone, it's two o'clock in the morning. I hear Ronnie's soft snoring. I use the remote and stop the video. I really need to pee. I get up quietly and go to the bathroom. We haven't seen anything strange or anyone familiar.

Jimmy from Little Italy has been at the ER desk or the reception area in a couple of the shots, but he was working. I didn't see him in any of the hallways or on the second floor. That kind of bugs me. If I were the hospital and had a policeman working security, I would want him taking an occasional stroll, checking all the floors. Jimmy seemed to have his ass glued to the chair. In most of the shots he was on the phone.

I turn the light on in the bathroom and am preparing to sit down. Suddenly I hear a knock at the front door. A chill runs down my spine, and as I hurry to pull my pants up, I hear Ronnie say, "I'll get it."

"Ronnie, no!" I try to yell, but the words freeze in my throat. My hand is on the doorknob when I hear her scream.

CHAPTER FIFTY

I come to face down on something hard and cold. I try to move but it feels like an elephant on my chest. I lie still and try to sense the rest of my body. My arms are stretched straight out from my sides. My legs are spread apart. Everything seems to be where it should be. I can wiggle my fingers and toes but my head and neck ache like I've run into a wall.

My eyes slowly focus, and I see I'm on the floor.

"What the hell?"

I can still speak, but the effort hurts from the center of my chest all the way to my throat. I feel the smooth finish of the hardwood. I lower my arm and feel for my weapon. The gun is gone. Panic rises. My heart is beating hard in my throat. And then I remember the kitchen counter. I put my gun with Ronnie's on the counter.

Ronnie? Memory starts flooding back. I was in the bathroom. There was a knock at the door. Ronnie screamed. I stepped out in the room. The front door was open. A figure filled it. Ronnie was being pulled up by her hair. A blow landed on her face, and I could feel the air being squeezed out of my lungs. It felt like an elephant slamming into me, rocking me back. And again. Then nothing. I've been shot. At least twice.

I listen. He may still be here. Waiting for me. To break my neck like the others. I'm not able to get to my feet anyway. I'm still wearing my clothes. I'm alone.

Ronnie?

I slide my arms up and try to push myself from the floor. Bolts of pain shoot through my chest and stars explode behind my eyes. The pain subsides. I pull my legs together and try again. This time I get to my knees, put one hand on the counter, and pull myself up. I don't know how long I've been down. My thoughts are jumbled. I keep seeing Ronnie being yanked from the floor by her hair. My breathing becomes steadier now that my weight isn't pressing against the floor.

There are two perfectly round holes to the left of center in my blazer, just over my heart. Unbuttoning my shirt, I find two mushroomed bullets embedded in my body armor. The steel plate I'd shoved in the front pocket protected my heart. *Saved my life.* It didn't protect me from the impact force of two large caliber bullets, but *I'm alive.*

I'm worried about Ronnie.

Looking behind the kitchen counter, I find both duty weapons. He has taken her but left the handguns behind. That was a mistake. I holster my .45 and tuck Ronnie's under my blazer and into my waistband before looking around the room. The television screen has been smashed. A pool of blood is on the floor. There is more blood on the edge of the door and on the doorframe. A bloody handprint is on the wall by the door.

There's more blood on the threshold.

I check for the thumb drive. It's gone. I'm sure now who I saw in the instant he shot me. I know where to look for him and I *will* find him. I will find Ronnie. If anything has been done to her, God can't help him.

CHAPTER FIFTY-ONE

Ronnie's car keys are in the kitchen. Her Smart car is tiny, less noticeable, quieter. I'll apologize for taking her car after I save her.

I drive to the bay. The *Integrity* is moored right where I knew it would be. The Port Townsend police car is tucked in between two boat trailers. He's here.

I drive down the pier with the headlights off and park. The *Integrity*'s cabin light is on and I can see movement. Just shadows. I try to take a deep breath before I get out, but it's impossible, as I've tightened the armored vest so much. At least it holds my ribs and chest together so I can finish what I have to do.

I get out and wince when the damn car's dome light comes on. The car is far enough away from the boat that I hope the light wasn't noticed. I shut the door as quickly and quietly as I can and extinguish it. Moving bent over is excruciating, but I make it to the ramp and from the ramp to the boat. Lights along the deck play on the water. I can hear the soft beat of music coming from somewhere. Maybe one of the other boats nearby. The Sheriff's Office has a separate mooring area for the Marine Patrol. A smaller boat I don't recognize is docked right next to the *Integrity*. No one is aboard it, but the cabin light of the *Integrity* is still glowing.

I move carefully, quietly, my hand gripping my .45 tightly. My finger isn't along the side of the trigger guard like they teach at the academy. It's on the trigger. I'm playing by *my* rules. I won't be shot again.

The rope stairs are just ahead now but my foot hits something and it clatters across the boards. I keep my eyes on the cabin. The light goes off. *Crap!* I rush to the boat and put my back against the hull, holding the .45 in a two-handed grip, muzzle pointed upward. I'm hoping he'll look over the railing. He doesn't. I can see what I kicked about ten feet ahead. It's Ronnie's cell phone. I'm motionless, barely breathing, not by choice. I stay that way longer than I like, but I want to let him make the first move so I can make the last one.

My shoulders are on fire from holding my arms above my head, and my chest is throbbing. I'm going to have to move. I switch the .45 to one hand, turn toward the ladder, and begin climbing. I stop after each rung and listen. With a boat the size of the *Integrity*, I don't think my movement will rock it and give me away, but I'm not sure. I guess it really doesn't matter. The light went off, and if Ronnie is in there, he could be doing anything to her.

I climb until I see the boat's rough deck. It's deserted. The boat is rocking gently against the rubber bumpers. I climb onto the deck. This is where I'll get ambushed if he's waiting for me. But I don't think he is waiting because he thinks he has already killed me.

I put my back against the outside wall near the cabin door and risk a peek through the door glass. There's a half-moon out. Just enough light to see Ronnie slumped on the floor against the far wall. She's not moving. I can't tell if she's alive or dead. *Please!* I can't even tell if she's hurt. I try the handle. The door is unlocked. It clicks and opens an inch. The muzzle of my .45 opens it another inch. There's no sound but the rubbing of the hull against the bumpers.

When I was young I was impetuous. I become that girl again now. All I can think about is Ronnie and my brother. I promised Hayden I'd protect him. Never leave him. I left to protect him. He'll never understand that. I made myself a promise to find Ronnie. I've found her. Now I have to bring her home.

I should never have let her get mixed up in this. I should have known the killer would come after us. Particularly her. She has the perfect profile. And she is dangerous to him. He had to know what we were doing tonight. What we did today. Who we talked to. What we know or have guessed. He's been a step ahead of us the entire time. He killed Boyd and Qassim to cover his tracks and put us on the wrong scent. He is ruthless. But I am too. I'm not afraid anymore.

I use the muzzle to push the door open and I go in low. Something hard and cold presses against the side of my head.

"Drop the gun."

"Hello, Little Italy," I say, and take my finger off the trigger. I can see Ronnie. Her chest is moving slightly. *She's not dead.*

"Where's Captain Marvel?" I ask.

"Marvelous Martin?" He laughs.

"Is he still alive?"

"You should be dead."

I'm scared, but I try to make a joke. "Yeah, I've heard that before. I think we should talk about your marksmanship."

The joke doesn't land where I hoped.

The muzzle of the gun presses harder into my temple. "Drop the gun, hotshot. I mean it."

"Or what? You'll kill me? You've already tried that once."

I can sense him putting pressure on the trigger.

"Okay," I blurt out. "I thought you Italians had a better sense of humor." I lay the gun on the floor. "Now tell me where the captain is." My voice is shaking, but not with fear. I'm too angry to be scared.

"Slide it backward to me with your foot," he says. "And if you value your friend's life, you won't be stupid."

Don't worry, asshole, you've got stupid covered nicely. I use my foot to slide the gun behind me. He is smart. He doesn't bend to pick it up and instead kicks it off in the dark.

"Now that you've got my gun, can we sit down and talk about this?"

He chuckles. "I heard you was a smart-ass. It's good that you can joke when you're going to be dead—again—in a minute. Too bad. I think we could've been friends."

"I thought we *were* friends," I say. "Tell me where the captain is. Did you kill him too?"

"He's down below," Jimmy says. "You think you're tough. He thought he was tough too. Gets me excited. Know what I mean."

"The captain got you excited? Okay. To each his own I guess."

He moves the muzzle of the gun around to the back of my head and presses it into my scalp, forcing my head forward.

"Get on your knees. I got something special for you."

"Okay. I'll accept your surrender. And you don't even have to get on your knees."

"I'm gonna let you blow me, and if you do it good, I won't blow you. Get it? *Blow* you?"

Bending lower like I'm getting to my knees I say, "Didn't you pay attention in the academy?"

"That's enough," he says, and I anticipate him shoving the gun into the back of my head again. As he does, I twist, slap his gun away with one hand, and draw Ronnie's .45 from my waistband with the other. I fall to the floor and hit it hard. Hard enough to start blacking out, but I don't. I pull the trigger. My bullet hits Jimmy Polito just above the notch in his throat. He lifts his face and I see an expression like *What?* His gun is again pointed at me. In the academy they taught me to shoot until the target is no longer a threat.

So I shoot.

Twice in the upper chest.

Once in the crotch.

Then a last one in the crotch, because of what he is.

He drops the gun. His hands jerk up to his throat and down to his crotch like he can't make his mind up. They end up at his throat. He slumps against the cabin wall and slides down onto his butt. I stand over him and watch blood seep between his fingers. His mouth is working like a fish's when it's pulled out of the water, and blood oozes down both sides of it. His eyes are fixed on mine. He's not completely dead.

I lean over and put the muzzle of Ronnie's .45 against his forehead.

"When you kill someone, make sure they stay dead, asshole," I say.

His eyes widen just before the back of his skull explodes against the cabin wall.

CHAPTER FIFTY-TWO

The ambulance had come for Ronnie. It was too late for Officer Jimmy Polito. Captain Martin's body was found belowdecks on the *Integrity*. He'd been shot once in the side of the head with his own duty weapon. Skull fragments and brain matter on the wall indicated he'd been shot at close range. His holster was empty.

His gun was in Jimmy Polito's hand.

I am sure the gun Jimmy used to shoot me will prove to be the captain's duty weapon. Polito knew from the police grapevine that Ronnie and I had been traipsing all over Clallam and Kitsap Counties, talking to people about Captain Martin. He was the perfect scapegoat. Larry had already planted the seed of suspicion when he told us about Martin's pregnant wife drowning. Martin was supposed to be reenacting the tragedy. But that made no sense. Because Martin had lost the baby when his wife died, he'd have wanted to protect Margie's unborn child.

Even if she was planning to sell it.

Polito intended to make it look as if Captain Martin had come to Ronnie's place, shot me, kidnapped her, and taken her back to the *Integrity* with the intention of dumping her body somewhere like the others. The other boat that I'd seen next to the *Integrity* would be towed behind. Jimmy would leave Ronnie's body on the rocks. He would leave the *Integrity* anchored where it would be found in the area of the murder with Captain Martin's body inside. He'd take the other boat back to Port Townsend, where his car was parked, and probably pull it up on one of the boat trailers I'd seen. It would be ruled a murder/suicide. He'd already tried that scenario with Boyd and his roommate, but when I didn't believe it, he had to try someone else more believable.

He made one mistake.

Not killing me.

He'd never make that mistake again.

I was released from the same hospital where Jimmy Polito had worked. And now I am sitting in Sheriff Gray's creaky chair; he insisted, saying it's the most comfortable. If I move or stand the wrong way it still feels like an elephant is standing on my chest. Sitting is worse, but I don't want to ruin the sheriff's chivalrous gesture. He's in full father mode and has made coffee for us. Ronnie is in the room with us.

Could use a little Scotch in it, but it's not too bad.

Ronnie sits next to me in the roll-around chair Sheriff Gray borrowed from my desk. She was banged up pretty good. Split lip. Broken wrist. Bruised ribs. Stitches in a cut on her forehead. But she wasn't raped, or killed, or posed naked on a beach somewhere with that ridiculous all-seeing eye watching her body be discovered.

Getting a deep breath is still difficult for me, so I let Ronnie do the talking.

"Megan and I were watching the hospital surveillance video at my place. She had the idea that the killer might have visited one of the victims when she had their baby. That's why she asked for the court order for records and video from the hospital."

The sheriff nods.

"We spent the day running down family and coworkers and friends of the victims in Clallam and Kitsap Counties. We were hearing different stories from what was in the detectives' reports."

Sheriff Gray turns to me. "Is that why you didn't want those detectives in on the debrief?"

"I'm still pissed at them," I say.

Not a complete lie, because I *am* pissed at them, but it isn't the only reason. I don't trust them, and Kitsap is in charge of the investigation on the *Integrity* and at Ronnie's place: the shooting of Captain Marvel—I need to quit calling him that—my shooting of Polito, and of course his attempt at killing me. Twice.

"Continue," he says.

Ronnie winces. Her lip—her whole face, for that matter—must hurt when she talks. But it's a good teaching tool. Never open a door blindly. Of course, it was Jimmy Polito who was at the door, in uniform; she would have had no reason not to trust him. And our guns were clear across the room on a counter. And we'd both been drinking for a couple of hours.

"I must have nodded off during the video," Ronnie says. "I heard a knock at the door and woke up. Megan wasn't on the couch. I thought maybe she'd left and what I'd heard was the door shutting. I got up and cracked the door to see if she'd left and a uniformed policeman was standing there. He looked kind of familiar. He forced the door open, said something like 'Surprise, bitch,' and kicked me in the stomach. He grabbed me by the hair and pulled me up and punched me in the face."

She has the black eye to prove it. Her cheek is swollen and shiny black. The stitched-up and bandaged cut on her forehead just above her eye is where his academy ring struck. That will leave a scar. Every cop needs one to tell stories and show to their grandchildren.

I should be so lucky.

"I heard shots and then he hit me on the head with something. I don't remember how I got on the boat, but I woke up in the cabin. He was bragging about how he'd fooled us all. He admitted killing Leann and Dina and Margie. I asked him why he did it and he said they had it coming. The all-seeing eye marked them. He was almost in a rage about them giving up their babies. He said he especially enjoyed killing Margie because she was selling her babies. Then he got quiet and kept looking at me. He said…he…"

Sheriff Gray says, "Go ahead, Ronnie. It's okay. You're with family."

I surprise myself and put a hand on hers. She's been through hell and survived. That gets her lots of gold stars in my book.

"He told me to take my clothes off. He said he had something for me that I wasn't going to forget. Then he laughed and said I wouldn't remember it, either. I knew he was going to rape me and kill me just like those other girls."

She swallows and I can see her lips trembling. She's about to come apart. She takes a breath.

"I remembered where I'd seen his face," she says. "He was the security officer on the hospital video we were watching. That friend of Clay's. He had a gun in his hand the whole time. He must have heard something because he looked out the window. I knew I had to fight to escape and I was getting ready to when he slammed me against the wall and hit me over the head again. I don't remember anything after that until I woke up on the boat with Megan sitting on the floor, holding me. She called for an ambulance and backup."

She gives me a look that I can't quite read.

"I'm sorry I let you down, Megan. I should have...I should..."

Tears start streaming down her cheeks.

The sheriff clears his throat. "That'll be enough for now. I'll need to get a taped statement from both of you, but it can wait."

Our guns were taken at the scene and there will be a hearing to determine if my shooting was necessary. My only regret is that I didn't completely castrate the son of a bitch. Sheriff Gray says he'll get in touch with Clay Osborne and Cousin Larry and tell them to leave us alone until we are ready to talk. He gives us both a week off, but I know I'll be back at work tomorrow. Ronnie, maybe not. She is still pretty shaken up about Captain Martin. She looked up to him. I thought he saw her as a conquest, but that's unkind. Maybe he wasn't a self-centered pig.

At least now she knows he wasn't a murderer and rapist.

Sheriff argues, unsuccessfully, that we be taken home. I insist that I take myself and Ronnie home. I don't like being coddled. I win. I drive.

I walk Ronnie out to my car. Someone picked the Taurus up at Ronnie's house and left it here at the station for me. I feel every jarring step from my ribs to the top of my head. I'm badly bruised and it still hurts to breathe, but I'm alive. One of Jimmy's bullets struck my body armor directly over my sternum. The doctor said if I hadn't been wearing the armor plate in my vest, I wouldn't have made it. I told him he should see the other guy and got a laugh.

Ronnie's car keys are still in my pocket. I hand them to her.

"I stole your car. Sorry."

Ronnie smiles and winces at the same time and her hand goes to her split lip. It has been glued and taped together. Another scar.

"I'm going to have a black eye," she says.

Guess what? You already do. "It gets better. Put some raw meat on it."

"Why do people always say that? I think it's a waste of a good steak."

She still has a sense of humor. That's good.

"Yeah. You ready to go home? I'll get someone to get your car for you."

Look at me: I'm being nice. It can happen.

"No," she says. "Let's get my car. My wrist may not be good for a while, but I can drive with one hand. I'm just thankful that I'm alive. If it wasn't for you..." She trails off and the waterworks turn on again. I'm starting to think the knock on her head did more than knock her out no matter what the X-ray showed. She hugs me with her good arm, and I let her. I clumsily hug her back. We shared a traumatic experience. Normal people bond after something like that.

Maybe I *am* normal...

When Ronnie dries up, I help her into the Taurus, buckle her up, and off we go.

I turn onto SR-19 and head home. I'm tired, sore, and sick inside that Ronnie almost got killed thanks to me, but I'm not satisfied that this is really over. Jimmy Polito bragged about the murders of the three women but not about Karynn, and not about Boyd or Qassim. It is probably nothing. He killed the captain but didn't admit to that.

Maybe Ronnie just didn't remember everything he'd said.

I think about all the assholes in this case: Jim Truitt, Joe Bohleber the Bobbsey twin. But there are good people, like Cass, whom I still owed; Lonigan, whom I've come to respect; Marley Wang, who has been a real trouper. My thoughts circle back to Hayden and my mother.

Good and evil.

Maybe it was her betrayal of me and Hayden—and my own betrayal of Hayden—that isn't allowing me to put this to rest? My mother lied, and then lied about the lies, and on and on. She was a supremely talented liar. She could teach politicians and lawyers a thing or two and pick their pockets at the same time.

Hayden still loved her.

He doesn't know what I know.

The road is fairly clear, and I drive on autopilot, my mind recalling everything I saw at Ronnie's; Jimmy standing in the doorway, holding Ronnie by the hair, shooting me; everything at the pier; everything on the boat. And then it hits me. I don't know why I didn't see it before. I was too focused on taking the asshole out. I didn't consider everything.

"We need to make a stop," I say.

"The Tides? Honestly, I don't think I can drink anything, Megan. They gave me some pain meds at the hospital and I'm not very hungry."

"Did they find your cell phone?"

She felt her pockets. "Yeah." She took the phone out and showed me.

I tell her who to call. To her credit, she doesn't ask questions. She dials and hands me the phone. The questions will come after the calls.

CHAPTER FIFTY-THREE

The Kingston substation of the Kitsap County Sheriff's Office has exactly three parking spaces in front. I have my pick. The front of Clay's motorcycle peeks out from behind the building. Larry Gray pulls in beside us in a brand-spanking-new Ford 500 sedan, not his assigned late-'90s-model Chevy Caprice. The Caprice is a beast. A land whale. It handles turns about as well as an ocean liner. He's in full uniform instead of civvies. We get out of our vehicles, and Larry stands in front of his new car, arms spread wide, an equally wide smile on his face.

"Thanks to you two the sheriff gave me a new car," he says. "I'm somewhat of a celebrity now that I cleared the Benton case."

You *cleared the case?*

"I'm happy for you, Larry."

But we're not quite done yet.

"What are you here for?"

Larry thinks he has solved the biggest case in his county, but he doesn't have a clue why we're here. Typical. He got a new car and I'm still driving the Taurus. Actually, I prefer the Taurus because I don't have to worry about wrecking it. It's already a wreck.

"I haven't told Clay we're coming yet," I say. I only called Larry because I knew it would take him longer to get there.

"Is this a surprise celebration? Well, now, I guess we deserve it for closing all these murders. You little gals did one hell of a job. Of course, us old timers helped."

Us little gals did everything.

I am a little ticked off that Larry got a new car for what Ronnie and I went through. But Larry is the kind of guy who can fall in a pile of manure and come up smelling like roses.

"Can I talk to you for a second, Megan?" Larry says.

Ronnie goes inside ahead of us and Larry speaks to me in a confidential tone.

"I heard you talked to Bonnie out at the Alibi."

I don't say anything.

"Now that you know who did all this, there's no reason for her name to come up."

"No reason I can think of, Larry."

"Does Tony know?"

"I didn't tell him and it's not in the police reports."

Yet.

He's all smiles again and puts a big paw out.

"You're okay. Darned okay in my book. If you ever need anything in Clallam—and I mean any little thing—you can count me in."

"Thank you," I say.

I like being owed favors, but I'm not sure if Larry will deliver.

"So," he says, putting a hand beside his mouth, hiding his words, "what are we here for?"

"Let's go inside. I have some news you're both going to want to hear."

"Okay. Surprise it is."

Larry, being the gentleman he sometimes is, holds the door for me as I enter. Clay and Ronnie are sitting in chairs that he arranged for our meeting. Ronnie is clutching her ever-present cell phone. Larry tries to hold my chair for me, but I beat him to it.

"I can do it, but thank you. I'm not as sore now."

It hurts like hell, but my mother taught me never to show weakness.

"Oh. Okay. I didn't know you got so banged up. I should have been there. I'da never let anything happen to you little gals."

"I know, Larry. I appreciate you saying so."

Even if it's just lip service.

I sit on the front edge of the chair trying not to show my agony.

Clay looks more relaxed than usual. He sits with one arm over the back of the chair, the Colt Model 1912 prominently displayed under his arm. Unlike Larry, he doesn't ask why we're here.

"I'm sorry about Jimmy," I say.

Clay doesn't move. His expression stays the same. "He got what he deserved. I'm glad it was him and not you. Either of you."

Me too. But I expected him to be a little more broken up over his chum's brains being turned into, well, chum.

"Did you ever meet Jimmy?" I ask Larry.

He seems to be thinking.

"No. I don't believe I ever did," he says. "What was his last name?"

"Polito. From Little Italy in New York."

Larry shakes his head. "I don't hold truck with crooked cops. Maybe someone not writing a ticket, but what he did wasn't human. I'm with Clay on that. The asshole got what was coming to him."

"What happened to your Caprice?" Clay asks.

"I'm not sure." Larry's smile slips a tad. "It was ready for the junkyard. Maybe it went to the crusher. I hope so."

I know you do.

"I might be in the market for a personal vehicle," I say. "Do you think they'd sell it to me?"

"Now, why would you want a piece of junk like that? You get to drive your department car for free, don't you? Stupid to have gas bills and repairs. And try to find parking with a personal car. Believe me, you don't want that headache."

"You're right," I say. His smile is back.

"What about you, Clay? You don't use that Harley for police business, do you?"

Clay looks at me. "I didn't know we were here to discuss vehicles."

I can see him tense up. His jaw tightens and the muscles in his neck ripple. His hand moves to his lap, directly beneath the .45.

"We're a team. Remember?"

He stays mute. I look from Clay to Larry. "I needed to get us all together to iron something out that's been bugging me."

It's perfectly quiet except for a ship's horn on the bay and the clanging from a buoy.

"Ronnie, tell them what you told me and Sheriff Gray this morning."

She looks nervous, like a kid in school giving a report in front of the class. I nod at her to indicate it will be okay. She begins and gives almost word for word the report she told me and Sheriff Gray. When she's done, it's still silent in the room. Clay hasn't moved but Larry has lost the smile. I can see a little tic develop under one of his eyes.

"Margie Benton. Dina Knowles. Leann Truitt. Robbie Boyd. Karynn Eades. Qassim Hadir. Captain Roy Martin," I say.

A stillness fills the space between all of us.

Larry breaks the silence. "Aww. You're not going to say we still have to investigate all of them other ones, are you? I mean, hell. This Polito guy confessed to three of them. He did the rest. Cases closed."

Clay's eyes never stray from mine. "I never thought I'd say this, but even though Roy was one of us, I have to agree with Larry."

"Well, kiss my ass, Clay," Larry says but he chuckles and relaxes. "Excuse my French. I mean, this is done. No one's unhappy. My sheriff even gave me a new car. I'm sure Tony'd like all this to just go away."

I'm sure someone would. But it's not happening.

"I don't usually tell people this"—I look at Clay—"but I have almost perfect memory. If I see something, I can see it exactly the same way even years later. You can call it my all-seeing eye, like the symbol that we found at all the scenes. I'm sure we would have found it near Ronnie's body if Jimmy had been successful. I can remember everything that is in a room. Exactly where it is, what was near it, colors, all of it."

No one speaks. I look at Larry. "I guess you could call it a blessing, but sometimes it feels like a curse. For example, I remember pulling down the road along the pier where the *Integrity* was moored."

Larry looks impatient. Clay is unmoved.

"I remember every vehicle, every boat, the hull numbers, boat trailers, everything. I remember everything inside the cabin when Jimmy thought he had the drop on me."

Still nothing from either of them.

I look directly at Clay.

"I remember seeing a motorcycle tucked in behind a trailer."

Clay grinned. "And?"

"It wasn't a Harley. It was a Suzuki. Not your style. Not Jimmy's, either. His police car was there. I couldn't see the back, but I got the tag number."

"I did too," Clay says. "I've got a copy on my desk. It's one of the dockworkers' bikes. He weighs ninety pounds wet. No way he could have done any of this. But if it makes you happy, I'll bring him in."

I turn my attention on Larry. "I guess you could say I have an all-seeing eye myself, because I also saw a faded blue Chevy Caprice. It had Clallam County government tags."

Larry's face goes pale before I even finish. He starts to jump from his seat, but it has been a few years since he's moved fast. Clay has already drawn the .45 from his shoulder holster and is pointing it at Larry.

"Sit," Clay says.

Larry's hand was going to his own gun, but he stops and sits back in the chair.

"I can explain that," Larry says. Some of the color is coming back to his face as his confidence grows.

We all stare at him. Waiting. *Go ahead and try*, my look says. My .45 is in my hand. It hurt like hell to twist like that, but not enough to keep me from blowing Larry's lungs out his back.

"You can't prove shit," Larry says. His voice has lost its playful Texas drawl. I hope he calls me "missy" again.

Clay says, "Move away, Ronnie." She does. "Now get up slowly, Larry. You can try to grab your gun, or you can turn around and put your hands behind your back. Your choice."

Larry looks from Clay's gun to mine. He shakes his head, stands slowly with his hands up at shoulder level, and turns around. He hesitates and lowers his arms. I tighten the pressure on the trigger. I can't miss at this range. Larry lets out a deep breath and puts his arms down, hands behind his back. Ronnie asked to handcuff him earlier but with a broken wrist it would have been awkward.

Clay places a handcuff on one of Larry's wrists and tells Ronnie, "It's all yours."

Ronnie uses her good hand to secure the other handcuff. I'm sure she'll always remember every click and ratcheting sound the steel made. It is her first arrest. She's had a big part in all of this. In fact, if it weren't for her being a target of these two killers, we'd never have caught Jimmy.

Or Larry, for that matter.

Clay takes Larry back to a holding cell and he isn't gentle about it, but I will swear in court I never heard the man fall down. Twice.

Clay comes back and we all sit again. Larry's yelling from the back that he wants an attorney. Clay gets up and shuts the door. "I didn't take his belt or shoelaces. I'll get them in a bit."

I have to smile even though it hurts behind my eyes.

CHAPTER FIFTY-FOUR

Larry was wrong about me not proving anything.

On our way to meet with the two detectives Ronnie remembered something she saw on the hospital video. I hadn't noticed, and she most likely didn't think it was too important, since we were looking for Captain Martin. In the view of the ER entrance she saw Larry standing outside the doors, talking to Jimmy. That was why Jimmy took the thumb drive at Ronnie's when he shot me. We'll have to go through the video again, but I am all but sure we'll find Larry and Jimmy together on other dates. It will take a lot of Scotch and pizza to watch all that video, but Ronnie and I will soldier through.

Since the kidnapping of Ronnie and death of Jimmy happened in his county, Clay said he would get a court order to obtain DNA from Larry. There is no way Larry is going to cooperate. Or confess. Or kill himself. He loves himself too much for that.

It was Ronnie who had the idea of calling in the FBI. We had six murders involving kidnapping covering three counties. The Feds had the clout, the attorneys, and the reach to get extensive records on both Larry and Jimmy and trace Jimmy's path across the country from Little Italy to Port Townsend, looking for other unsolved murders. Plus this was all very high-profile and news media were showing up from across the country. From other countries. Sheriff Gray said he'd neuter or spay anyone who gave the news people my or Ronnie's address. When he said it, he was looking at Nan, who kept her back turned, but I knew she'd heard every word. The FBI were more than happy to get in front of the cameras and microphones. I like news people only when they tell me something I need to know.

There was only one other matter to clear up, and I wanted to do it. Ronnie got into county tax records. She found property owned by either Jimmy or Larry. Larry owned a house in Port Townsend that had belonged to his birth mother. Apparently he had tracked her down and she had not been heard from for the last ten to twelve years. Probably dead.

Sheriff Gray acknowledged that Larry was adopted as a baby but said he knew nothing about Larry's real parents.

We got a search warrant and found the room where the two killers had kept their kidnapped victims. Deputies Davis and Copsey went through the house with a fine-tooth comb and found jewelry, purses, clothing, identification, and evidence of the horrific conditions the women had been kept in. There was a single bed with a steel frame. A chain was attached to the bottom rail and an ankle cuff attached to the other end of the chain. A set of bloody handcuffs was on the mattress. A leather dog leash was on the bathroom floor. The entire house was a hoarder's dream.

DNA left at the scene was Marley's dream.

We weren't needed at the house anymore, so I took Ronnie to get her car. We agreed to wait until the next day to do any reports. The FBI had enough evidence to put Larry away forever. If he gets out, I'll be waiting for him.

I follow Ronnie to make sure she gets home, then go to my own place. We are both beat. Physically. Inside, we have won.

I park in front of my house and sit for a minute. I'm not thinking about anything except how much it will hurt to get out. I have to pee. Code 3. I get out.

Inside, I drop my keys and purse on the table and head agonizingly slowly for the bathroom. It's still mid-morning but I want something. Wine, maybe. The hospital gave me painkillers, but I pocketed them. I need a clear head. My stalker is still out there and seems to be keeping current on Megan Carpenter. I think Scotch will work better. I have nowhere to go and plenty of time to get there.

Before I leave the bathroom, I look at my face in the mirror. Blood spatters look like freckles, only redder. I run a brush through my hair, hoping it doesn't come away with bits of Jimmy in the bristles. My blazer is marked with blood spatter and was taken by Crime Scene. They wanted my shirt as well, and my body armor. I drew the line at my pants. I was wearing a Washington State University T-shirt Clay loaned/gave me with my shoulder holster. They took my body armor, but Sheriff Gray gave me and Ronnie loaner .45s to keep until the shooting inquiry and ballistic tests were over. It wouldn't be long. We're both on administrative leave, but I plan to go to the office tomorrow if I can get out of bed. There's a ton of forms to fill out.

Killing Jimmy will take less paperwork than arresting Larry. There's a lesson in there somewhere.

I get the Scotch and tumbler with the Idaho motel logo out of my desk drawer. I'm drawn to the box of tapes on top of my closet. I keep the loaner gun in my holster. The weight under my arm is comforting, reassuring. I get the tapes down and put them on the desk with the recorder. I can smell myself. The smell of blood is still in my nostrils. Blood is still under my fingernails. I want to take a shower but I'm too tired. I'll wash my hands and face later. I'll take a shower after I sleep.

I pour the tumbler half full. No ice. The Scotch is cheap. After the first sip, they all taste the same. Something on an old tape of a session with Dr. Albright comes to me. Of course, I remember it word for word.

I can picture her white hair, her kind face, as we talk.

Dr. A: But you're here now. You're safe.

Me: I think so. But I don't know for sure. No one really does.

Dr. A: I suppose that's so. But you're no longer in imminent danger.

That's what you think. What was true then is true now. I have a stalker. I'm not conscious of moving my hand, but I've drawn the loaner .45 and am holding it on top of the desk. Again, I don't know why they need to test my gun. I told them I shot the asshole. I know I'll sleep with this one for a while.

I look at the top of my desk. Cheap tumbler. Cheap Scotch. Cassette tapes in a box. Cassette player. Two framed pictures of my brother. One was taken at my aunt Ginger's house in Idaho. The other is of Hayden when he graduated from high school. On the back of that one is a handwritten note:

Rylee, I'm graduating today. You are not here (as always). My foster parents are nice people, but they don't replace my family. Thanks for taking all of that away from me.

I deserve his hate. But still I send emails and check for emails several times a day. I've written him dozens of times. He hasn't written back.

I punish myself by listening to the taped sessions with Dr. Albright. I guess they've helped to open me up, as she was fond of saying. Giving me a new life. I don't think so. I slot in a new tape and my finger pauses over the "play" button when I hear a knock at the door.

There's a sharp pain in my chest because I've jumped up, and my weapon is in my hand. I don't think a killer would knock first, but Jimmy knocked at Ronnie's before he shot me twice. I move to the door and stand to one side, gun held in both hands, muzzle pointed at the middle of the door. I wait. Another knock. Not forceful. I move to the other side of the door where the doorknob is. I unlatch the door, twist the knob, and pull it open.

My breath catches in my throat and I consciously have to ease the pressure my finger has put on the trigger.

"I figured I'd get a reception," Hayden says, "but I didn't think it would be this."

I can't stop staring. My mouth is hanging open. I will my arms to lower the gun.

"Can I come in?" He smiles that same stupid lopsided smile of his and that breaks the spell.

I stand back and he enters. I close and lock the door behind him. He walks into the sparse room where I have a couch and a kitchen chair. I still don't have a television. Too many of the programs still trigger bad memories. I only think of the TV because Hayden spent hours in front of it.

My brother is more than six feet tall and his skinny ribbed chest and slumped shoulders have broadened and filled out with muscle. He's wearing khaki cargo pants that are a little too snug and a blue-and-red T-shirt with Spider-Man on the front. His hair is short and sun-bleached the color of beach sand. His eyes, however, have changed. The color is the same, but they aren't the scared-shitless eyes of a little boy. They exude confidence. Experience. Danger. They've seen things even I haven't seen. He's me, only maybe more messed up.

"How have you been?" It comes out of my mouth and I cringe inwardly. *Stupid. Stupid.*

"I'm home. That's all that matters. Right, Rylee? Or is it Megan now?" He grins, but I can't tell if it's a humorous grin. It's more accusing. Sharp.

"You're home." I can feel my eyes tear up, but I don't want to cry. It would be wrong. I'll never cry in front of Hayden. I was the strong one. Regardless, I don't trust myself to speak.

"Are you expecting someone else?"

He's looking at my gun.

I put it in the shoulder holster but don't take it off. "No," I lie. I'm always lying to him. "I just had a tough couple of days. Still haven't wound down, I guess."

"I heard all about it on the news. You're on paid leave?"

"I guess I am."

"The case is over?"

"Yeah. It is." Except for my stalker. "How long are you home?"

The look he gives me is indifferent. Not the Hayden I remember. But what did I expect? He's been in Afghanistan. That he's in one piece is amazing.

"I'm done. Out. Honorably discharged."

He is so grown-up. So sure of himself. I missed all of that because I left him. It's like the note on the back of the picture. I glance at the picture and so does he.

"I see you have my photos out."

I nod.

"And Scotch. When did you start drinking Scotch?"

"It's a police thing." I don't tell him it's to numb the pain of losing him.

I forget the pain in my ribs. My heart hurts worse. "Hayden, I'm so sorry. I truly am."

He looks up at the tall ceilings and sees the cobwebs, I'm sure. I'm not much of a housekeeper. I don't want to tell him it's because our mother treated me like a slave. I did everything while she coddled him. I held it against him when I was younger, but then I started to become his mother. I loved him more than she ever did.

As he turns his head I see a scar under his chin that runs to the back of his jaw. "You were hurt."

He puts a finger on the scar. "Want to see?"

"Yes," I say, but my voice is so weak, I'm not sure I actually said it. I can feel tears threaten to come.

He turns sideways and pulls his T-shirt collar down. Another scar, this one the size of a half dollar, mars the skin at the nape of his neck near his spine. I could cover the one in the front with the tip of my pinky.

"I love you, Hayden."

He looks at the pictures on the desk again. "I guess that's why you left me. Because you loved me so much."

His words are angry, accusing, but his face is a mask. His eyes give away nothing.

"I wrote you. Dozens of times. You never answered. Not once."

"I didn't need your emails," he says. "What I needed—what I need—is a family. I've found that in my foster parents. You have never been there for me. You promised me."

I can feel a tear slide down my face. I can't stop it. He's right and I hate myself more than he could possibly hate me. I start to say I'm sorry again but hold it inside. It's meaningless in the face of all his pain. I should be ecstatic with joy that he is here at all, but he really isn't here. Not in any meaningful way. He is here to punish me, and I know I deserve it, but I gave everything to protect him. I was almost killed trying to protect him. I wanted so bad to tell him the truth, but I can see now it wouldn't matter. His hurt runs too deep.

So does mine.

The tears are coming freely now, and I hate myself for letting it happen in front of him. I was his only family. And I abandoned him. He wasn't old enough, didn't know the truth, and I couldn't tell him.

His stare is a hard one.

"Look," I say, "I've thought of you every day."

He doesn't speak.

I go for broke. "Please stay and let me make this right. Please."

"Did you ever think about me when you left?" he asks.

"You know that I did."

"I don't know that, Rylee. All I know is that you left me with Aunt Ginger, a perfect stranger."

"She was our aunt."

Was is the right word.

"Can we not discuss this right now?"

"What else are we going to talk about, Rylee? Mom?"

I will never talk about her. I stay mute and just stare at my long lost brother.

"Rylee, she misses you. She asks for you."

My heart drops. It nearly makes a sound on the floor. A thud. I wonder if Hayden felt the vibration.

"Oh, God, are you telling me that you've seen her?"

He keeps his eyes riveted to mine. Testing me. "Once a week since I've been back."

The room starts spinning and I steady myself. "She betrayed us, Hayden."

"She's our mom," he tells me as though I need a lesson in biology. "You've never bothered to hear her side of what happened," he says as though he's her understanding lawyer.

I don't say so. Not out loud, anyway. I've never needed to hear her side of any story. I knew who she was and what she did. Right then, however, my mind goes to Alex Rader. My serial killer father.

Hayden's father.

A secret I've kept.

"Let's table this for now," I finally say. "I have a spare room. Will you stay?"

He doesn't answer right away. He lets me twist in the wind for a beat.

"Yeah. I will."

I hold my breath. Despite everything our parents did, I want nothing more than to make this right with Hayden. Suddenly it feels as though he's no longer just a link to the past, but a pathway to what I need to do. And that gives me hope. Hope is a very good thing.

A LETTER FROM GREGG

I want to say a huge thank you for choosing to read *Water's Edge*, the second in the Detective Megan Carpenter series. If you enjoyed it and want to keep up to date with all my latest releases, just sign up at the following link. Your email address will never be shared and you can unsubscribe at any time.

https://www.greggolsen.com

These are strange and scary times we're living in. I hope this message finds you safe and making the best of the new normal. One thing, I'm sure, is that nothing passes the time and takes our minds off whatever we're facing like a good book. When I finished this novel, I thought about all of you. My hope that *Water's Edge* provides you a distraction, even if only for a little while. Reading can be a source of connection in a time when we really need it.

Of course, since I wrote it for you, I hope you loved *Water's Edge*. If you did I would be very grateful if you could write a review. Reviews are your way of introducing others to books that have intrigued or maybe even scared you. ☺ I'd love to hear what you think, and it makes such a difference helping new readers to discover one of my books for the first time.

It makes my day hearing from my readers—you can get in touch on my Facebook page, through Twitter, Goodreads, or Instagram. Take care and be well.

Thanks,
Gregg Olsen

GreggOlsenAuthor

@Gregg_Olsen

@GreggOlsen

ACKNOWLEDGMENTS

I'm thrilled to bring readers (new and veteran) the second in the Detective Megan Carpenter series. And as tough and resourceful as Det. Carpenter is, she doesn't get to the page without a lot of help. I am grateful to the awesome Bookouture, especially publisher Claire Bord, who saw the series' potential and has been its guiding light ever since. Much appreciation also goes to each and every member of this amazing team: Leodora Darlington, Alexandra Holmes, Chris Lucraft, Alex Crow, Jules Macadam, Kim Nash, Noelle Holten, and Caolinn Douglas. Much appreciation to my copyeditor Janette Currie, proofreader Tom Feltham, and, last but not least, cover designer Lisa Horton. And to David Chesanow, you always get the best out of me. Thank you!

I'd like to pay tribute to my agent Susan Raihofer of David Black Literary Agency, NY, and my personal assistant, Chris Renfro, for all that you do to keep things moving at a rapid-fire clip. I'd be lost without the two of you!

And to Tish Holmes, I hope you are enjoying that well-deserved glass of wine. Thank you so much.

Detective Megan Carpenter's explosive first case from the #1 *New York Times* bestselling author Gregg Olsen!

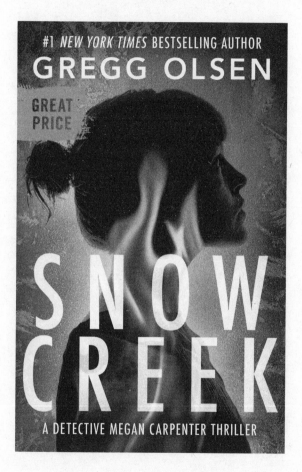

Footprints were scattered about like fallen leaves. She looked down into the ravine, and once more her lungs filled with fear. A body lay silent and unmoving in the bushes.

Please turn the page for an excerpt.

PROLOGUE

No deviations interrupted Regina Torrance's daily routine.

She simply couldn't allow it.

To permit any was to risk everything.

Regina had a strict mode of operation that was so rigid, so unyielding, that any, even the slightest change, could send her back to bed for a week. She lived with her wife, Amy, in a leaky cabin with an outdoor shower and an outhouse in the hills above Snow Creek. Completely self-reliant. They raised vegetables. Trapped squirrels for meat. Despite the fact that she had only one eye, Regina was an expert with a rifle.

Doves were lean, but tasty. Squirrels were oily and frequently on the chewy side. For protein, the couple relied mostly on nuts, eggs, and goat cheese from their trio of Nubians. Each had a name, though she never said them aloud.

Amy was on the sofa. She had been ill for quite some time. Her hair was long and braided, a pretty chestnut swag that ran over the pillow like a northern Pacific rattlesnake. She wore a blue nightgown trimmed with white piping. Both were convinced it was her best color, and it rotated frequently in and out of her wardrobe. She lay still while a conversation passed between them on a familiar loop.

"Brought coffee for you."

"Boy goat is rangy."

"Broke a jar of tomatoes."

"Darn it all! I'm feeling a change in the weather."

"You look like you're feeling it too."

Regina touched Amy's cheek and then bent down to kiss her. Like Regina, Amy was lean, sinewy. Her shoulders were cabinet knobs and her legs were a web of veins and scars. Amy's eyes caught the light streaming in between a narrow gap in the curtains at the window.

"Beautiful morning!"

"Indeed! Going for a walk now. Wish you were feeling up to it."

"Next time! Promise."

Regina pulled the curtains tight and went outside.

The ground around the barn was spongy from a nighttime rain, and the clouds dragged over the top of the trees, holding them up like circus tent poles. Regina fed the animals and started her walk, first along a narrow path that had once been a driveway. It had been at least a decade since cars had access to the ramshackle home the women shared. That was fine. No one lives in the hills above Snow Creek if they don't want to be alone. It's all about being isolated. It's solitary, not solidarity. People there mind their own business.

When Regina and Amy first fell in love, they just wanted to live and love. It was about being with each other. No constant avoidance of stares if they should hold hands. They didn't join in the Pride movement, because their love was about them, not about being part of a group.

Snow Creek wasn't far from Seattle, but it took a ferry ride to get there. And don't even think of finding their place without detailed directions. That's the way they liked it. Sure, in the beginning, the pair made frequent trips back to the city. In time, however, they just stopped returning to their old home.

Their abdication of city life was complete.

They said their wedding vows under a mammoth cedar that they eventually cut down for the house they built. Friends still came over at that time, though not many. Some came with skills to help with the farm, others to remind them that they were giving up the city and all that Snow Creek had to offer for a drippy forest and a meandering creek.

"We like the drippy forest," Amy told one of the doubters.

"Creek's not too bad, either," chimed Regina.

Their friends stopped coming after a couple of years, but the women didn't mind. Especially Regina. She'd been the one to first broach the subject about living off in the wilds, and Amy considered it merely an adventure. Something they'd do only for a while.

A while became forever.

As Regina continued her walk along the creek and then down through the woods, she paused for a beat. She thought she'd heard something. It was a familiar noise, but not one she'd heard in quite some time. It was the sound of traffic.

Two cars.

By Snow Creek standards it was beyond a traffic jam. Gridlock, really. Completely annoying too.

Regina looked up toward the noise, remembering that there had been a logging road in that vicinity at one time. She wondered if the loggers were scouting the area for another big green bite out of the hillside.

Please no.

She stood still. Like a deer. Her eyes scanning through a veil of evergreens. The wind picked up and the fringe of forest cover parted a little, though not enough to afford a better view. She moved a few steps closer.

Arguing.

What are they saying?

She couldn't quite hear, yet fear gripped her anyway. Something bad. Something terrible was happening.

What are they fighting about?

Next, there was the sound of a car door slamming, then another, and branches snapping and, finally, a loud whoosh as something rolled from the road down into the ravine.

A beat later, flames shot upward into the soggy sky.

Adrenaline surged through Regina's thin frame, jolting her, playing on her bones like some kind of macabre xylophone. She put her hand to her lips as though she needed to stifle a scream.

Don't want them to know I'm here!

Regina wasn't a screamer. Amy was.

Then the fireball gave way to a column of black smoke rising above the treetops. It was heavy, oily, and very scary. It took her breath away.

I need to get out of here. Wait until I tell Amy. Oh God. She probably won't even believe me.

Regina turned to leave and a voice called out from the logging road above.

"Someone's down there."

Another person called out.

"Shit no!"

"I saw something move," said the first one.

"You're crazy. You saw a deer."

"No, it was more than that."

"A bear. A cougar, then."

Regina didn't move. She wore a dark shirt and khakis that she rolled up above her dark blue Crocs. She didn't know why for certain, but she was terrified.

Stay still. Still will make it go away. Make them go away.

She wondered if the animals she'd trapped felt the same way when a snare caught their little legs.

She turned and took in a big puff of air and ran as fast as she could. She never looked back. Not even when she lost a Croc to a root over the trail. She was the rabbit that got away, though she still wasn't sure what she was running from. She carried that puff of air in her lungs, forgetting to exhale until nearly passing out. When she returned home, she noticed that her bare foot was bleeding. She'd cut it somehow. Sweat had drenched her back, leaving a racing stripe from her neck to her waist. She removed her clothes on the front porch, then let the water of the outdoor shower run over her. It was cold, spiking her body, mixing with her tears.

She hadn't cried in a long time.

There hadn't been any reason to.

Regina thought she heard Amy call out. She turned the faucet from her face, twisted off the water and retrieved a stiff, formerly white towel from a peg, wrapped it around her and went inside. She poked her head into the living room. Amy was still asleep. She didn't like to be wakened. She needed her sleep. Sleep would return her to her old self.

She'd tell her everything tomorrow.

She'd also go back and find out what had happened on what the couple had long believed was an abandoned road.

The next day, despite the excitement, as she now called it, Regina went about everything as she did every single day. No deviation whatsoever. She checked the stove and added an alder log because a good one could last all day. She went into the yard, down a slight incline, to the outhouse and relieved herself. She made a pot of coffee on the woodstove. Dressed. Returned outside and fed the animals. The female goat needed milking, so she did that too.

Back inside she told Amy everything and implored her to stay put.

"I can handle this. Don't give it a second thought. Something bad went on out there, but nothing happened to us. We're fine. We're good. Do not worry."

Amy nodded.

Regina kissed Amy and went for her long walk, her heart beating harder the closer she got to the place where everything had happened. She kept her eyes peeled for her missing Croc, though it was nowhere to be found.

That's my last pair. Maybe I can use Amy's old pair. Purple's good.

The forest was quiet, and the air had thickened. The change in weather had come. Early summer rains had finally given way to the warmth of high summer. Regina's garden had a chance now. The growing season in western Washington is somewhat short and unpredictable. Last year Regina and Amy had a bumper crop of ripe tomatoes. The year before, nothing but a bounty of the fried green variety.

She stood still and listened. *Nothing.* Then she started to climb up to the road, her eyes searching for the spot where she'd heard the couple arguing, where she heard the car and saw the channel of smoke filtered through the trees.

Tires had cut ribbons of mud, and footprints were scattered about like fallen leaves. She rested a moment, taking it all in, before making her way to the obvious location where the crash and fire had occurred. Tracks led to the edge of the rutted road.

She stood there looking down into a ravine, and once more filled her lungs out of fear.

A body, blackened and motionless, lay splayed out in the bushes.

Oh no. Oh God, no. This is horrible. Someone will come.

It took only a moment before she went into action. Regina concocted a plan to make sure that no one could find the burned-out truck or where it left the road on its way to oblivion. It would be no easy task. Concealment is hard work. She knew that from experience. She and Amy didn't want visitors. They just wanted to be left alone. Live their lives without the intrusion of the outside world.

How to do this? How to stay safe? Keep people away?

The slash pile left by the loggers beckoned her.

Erase.

She selected a skeleton-like fir tree branch from the slash. She surveyed the scene one more time, scanning for every telltale sign that someone had been there. Walking backward from the furthest edge of all indicators, she began to sweep away the muddy tire tracks. Methodically. Forcefully. It took some doing, but she worked her way to the edge of the logging road where the truck had plummeted downward. Back and forth, the fir branch swished away everything. It was sandpaper. It was a cleaning cloth. A vanishing act.

She stopped and regarded her handiwork. It wasn't perfect. Regina was fine with that. Nature isn't perfect, after all.

Brushing her forearm against her sweaty brow, she looked one last time, before disappearing down the trail, still walking backward and adjusting forest deadfall to vanquish her own tracks.

A hundred yards in, she turned around and started for home. Everything would be fine.

And indeed, it was.

That night Amy returned to their bed.

"I was so worried."

"Me too."

"Are we going to be all right, Regina?"

"Yes, love."

"No one will take me away."

"Never."

"Are you sure they won't come back?"

"No. I have a plan though. At least I think I do. I have to do something. I'll go back for the body and get rid of it once and for all."

"Too risky."

"Not now, Amy. Later. I'll wait awhile. When I'm sure that no one is coming back. When no one is looking for him."

Amy snuggled against Regina's breasts, and Regina stroked her long, shiny braid. She pulled the faded blue eiderdown to cover their shoulders. In that moment, all seemed perfect. Like nothing bad had ever happened. Or ever could. Safe and sound. Secure. Regina's hands traveled downward, pressing so lightly, so tenderly against her wife's body.

Regina breathed in Amy's sweet scent.

"I love you, Amy. Stay right here."

She kissed her tenderly.

"You are everything to me and you will always be my love."

"I love you, Regina."

"Always and forever."